All's Fair in *Love* and Construction

COFFEE SHO

DOLLY'S SALON

Ali's Fair in *Love* and *Construction*

By Zia Tyree and Kristen Sandmann

To all of the Type-A overachievers
who love to be called "good girl"...
This one's for you.

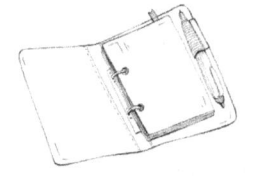

PROLOGUE

Iris

Age 6

"Ouch! Get away from me, butthole!" Iris yelled, clutching her soaking teddy bear and staring down at her favorite red polka dot dress, now covered in mud.

Today was show-and-tell day at school, so of course she was going to "show-and-tell" her best friend, Albert.

Momma always says Albert is a silly name for a bear that dad brought home. Why does she care if dad's the one who got it for me?

She didn't need to look up to know who just pushed her face first into a puddle with her favorite brown teddy. A group of older boys had been finding new ways to push her buttons since she started school. Last week, Eddie snuck into her desk and snapped all of her favorite pink and red colored crayons in half. Yesterday, Thomas and Michael snuck actual worms in her pudding during lunch. If they were the sour gummy kind she loved, it would have been a different story. Normally, it would be easy to ignore them. Normally, she could handle hiding during recess, constantly looking over her shoulder to make sure they weren't trying to mess with her. But today, she was tired of pretending to be stronger than she really was. Little Iris peeked at Albert for the first time since getting thrown into the puddle and her heart stopped.

Both ears were caked in mud. There was even a small tear through his round belly.

Does getting older mean getting meaner?

"Why do you keep hurting us?" Iris screamed while tears struggled to break free, "Albert does not deserve to get dirty on the biggest day of his life!"

"Awww is she going to cry?" yelled Eddie.

"Wahhh wahhh wahhh!" mocked Thomas.

"What kind of baby brings a stuffed animal to school?" Michael laughed, towering over her.

As Iris looked up at the three older boys who had been tormenting her for weeks, she battled sadness and thick mud. The tears she fought back started falling down her cheeks as she saw past her three tormentors, noticing the one person she never expected to see hiding behind Michael.

"Ren?" Iris whispered as she watched him nervously chuckle. He even stepped forward to high five his three new friends. She almost rubbed her eyes to make sure she was seeing this right until she remembered she was covered in mud and it would probably make her current situation worse. This was no mistake- her best friend's older brother saw her being tossed into a puddle and was laughing at her.

"Don't worry about Ren. He's with us now," Thomas laughed, elbowing Ren in the side.

"Yeah and don't tell your parents about this because we're having too much fun. You wouldn't want to get dirty again tomorrow, would you?" Eddie laughed.

"You mean her mom. Last I checked she doesn't have a dad," Ren said.

She paused for a moment, begging her eyes not to release the tears building quicker at the mention of her dad. She thought Ren was her friend too because she was friend's with his sister, Sage. He always carried Iris's backpack home from school and made cheese and crackers if she stayed at their house while her mom was still at work. He knew cheddar was her favorite. Once, he even made Albert a snack too after strapping him into an old high-chair that was in storage in the garage.

That's what a friend would do, isn't it?

Iris didn't have much to go on because Sage and Albert were her only friends. She supposed the entire Anders family was like a family to her, too. She didn't know much about the pillars of friendship, but she did know that friends don't laugh at you while caked in mud. Friends don't stand by and watch while something bad happens to you.

Iris glared at the back of Ren's head as he walked back across the playground, hoping he could feel how much anger she felt in that moment. Suddenly he turned around, his eyes locking with hers. She thought she could see something in them, maybe guilt? Just as quickly as she saw it, he was gone. After another minute, she realized Ren really wasn't going to come back and rescue her.

Well I'll just have to save myself then. I wonder what Sage will think of her brother being a big, stinky jerk.

Iris grabbed her mud-soaked teddy bear, picked herself up from the puddle, and walked away without another word to the other boys.

CHAPTER 1

Iris
21 years later

THUD!

Iris O'Connor woke up to Sage Anders nearly tackling her out of the fluffy guest room bed. Iris had stumbled into her best friend's house the night before after taking the red eye from Boston back into their mutual hometown of Shelburne, Vermont. After so many years spent away, she was surprised to see not much had changed as she drove through the star filled town late last night. Swiping at sleep-addled eyes, she attempted to stifle the yawn that encompassed her after only four hours of sleep.

"Let's go, Riss! Today is the day!" Sage proclaimed, her dirty blonde hair bouncing up and down before she jumped up and quickly bolted downstairs to the kitchen.

"I know, I can't believe it! Right behind you!" Iris replied after her, desperate to keep her eyes open and cheery in order to keep the good energy going.

It was hard for Iris to fault her best friend for being excited, but she was just so damn exhausted. Sighing, she pulled the comforter back over her eyes to give herself a few extra minutes of sleep. Iris had dropped everything in Boston to help renovate the shop space Sage has been so passionate about. When she got the call a month ago that

Sage's dream was coming true, how could she refuse? Sage has been a vintage collector and refurbisher their entire lives, and opening a brick and mortar in order to properly sell her wares in downtown Shelburne just made sense. The Anders home was overflowing with projects, and Sage could hardly handle her ever-expanding clientele as it was.

Sage had fallen into her career path as an entrepreneur effortlessly, getting her hands dirty with projects, just as Iris fell into event planning. Iris adored her job, the way she helped people feel excited about a new space opening, whether it be a restaurant or an office building. The company she worked for back in Boston, Not Your Mother's Events, even curated celebrity baby showers and TV show premier parties. But Iris knew that planning the first day of a shop opening was where she did her best work. The curvy redhead loved being around people, and the fresh smell of paint on the walls of a new building was icing on the cake.

Even as kids Iris was always the planner, and Sage was the dreamer. In adolescence, they were constantly trying to figure out how they fit into their small town. She lost count of the number of times Sage forced her to come over and look at every new strange and funky antique find growing up. Iris was always a good sport, "oohing" and "ahhing" at things like velvet Victorian lamp shades, and old brass food scales- which now resided in Sage's personal collection.

After Iris finished a charity event in Boston with her event planning company, she found herself relatively free to do remote work for the next several months. No amount of cranky vendors or potentially strained relationships with clients in Boston would get in the way of Iris helping Sage. Besides, she was overdue considering the amount of free furniture Sage managed to get sent to her most recent apartment in Beacon Hill. For example, the chaise lounge in her office, walnut entryway table with refurbished handles, and numerous throw pillows that Sage swears she "steam-cleaned to cootie-free perfection".

She was actually glad to have a reprieve from the hustle and bustle of Boston. She had a great group of girlfriends from work, but it was always some event, some shower, some party, that pulled her attention away from her own passion projects. And don't even get her started on the single's meetups she had been forced to attend every weekend since her last breakup. Iris was always happy to participate in each event, but the prospect of easy-going Shelburne had its appeal after years spent at her stressful job.

Tossing her mess of tangled red hair into a heaping bun, Iris rolled out of bed, following Sage downstairs to the kitchen. Meeting her chosen sister with a soft smile, she graciously took the cinnamon roll and caramel-flavored coffee bribe.

"I can't even believe this is happening! You're here! And Vintage Vixen Espresso is coming to life!", Sage exclaimed before taking a huge gulp of her own cup of caffeine. She was always testing different names out loud, hoping that if she said it with enough fervor, a name would actually stick.

"Wait when did you finalize a name? I need it for opening day signage! Also - where the fuck did the 'espresso' come from? I thought this was an antique shop?" Iris tried to keep her voice even. She hid her confusion by taking a sip of her too-hot coffee.

"Oh, did I not tell you? I was laying in bed a few nights ago and realized the shop was actually missing something. Or maybe even a few things! But we definitely need a coffee shop so everyone has something to sip on while they shop. Don't you love it?"

Iris watched Sage hop from one foot to the other, spilling little sips of her drink as she went. Iris pulled deep into her professional mindset, trying and failing to keep a smile on her face while watching Sage fly around the kitchen.

"Sage, don't you think you should have run these ideas by me or maybe even the construction company? I have a feeling some structure and design elements may change if we add an entire coffee shop into the existing store."

"Yeah of course I did! I mentioned it to Emmett Leif once at the grocery store. I saw him buying coffee beans and figured it would be the perfect time to approach," Sage said confidently.

Emmett was the owner of A New Leif, the major construction company in town, and happened to be Sage's older brother's best friend from high school. The company was based in Vermont, but was expanding into having remote contracts across the country.

Iris felt herself frown. "Jordan didn't mention it in any of our correspondence, so I'm glad at least someone knows!" Iris gave a playful tap on her best friend's shoulder.

Sage was brimming with ideas so there was bound to be a dropped line in communication somewhere. Not everyone lived their lives in an hourly planner with personalized to-do lists like Iris did.

Sage walked around the island counter to top off Iris' drink. "I've already been meeting with the other shop owners to give them a heads up on all of the construction and commotion, so this morning we can focus on meeting with the actual construction crew. Also, who's Jordan?" Sage stood still for a rare moment, pinning her with her eyes.

Iris wasn't prepared for this round of questioning, blushing as red as her hair.

"Um, Jordan Poulter? He's just one of the project managers at A New Leif. Emmett sent me his information a few weeks ago, and I reached out to make an introduction. Anyways...think any hot construction guys will be there?" Iris replied quickly, hoping Sage didn't notice how flushed she had gotten at the mention of the lead construction manager.

"Construction guys are always hot... Except for my brother. Oh, and Emmett Leif. What a sleaze," Sage pointed to her mouth and made a gagging noise, "At least he's been helpful. I wanna know what's been said between you and Jordan that's making you blush like a little school girl," Sage said with her eyebrows raised.

Iris should have gotten a first place award for how well she held in her eye roll at the mention of Sage's older brother, Ren Anders. Ren was the devil to Sage's angel. Loud, cocky, and not at all as hot as he seemed to think he was. Iris had learned years ago to keep her opinions of the older Anders sibling to herself. Sage loved him despite his flaws, so Iris kept her mouth shut.

Knowing she'd never hear the end of it, Iris trudged back up the stairs to grab her laptop. Sage was waiting for her at the kitchen counter, and the two girls saddled up side by side in what felt like a live-reading of Iris' private diary.

To: Jordan Poulter

Subject: Introductions for the Sage Anders Project

Date: August 23rd

From: Iris O'Connor

Hi!

My name is Iris O'Connor, and I'm already pleased to make your acquaintance. I hear you're the project manager for the project in downtown Shelburne. Emmett Leif gave me your contact information on behalf of Sage Anders, the new owner of 275 E Spruce (name is TBD).

I primarily work for an event company in Boston, but happen to be Sage's long-time friend.

I have a few ideas for the store to really elevate the space, as my specialty is in Grand Openings. Realistically, I know I'm hired on as the Creative Director, but I'll additionally be running point on any future events for the space, and would love continued involvement.

Attached, you'll find a green and blue color palette alongside a mock design of the layout working from the entrance, all the way to the back office to create the best flow possible. Let me know your thoughts on our collaboration.

Sincerely,

Iris O'Conner

From: Jordan Poulter

To: Iris O'Connor

Subject: RE: Introductions for the Sage Anders Project

Date: August 24th

Hey there!

Emmett mentioned you might be reaching out, so I'm more than happy to go over what you send electronically until we meet in person. Once you're in town, we can establish timelines and blueprints at the office.

Our client seems lucky to have a friend like you. (I heard it was going to be called ReWIRED...but I can keep "TBD" on the documents)

Give me about a week to see what I can do about this... interesting... paint scheme, and I'll get back to you.

Best,

Jordan Poulter

Over the past several weeks, the emails she and Jordan had been exchanging grew increasingly flirtatious, but she didn't want to gether hopes up.

He'd write things like-

Sure, I'd love to get coffee while we're both in town. I know of a great spot. What's your go-to order?

Surprisingly-

Oh yeah, I've been to the infamous Fall Festival. It's not too far from where I live. Maybe I can help out and we can dress as ... Frankenstein. And his Bride.

And most recently-

Do you have enough warm clothes packed? It still gets cold in this part of Vermont...

She decided against stalking him on socials because knowing her luck, he was probably just an easy-going, blue-collar guy, who happened to be funny and perfect, and was trying to help out on a remote project. He didn't try to add her on anything either. Which was just fine. The fantasy of who he could be came back and forth into view like the Boston Harbor tide. Iris found taking care of business using what was in her bedside drawer was easier than putting herself out there.

"Oh man, I can see why you're into this guy! I can't believe you haven't social-stalked him already!" Sage said, excitedly.

"I'm a consummate professional. I'm here on business," Iris said, fidgeting in the barstool.

"There's nothing wrong with a little bit of pleasure too," Sage winked, and set down her cup of joe to head up the stairs and start getting ready for the day.

While Iris tossed back the dregs of her coffee, she daydreamed about cooking dinner for a faceless man she never met after he had a long day of work. In her mind's eye, he was everything she wanted. Tall, perhaps a little brooding, with dark hair. Jordan Poulter probably smelled like heaven and a few bad decisions. She dreamed of a sizzling steak with tiny fingerling potatoes and charred asparagus, the smells wafting together around her small but cozy apartment. He would open the door in a big "Honey, I'm home!" sort of way, and sweep her off her feet. Her receiving love language was acts of service, so she'd be happy to impose a few traditional values if it meant being loved and protected in return.

Too bad the last time I did that for someone he ended up being married already. So very traditional. Great values.

Sage pulled Iris out of her reverie while wrapped in a hotel-style towel, steam billowing after her at the top of the stairs.

"You need to shower! Time is ticking! "Sage pointed down at the grandfather clock she refinished a few years ago that lived in her living room. She signaled for Iris to hurry up with her pointer finger circling in the air, anytime she was feeling particularly impatient. Iris loved that about her.

"Fine, I'm going! I was just thinking I could really work a hard hat," Iris called back. "Oh and I've been working on my wolf whistle! 'Hey little lady, whaddya doin' this weekend?'" Iris put on her heaviest Boston impression, feeling some level of the coffee taking hold of her. She found herself missing the group of gals she had from work, noting that she was missing their Monday morning coffee-sesh. They'd start their day off with a Dunkin iced coffee, and the cheesiest pickup line to distract them from the misogyny near construction that seemed never-ending. She quickly shot off a text in her group chat to tell them she made it there safely, and she got, "YAY, be safe!" and "Send us pics of the progress, you got this!", and "Miss you already! We can't wait to be there for the opening in Jan!" in response.

"That was halfway decent, you should keep the plumber's crack as long as a g-string pops out!" Sage poked her head out of her bathroom again.

Jokes aside, there's no way the girls would be able to mix business with pleasure. With the addition of the coffee shop, there was no telling what hurdles might lie ahead. They were both too busy for men. Besides, Iris had never been into Emmett growing up. He'd always been too... hairy? And self-assured? Especially when he absorbed Ren Anders into his little lacrosse crew. Emmett managed to turn the biggest dick-and her personal childhood bully- at their school into a winning machine, so she had to give him that.

Teenage guys only seem to listen to other guys, which is archaic and stupid.

Sage had always been into burlier men. Growing up, she was constantly trying to pretend she didn't think her brother's lacrosse friends were attractive, so Iris guessed she would have a hard time not ogling the crew.

Maybe the main construction crew has a bunch of older married guys? With families? And plumber's cracks... Gross.

She swiftly rinsed out her mug and heeded Sage's call to "glam the fuck up". Iris jumped into her own steaming shower, complete with all of the amenities she could ever ask for. She knew staying with Sage was a good idea when she found an extra fancy blow dryer was under the sink when she got out. She adored knowing that her oldest friend, queen of budgeting and thrifting, could still splurge every once in a while just like her mother always had. Iris smiled as a memory formed, putting some heat protectant in her damp hair.

Mrs. Anders was a strong lawyer who always believed in putting your best face forward. She taught Iris how to do makeup, hair, and the importance of a blazer. Iris' own mother was always stuck at the hospital working, so Mrs. Anders became like a second mother to her, always showing up in ways her own mother couldn't. Dr. O'Connor knew what she was doing, choosing her best friend to be Iris' godmother. In turn, Mrs. Anders gave Iris a built-in best friend- Sage.

Iris finished styling her curly mane, opting to leave it fanned out and away from her face. She tiptoed into her go-to "first meeting" outfit- a light blue chiffon blouse and her favorite pair of black slacks that hugged her hips, right at the crossroads of business and sexy.

She finished the look with her signature 3-inch black stiletto heels and strutted back down the stairs, giving her best prom queen wave. Sage giggled back up at her by the front door, both of them remembering countless "fashion shows" they hosted for Mr. and Mrs. Anders.

Sage was in her typical overall, t-shirt, and sandal combo, which Iris dubbed "the uniform", because "Why come back home to change when I just have to work more later?" Sage let her own wavy, dirty blonde hair pulled together in low pigtails and sea blue eyes do the talking. She was a natural beauty, through and through. The most unput together, perfect cyclone of an artist you could ever meet. Iris, on the other hand, was simply more regimented, like her doctor for a mother.

"I just never know when I'm going to see a patient out in the wild, Riss," she remembered her mother telling her twelve year old self, while applying Clinique's classic Black Honey lipstick.

On her way out, Iris looked up at the entryway mirror that had been there for decades. The large walnut frame always seemed perfectly oversized for the space. She took stock of herself, believing in the woman she had become in the professional world. Someone Mrs. Anders would have been proud of.

If only my love life had the chance to catch up.

Iris knew she wasn't brave enough to visit more than a few times over the years. Sage opted to road trip up to Boston more frequently for some much-needed night life. Iris knew it felt a little unfair, but both girls knew why it was harder for Iris to come back to their hometown.

Iris pushed open the passenger side door of Sage's hot pink lifted Jeep and hopped out of the side. Sage stood at a strong and lean 5'5", and she insisted on having a Jeep to accommodate the furniture she would find on the side of back roads and sketchy Facebook Marketplace deals. Despite her best ecological efforts in thrifting and antiquing, she insisted on having the most obnoxious looking car for the show of it all.

Iris didn't have a leg to stand because she didn't even own a car-she walked everywhere in Boston. She was glad Shelburne wasn't too big, because she planned on maintaining her running and walking routines. But for now, living life top-down in the Jeep should cover it.

She became eager to flip into work mode as she stared downtown Shelburne right in its cobblestone lining. As she walked along the unsturdy and personality-filled sidewalk of the too-familiar Spruce Street, she took a breath to remember that she was capable of a project like this. Masterminding events on the busiest street in their hometown would take her career to the next level.

Iris was still working for the first "big girl" job, working her way up to bigger and bigger events over the past five years. She more than earned her place at Not Your Mother's Events. After years spent juggling internships and planning college-wide pep rallies, during her time at the University of Massachusetts, she yearned to get away from college administration and into the hands of the East Coast elite. Their attitudes were worse, but the pay was significantly better. She might have gone from completely green to regularly jaded, but she loved what she did.

Growing up is realizing most people fucking hate what they do for work, but "responsibilities" and "children" get tossed into the mix and they can't leave. I do this because I want to, not because I have to.

Iris yanked the binder containing the blue and green color scheme and blueprints from her Gucci bag, turning to Sage pointing out the inconsistencies that she noted from Jordan without saying his name directly.

And just then she ran smack into what felt like a brick wall, preoccupied with the need to be right.

What the fuck was that?

Much to her surprise, the brick wall turned around to catch only the schematics before she fell ass first onto the sidewalk in front of the gutted shop. Iris looked up, ready to freak out on the person who was so clearly in her way. Anger flooded her body as the bane of her existence stared down at her laughing, examining her binder. She knew her skin matched her fiery red hair, feeling her pale cheeks prickle with heat.

Ren.

Fucking.

Anders.

The reason she almost never visited home, anymore. The reason she left this quiet town so quickly after graduation and stayed in Boston after college.

"You're such a bastard!" Iris yelped, her curls shaking in anger.

"Well good morning, sunshine! Why are you wearing heels when you know about the cracks? And you weren't even looking where you were going!" Ren said, trying to hide his laughter with mirth.

"Why are you here? We're busy needing to meet with actual professionals," she said while slapping his upturned hand away to stand up on her own, and hoped she didn't bruise her tailbone.

"Lucky for you ladies," Ren drawled, "I'm back from my trip to Texas, and I just so happen to give out a family discount. And a generous one for my perfect little sister. But I'm still a professional at the end of the day."

Iris grappled for the binder to get it away from Ren. After several jumping attempts he taunted her, keeping it just out of her reach.

Was he always a *professional* giant like this? Or am I finally shrinking? At what age do we start shrinking?

"Printed emails? From... oh who is this? And what are these colors?" Ren teased.

"Nothing! Just give me back my notes," Iris said, hands firmly on her hips.

"Say please," he responded, looking down on her.

"Excuse me? Are you twelve? Give me my shit back," she swatted at his chest.

"Say please and you can get your precious journal back," he said, faking a wince.

"It's not a journal! I keep correspondence printed in case my phone dies or something. I can kick your ass with both hands tied behind my back," she said, going for a behind-the-knee kick to prove a point. The kick lands, and Ren muffles a grunt.

"Only if you ask nicely," Ren teased, rubbing the back of his knee and dropping his voice a little too low, throwing Iris off.

"Wait-is it from Jordan? Sage chimed in, ignoring the assault Iris promised to reign on her brother.

So maybe she did know I had a small crush on the project manager. I couldn't have been talking about him that much, right?

"Can the both of you leave me alone?" Iris turned around to Sage in pure shock. She felt gutted, how could her best friend have left out the part where her childhood bully was coming back into town?

"Right okay so Ren is just here kind of sort of... to help? This is what I meant when I said I got a good deal on the labor" Sage said sheepishly, gesturing to the entrance of the shop without any luck.

"Some of this is good, Riss. Really good," Ren flipped through design mock-ups. He had no interest in giving it back unless she caved.

"I need that to take notes. It's been a while since I've been in here," Iris pouted.

She was disappointed that she resorted to old-school guilt tactics.

"You know the magic words," Ren responded, pinning her with his eyes.

Always with the taunting.

"Please," she said through gritted teeth.

"Say it again." Ren shifted his body to lean against the front door, tilting his head back slightly.

"Please!" she shouted, angrier than ever. She noted him peering down at her through heavy-lidded, icy blue eyes.

Ren Anders continued to assess her a moment before he bowed and handed her the binder as if it were on a silver platter, laughing as he did so.

"After you, ladies," Ren drawled once again in feigned chivalry, opening the door for both girls. He was speaking to both of them, but she felt his eyes on her alone.

The fact that he seemed to be offering assistance for once was a fact she and Sage could discuss at home later. Too bad for Ren, Iris became even more closed off and suspicious of others after moving to Boston. No amount of fake southern hospitality was going to make this little surprise visit okay.

"When are you going back to Austin? We're working with a local contractor, A New Leif," Iris found a table to set her purse down on. She continued, "If you're still best friends with that massive lumberjack, Emmett, shouldn't you know that by now?"

Of course he is, they're always flying back and forth to see each other. The greatest bromance known to mankind, plastered for all of Instagram to see.

Not that she had stalked his Instagram or anything.

She rammed her hand into her purse, furiously dumping out the contents of the purse looking for a pen, so she could start taking notes on how the space "spoke" to her. There was nothing wrong with taking a manual approach to things in an age so... techno. With a few expensive personal pieces like her bag and gold jewelry alongside her near flawless track record with event structuring, every vendor she worked with had a healthy amount of fear and respect for her. She wanted to establish an aura somewhere between "I'm stylish and fun" and "Don't fuck with me".

Iris had a lot of ground to cover, with a multi-step process with each new project. She'd write a first impression using a fresh black-ink pen and a fresh spiral notebook, which would in turn, give her the perspective of a first-time client attending the shop, auction, or event. Each impression would give her a design idea or inspire space for the next event to lure guests in. She'd do anything to secure a successful grand opening. She was used to using work as a distraction, so no better time to continue the tradition.

"The fun part about that is my company *is* A New Leif. I've just been working on our remote projects in Austin. And I never said where in Texas I was," he pulled out a pen from his own pocket when Iris started to get heated again, "so you're stuck with us."

"The only thing I'm stuck with is a great ass and you can fucking kiss it on your way-" Iris got rudely interrupted by Sage putting a hand on her shoulder, always the mediator between the two.

CHAPTER 2

Iris

"Now now children, everyone just calm down," Sage said while holding her hands in front of her as if she was surrendering to a burglar. "Iris don't be mad, but my brother is, maybe... potentially... the head contractor for the project. In my defense, I thought you figured it out once you signed the contract last week." Between Sage's wide eyes and slender legs, she looked like a deer caught between competing hunters.

Oh no I was not stupid enough to do this to myself... Iris thought while she skipped to the back of the binder. *Where the hell is the contract!*

"No way Sage, I know for a fact I would have noticed that stupid, obnoxious, overbearing...." All words left her as she stared down at the printed and signed name in front of her.

I hereby sign that I will be informed of and will personally sign off on all project decisions for 275 E Spruce St. (Name Pending) **Ren Anders.**

This could not be happening. Iris couldn't even stand being in a room with Ren for more than two minutes let alone get him to sign off on all of her design plans. Sage brought her in on the project because they shared a dream of seeing one shop finally stand the test of time. Most shops in their hometown barely make it a year.

Iris assumed she'd have creative liberty given her recent background with what spaces work the best when it comes to community-building and getting people off of their phones. After shoving the binder back into her bag, she felt a mix of emotions for the scene playing out in front of her.

"I know this is a lot to take in but I swear to you Ren is only here to help and he will love your ideas - isn't that right Ren?" Sage said while not-so-subtly nudging Ren with her elbow. Sage sounded like she was trying to soothe her like a child, which was ridiculous considering Ren was the only child in the room.

"Absolutely, after all I am a total gentleman," Ren said, tipping his A New Leif baseball cap her way before walking into the crumbling building, which made Iris roll her eyes so hard she was lucky they were still attached to her head.

"Oh please, don't give me that shit," Iris said, attempting to flick Ren's baseball cap off his head.

"Careful Riss, remember I sign off on everything you do from now on," Ren smirked with baby blues that matched his sister's, while adjusting his cap. "Come on girls, enough chit chat let's actually take a tour of the store we've been standing in. I need to assess the water damage and any additional structural issues," he said leaning against a withered former coffee bar.

It had been years since she saw Ren in person. Pictures on social media simply did not do him justice. Iris suddenly couldn't help but notice his bicep muscle bulge as he shrugged on a blue and gray flannel. She could have sworn there was a whisper of black ink under the sleeve by his wrist.

Dear God, what are they feeding men these days? What were those veins on his arms? It must be so easy for phlebotomists to get annual lab work. Why do the hottest guys have to be the biggest assholes?

She had always objectively known that Ren was fit from sports while they were younger, but there was nothing boyish about him now. Ren developed the kind of tan that only true outdoor, hard working folks possessed. Iris only hoped he had a farmer's tan line to under-cut the rest of his glowing skin. It also seemed like he had somehow managed to get taller, going way above an acceptable six feet.

Not that I care.

She realized she was still staring at his arms, internally cursing herself. She quickly looked back up to meet Ren's striking eyes hoping he hadn't noticed. After a beat she realized both Ren and Sage were still staring at her expectantly.

Shit - what was it that they were talking about anyways?

"Of course, let's go take a look at the building that has been causing me so much trouble and haunting my dreams," Sage said, thankfully saving Iris from her embarrassing lapse in judgment. There must be some strong fumes in the air, because there was simply no other explanation for her checking out her best friend's brother.

CHAPTER 3

Iris

Iris hid her gasp as she processed the crumpled mess of wood before them. Because of the debris, it took an entire hour to walk around the shop. The walls still had massive holes from the last plumber looking for the original source of pressure in the system. The last disaster happened while it was a basic coffee shop. The pipes froze last winter, and then exploded right at the front of the store, causing half the shops on their side of the street to shut down for a week. Sage said that a group of local kids smelled like a combination of sewer water and the hot chocolate they dropped on themselves at the sight of the flood.

It came as a shock to no one when the city council closed the coffee shop soon after, citing faulty infrastructure. Sage only knew of the incident because several of the middle schooler's parents were frequent customers of hers. Whether she was flipping furniture or scouting out vintage finds all over the state, Sage knew everyone in their town.

And because she was the social butterfly of the town, Sage couldn't help but leave the store to interact with every passerby to let them know of her upcoming plans. While she was chatting up Cherie, the owner of the local organic grocery store, Iris made her way to the front of the store to finish her last lap of notes and picture-taking so she could concept map the area.

Iris sighed as she noticed a small puddle next to the front window.

That spot was one of her favorite things about this shop growing up, you could see practically every shop on Spruce Street right from the front of the store. Once, back when the store was a bakery, she skipped school and sat directly beside that window for hours with a warm croissant and her favorite book. The simple pleasure of watching the people of the town go about their day brought her insurmountable peace. She remembered thinking at the time how great it would be to get to see that everyday. She thought she could still smell the yeast rising and dough cooking in the old brick ovens.

"Hey Ren!" she called to the back of the store, "What is this puddle doing here? What did you spill when you got here?" Iris continued while walking up to inspect the puddle. Her black stilettos suddenly turned brown when she accidentally stepped into a puddle much bigger than she realized.

That's strange, she thought while bending down to get eye level with the exposed pipe that she could now see was slowly dripping onto the floor, behind the plaster wall.

"Ren, I think this one is leaking too. Better add that to your ever growing list of shit to fix" Iris yelled without looking back this time. "Hmm... it's so weird. It looks like the pipe is shaking a bit."

"Wait, what did you just say?" Ren's voice echoed from the back office where he was studying the updated permits. His chair groaned as he got up, about to shout back again. He barely arrived before disaster struck.

"Iris! Get the fuck away from that right now!" Ren yelled, attempting to cover the rest of the distance to her, but he was too late. All at once, the pipe in front of her shook violently and burst. A current of water crashed directly into her face and knocked Iris on her ass.

She thought she heard Ren shouting something, but she couldn't hear with all the water in her ears. Too shocked to speak, all Iris could do was stare down at her favorite outfit. Her baby blue blouse was completely soaked through and in her struggle to get into a sitting position, her shirt had pulled down off one of her shoulders creating an awkward "off the shoulder top" situation and was now showcasing one side of her hot pink polka dot bra. The pants that fit her perfectly this morning were now soggy and stained with rusty water. Her cheeks heated, she refused to look up and see the humiliated look on her friends face or the snarky laugh Ren would undoubtedly have at her expense. Water clogged her ears and she could barely make out what Ren was saying as he reached behind her to shut off the buildings water supply.

This is almost like what happened to me as a kid. All that's missing is Albert...

She expected to feel rage, but instead a different emotion rose to the surface. She was suddenly transformed back to her six year old self, remembering how humiliated and lonely she was lying on the ground staring up at what felt like the entire school laughing at her.

She remembered watching the way Ren's eyes change from open and kind to closed off and indifferent as he decided to join everyone else in school in their goal to bully and belittle her. The incident started Sage's anti-bully tirade, making it her mission to single hand-edly stick up for her and threaten every bully in school until they finally left them both alone. It took Sage a few years to build up her own reputation in order to overcome the "Aren't you Ren's little sister?" allegations. Even though it was the truth, Iris felt like Sage's familial relationship to her asshole brother shouldn't have meant so much to so many.

He fucking planned this, didn't he. We have a massive project to get going on, and this is what being helpful gets me. I guess time doesn't always change people for the better.

She knew Ren always took pleasure in making her life miserable as a kid but she had thought surely he would have grown out of it by now. Gathering her strength, Iris put on her best "I don't give a fuck" face and forced her stare back up to Ren.

"Happy now?" Iris yelled from the floor while blinking back tears. Once again she watched his eyes change to a hard, indifferent gaze.

"Why do you think this would make me happy, Iris? Do you think I enjoy watching the building fall apart right before my eyes? The wa-ter must have frozen and expanded the pipes, leaving them faulty and prone to... well... this," Ren said, shifting his gaze from her to the pipe and exposed drywall.

Iris couldn't take not knowing. Before she knew what she was doing the words were coming out of her mouth.

"Did you plan this? Is this just another prank to humiliate me? I could handle it when we were kids but if taking this job was some ploy to restart your old game you can kiss my ass goodbye."

Ren studied her for a moment then slowly lifted his hand, palm turned up. It took Iris a minute to realize he was offering to help her up. Knowing Ren, he would take it back at the last moment in another attempt to embarrass her.

Iris lifted herself up, like she always did, pushing up with both hands landing in the murky puddle. She quickly shifted her shirt back into place.

God, me here, why am I wearing my most embarrassing colored bra today? There's no way you're a woman like I always hoped. A girl's girl would never do this to me.

"I did not plant faulty pipes in this establishment Iris, despite how impressive you believe me to be. I don't even know how I would have pulled that off considering this is the first time I've been in this place since Sage bought it." Ren said calmly while putting his hand in his pocket, appearing to feel the small twinge of rejection. "And to your earlier point... what reason have I given you to believe I am not dedicated to this project?"

He slowly moved closer to her, and she watched his eyes rake over her body in a way she so didn't want to admit to appreciating. He was suddenly very close- scratch that- too close to her. So close she could smell him. He smelled fresh, like he had just done laundry. He leaned closer, and Iris noted a woodsy scent wafting from his hair that reminded her of the leaves changing during fall. She wondered what she must have smelled like.

"Besides, this is not the way I would want to see you wet and on the ground in front of me, Iris," Ren whispered so softly she knew only she could hear him. She tensed, Ren had never said anything like this to her before. She expected to feel disgusted but instead her stomach clenched and she desperately wanted to rub her thighs together to relieve the pressure that his words caused.

Iris didn't even like dirty talk. Some men had tried to use it on her in the bedroom, and each time she thought it felt forced and unentertaining like a badly produced porno. No way in hell was Ren getting the upper hand in this conversation. Iris met his eyes, willing herself to forget her body's foreign reaction to his words and decided her best course of action was to ignore them completely.

"What were you even doing so far behind me anyways? You were insistent on writing down everything in that stupid little book of yours before we moved onto the next task." Iris said and she swore she could see Ren flush a little.

"I wasn't far behind you. Apparently, you're just faster than the rest of us at finding the worst possible moment to bend down," Ren said while avoiding making eye contact with her.

"Oh whatever. Well, I am now completely soaked and smell like sewage." Iris sniffed at herself as she heard the shop bell tinkle, revealing a shocked Sage.

"Holy shit, Iris, you smell like ass! I knew I couldn't leave you two alone," Sage said, trying not to laugh at her best friend.

"I think I've done my duty for the day and deserve some ice cream and wine- what do you say, Sage?" Iris quipped back.

"I say that I need a tarp for the Jeep before I let you in! And Ren, let's just pick this up tomorrow," Sage concluded, gathering her and Iris's belongings so they wouldn't get soaked.

Iris was glad the water doused some of the heat between her legs, because she would have died of embarrassment if Sage had heard any of that conversation. Even so, Iris could have sworn she saw her move back to give them space a few times during the walkthrough.

Typical Sage. After Ren's senior prom, Sage tried to repair their relationship through the years. Iris had never hated him more after the incident, but Sage softened around him. Iris had to trust she had her own reasons for reconciling despite a mutually horrific high school weekend. During a Spring Break visit, just when Iris thought Ren would be partying elsewhere, Sage locked them in a closet for 10 minutes to "talk about their feelings".

Any and all advances she and Ren made slid right back to them hating one another. Reconciliation was temporary, but Iris's spite was forever. She gave up trying to be friends with Ren years ago because fighting felt better than talking through anything that happened growing up.

"Of course. I'm going to stay a while longer to finish my notes and gather supplies for tomorrow. See you at home ladies." Ren said and winked at Iris.

"In your dreams," Iris rolled her eyes and locked arms with Sage, despite the dampness. She couldn't imagine a worse fate than having to live with Ren. Working together was one thing, but living together would be mutually assured destruction. An involuntary shudder went through her just thinking about how awful of an idea it was. Sage led them back to the jeep while remaining suspiciously quiet. Usually, she would be talking Iris's ears off about her latest thrift haul or even what movie they would watch tonight.

Maybe she's just nervous about the building after seeing the pipe burst. I would be too.

Iris decided to stay silent about it in case that was what was causing her friend so much stress today. She hoped a change of subject would lighten the mood.

"Sooo... what flavor of ice cream are we choosing tonight?" She targeted the pointless question to make Sage laugh. They had both been eating the same flavor of ice cream since they were kids. Strawberry for Sage, cookies and cream for Iris.

"Shit, I think I ate the last of it before you came actually. Let's stop at the store and pick up supplies for dinner while we're out. And by supplies I mean what wine pairings go with our ice cream," Sage said while dramatically switching lanes last minute to pull into the parking lot of the local grocery store. People in Shelburne didn't bother with road etiquette. Or blinkers.

"I literally look like I got in a fight with a lake and lost, there is no way I am showing my face in that store, Sage."

"And don't forget about the stench that's coming off you," Sage replied, trying to hold back laughter yet again. "You can stay in the car while I head in, but roll down the window! And you better be ready to watch a rom com when we get home because I've been waiting to watch the classics!"

The only person she felt comfortable with making jokes at a time like this was Sage, because Iris knew the intent. Ren, however? She wasn't so sure.

CHAPTER 4

Ren

"This project is going to be the fucking death of me," Ren stared blankly ahead as he sipped his second IPA of the night.

Emmett, his best friend and notorious town playboy, slapped him a couple of times on the back. "Cheer up buddy, it's only for a few months.

Ren had gotten into Shelburne a few days prior in order to pour over the blueprints with Emmett before meeting with the new Creative Director. Sage insisted the woman she picked would help solidify her vision, but Ren didn't trust anyone but himself to make sure everything went right for his little sister. Even though she was younger, she raised him in a lot of ways because their mom was often sick growing up. He knew that her asking for his help was a big deal, considering how apt she usually was to act independently.

When Emmett told him that the creative director was Iris, Ren was nervous. He thought he was going to spend the whole project miserable because of some under qualified creative director. Now he knew he would spend it miserable because the insanely talented creative director hated him.

I am not who I used to be. I'm not a sad kid with something to prove anymore, he kept reminding himself.

He wanted to act like he had to the other women he'd dated in adulthood- stable, reliable, and definitely not a bully. Ren knew whatever he said never came out right. It didn't help that the banter they had sparked a fire in his blood that he hadn't been able to put out since he started developing hormones in middle school. He loved to get a rise out of her, because he'd do anything to see that pink blush creep up her neck and into her cheeks. Why did he affect her so badly? She stopped visiting Shelburne, even though her mom and Sage were still living there full time.

Slamming the rest of his own stout, Emmett called out to Ernie, his "favorite" bartender, so he could buy the next round. Ren was grateful for the guy who was more of a brother to him than anything. When they met in his freshman year of high school, Emmett was actually nice to him. The big jock didn't pity him and his sister for their mom's recurrent breast cancer diagnosis.

Instead, he introduced him to a well-meaning group of lacrosse players who happened to get decent grades. Emmett helped Ren realize his own potential, and he decided to slowly drop the guys who were toxic from his friend group. But he had realized their toxicity all too late in Iris' eyes. In return to Emmett's help, Ren helped Emmett learn the art of a good prank. Not quite a fair deal, but Emmett never complained. Unless he was on the other end of the prank...

He buddied up with Emmett's crew of lacrosse guys, creating his own found family in the process. Ren's long-standing rebellious streak needed a different outlet than picking on others for no reason. Girls picked up on the bad-boy-gone-jock after the summer going into their sophomore year, and that reputation followed him. Being the reformed rebel had its perks- girls who went to church on Sundays looked at him differently. Everyone looked at him differently, and not just because he was 6'4".

Sage had a much easier time in school. She fit in with the artists, the AP kids, and the theater group. She had so many talents that it became a game to see how many pictures she would be featured in when they opened their yearbooks. Her record was 11. She was- and continued to be- so open with people while Ren just wanted to run away.

Luckily, Emmett didn't let him skip class because "you never know when a scholarship could be waiting around the corner". His 65 year-old therapist named Shyla would later tell him that this was called "avoidant attachment style" and that he "should try to not run away from his problems".

While Emmett left him alone at the bar to use the restroom, Ren reflected on his childhood like he typically did when visiting their local haunts. He swirled his beer like a vintage wine, thinking about his high school rage over the unfairness of his mom's diagnosis. He thought the sickness in her body was managed well enough until she passed, two days before he accepted a full-ride sports scholarship to UT Austin.

Emmett got in on an academic scholarship, due to a knee injury in the first game of senior year. No big schools wanted to take the risk, and he didn't want to go D2. The loud "FUCK" yelled from the middle of the field was burned into Ren's mind, as was the imagery of his best friend rolling around in agony, clutching his right knee.

They made the most of things and the friends found themselves having the time of their lives in ever-growing Texas. Together with Ren as the Structural Engineer, and Emmett as the Civil Engineer, they pioneered new ways to enhance the beauty of current structures, and keep the best interest of the public while doing it.

Although known for phenomenal work with the Texas-based company they signed on to after college, they would get into spats with the Austin city council for ambitious planning. This finally came to a head, and they decided to go it alone. They opened A New Leif in Vermont just a few years ago and were rapidly growing. Since they were already familiar with Austin's landscape, Ren would go back on occasion to consult on contracts.

When they weren't working on a massive project, the overgrown boys were determined to give back. Ren used his portion of his mom's life insurance policy payout to create a charitable organization designed to give back to the Shelburne community and beyond. One portion of the charity program helped cancer survivors with housing costs after finding themselves in debt from treatment. Another program worked to beautify hospice centers, giving the dying a peaceful place to pass. They even hosted auctions where all of the proceeds were donated to women's health clinics.

He hoped that enough good deeds would make up for the little asshole kid he grew up as.

Ren's dad grew distant from his kids after their mom passed for a few years. It wasn't until Mr. Anders found out about the charity that he started to fly out to events for Ren. As a little kid, Mr. Anders often warned Ren about the dangers of falling into the wrong crowd. He could tell he was proud, but every time they met up there was a strain behind his dad's eyes. Every time Mr. Anders looked at his son, he found his wife's eyes.

Beyond watching out for his friendships, Mr. Anders never knew his only true victim was the annoying little redhead across the street. Ren supposed his dad never thought to warn him about becoming obsessed with a strong woman, because he grew up with two. The same girl- no, woman- who showed up wearing the most outrageous heels in the middle of construction.

Who was the pretentious tool, now?

"So, tell me again how Riss managed to find the one pipe in this whole town that was a second away from bursting? I swear, that's almost unheard of in the fall, especially considering it's what... like 60 degrees outside right now? Are you sure she didn't tamper with it hoping it would be you who found it" Emmett chuckled while sliding back into his bar stool.

If anyone knew the complicated relationship between Ren and Iris it was him. He had been with him through it all over the years, rivaling his sister in the amount of times he tried to help repair the friendship.

"I swear that woman goes out of her way looking for trouble. I had been on site the entire day, personally inspecting every pipe and exposed beam, while Sage and Riss trailed behind me. I was in the back office for a few minutes, and she managed to get ahead of me for that final pipe. I wonder if one of the guys inspecting before we got there fucked with the water pressure to test it at different points," Ren said begrudgingly.

He didn't have the heart to tell his friend the real reason why Iris managed to get ahead of him to inspect that final pipe. He hadn't been able to take his eyes off her the entire walkthrough. Those ridiculous high heels were so inappropriate in a construction site he couldn't help watching her every move to make sure she didn't fall. But when she walked ahead of him and he got an uninterrupted view of her ass, he froze.

He was a damn site manager for god's sake, working his way up in the company to become the best, working the longest hours both in the city, and in places like Midland building massive office spaces for oil tycoons. He's earned a small fortune, and now he's earned this time with family. But all it took was Iris strutting in front of him in those skin tight black pants showcasing her perfectly round ass and toned legs and all rational thoughts left his head. He couldn't own up to the fact that he didn't make it over to that pipe quick enough because he was busy envisioning sinking his teeth into Iris's ass...

"And if that wasn't bad enough, she had the nerve to suggest that I had orchestrated the whole thing just to humiliate her," Ren said, signaling to the bartender that he needed another round. He would need a whole lot more than three beers to get the image of Iris soaking wet in a pink polka dot bra out of his head. He gave in and let his mind wander just for a moment.

He imagined Iris kneeling in front of him in that soaking shirt staring up at him with admiration and lust in her eyes. Slowly, she would grab her wet shirt and lift it up over her head giving him a full uninterrupted view of that polka dot bra he couldn't get out of his head. Her hands would slide up his legs, taking her time to make sure he felt every second of her ascension to his belt. He finally allowed himself to grab her bra straps and started to slide them down her arms. She shivered when his fingers made contact with her skin, making sure she kept eye contact with him while she moved her arms to her back to unclasp her-

"I mean... Don't take this the wrong way but can you blame her? You two have done some pretty messed up shit to each other throughout the years." Emmett interrupted his daydream while grabbing the two new beers from Ernie. He coughed, thrown out of his fantasy.

Jesus, what the fuck was that. What was he, some middle schooler who can't control their urges? Iris was literally the last person to be having some ridiculous sex fantasy about. He internally scolded himself and tried to return his focus back on the conversation.

"Look, I know how hard you have worked to get back to a good place after your mom died. I have seen how hard you worked in the company to make a name for yourself and the hours of therapy you went through to become the man you are today, but Riss didn't. She has no idea and likely still thinks you're the same dumb boy that pranked her as a kid."

Ren sighed, he knew this to be true but he didn't know how to fix it. "So what, I should just write her an apology letter and slip it under her door" he said with a bit too much bite.

"All I'm saying is give her some time to see that you have changed and aren't some stupid kid anymore." Emmett said, completely ignoring Ren's attitude.

"You're right. I just can't stand to see the look in her eyes when she sees me, like she's waiting for me to hurt her. She wouldn't even take my hand when I offered to help her up." Ren said, taking a huge drink of his beer to try to settle his nerves over the topic.

"Then it's simple, show her the man you are now and make her change her mind about you." Emmett said while smirking at a girl across the bar. Looks like his friend had found his next target for the night. Emmett had always been a ladies' man. Everyone in town was familiar with his reputation but seemed to love him even more for it. He had probably hooked up with every eligible female in town. Everyone except his sister Sage who Ren had made sure his friend knew was strictly off limits.

Sensing Emmett was about to become preoccupied for the night, Ren slammed the last of his drink, closed his tab, and said goodbye. He hopped into his truck to head back to his sister's house for the night. Ren's apartment was currently rented out because he thought he would be taking over a project in Austin for the later half of the year, but his plans changed the minute he found out Iris was on the project. He had planned to stay with Emmett on his living room couch, but after being kept up the last five nights hearing Emmett's latest flings proclaim quite loudly how amazing he is in bed, he realized he couldn't stay there long term. Sage half-heartedly offered to let him sleep on her couch and he accepted before she could change her mind. Knowing his sister, he would bet Iris didn't even know he was staying with them until the Grand Opening.

Here goes nothing.

Ren pulled up to the house, heart beating out of his chest.

CHAPTER 5

Iris

After a thorough shower to wash off what she hoped was clean pipe water, Iris headed back downstairs for dinner. She and Sage ate quickly, eager to get to their favorite part of the night. Iris plopped on the couch and started up the TV to put on their favorite movie while Sage brought over the main course, strawberry and cookies and cream ice cream.

"Is that what I think it is?" Sage said while joining her on the couch.

"You bet it is! Can you believe it's been this long since we watched it" Iris said while clicking play on their favorite movie. *10 Things I Hate About You* started playing as Iris opened the ice cream containers, eating hers straight from the pint. Over the years this movie had become a constant between her and Sage. Whenever either of them was feeling sad or overwhelmed they would have a good old fashioned sleep over and watch the iconic classic. After the events that went down today, Iris was ready to sit down with her best friend and relax. She didn't even want to think about seeing Ren tomorrow, unsure how they were going to make it through his project without killing each other.

"Hey, I just wanted to say that I promise to be on my best behavior when Ren is around us at the site. It seems like he's helping and I don't want to continue to stir up old shit. I think as long as he listens to your design ideas and my event expertise we'll be okay. It's still hard for me to let things go with him sometimes. We always fought, but we're adults now. So it should be fine," Iris said to her best friend, trying to convince both of them it would be okay.

"I'm so glad you feel that way, because there's actually one more thing I wanted to talk about with you..." Sage trailed off suspiciously. She was doing that a lot lately.

Just as Iris shoved a bite of ice cream in her mouth, waiting to hear the latest cherry on top of the shit storm sundae, she heard a knock at the door.

"Are we expecting someone?" Iris said, taking another bite.

"Okay well at least his timing is impeccable," Sage began but an explanation was cut off by her hulking brother bursting through the door, looking a little too comfortable already.

"How did you know this was my favorite movie? Thanks for waiting for me to start it!" Ren said while sliding in between Sage and Iris on the couch. He disrespectfully snatched Iris's spoon, stealing a bite of her ice cream.

"Sage, can you ask your brother what he's doing here this late?" Iris said ignoring Ren, even as his cologne wafted over her. She could have stared a bullet hole into Sage's forehead with how piercing the question was. After a minute of Sage refusing to meet her eye Iris couldn't take it anymore.

"Okay what is going on here? Did something come up with the building that couldn't wait until tomorrow? If you don't get off this couch it's going to collapse with your added weight!" Iris couldn't keep the anger out of her voice. All she wanted was one night away from him to get her head straight. She hadn't been able to stop thinking about what Ren whispered to her at the construction site all night. She was ashamed to admit the heat rising in her body was from more than just anger.

"Nope, nothing work related at all Riss. And I helped Sage re-inforce the legs. Happy to hear you are willing to work late hours though" Ren said and winked. "I'm home for the night and you happen to be sitting on my bed. Howdy roomie!" Ren spoke with that fake southern drawl, stealing the container of ice cream from Sage.

"No. No that can't be. I think I would know if you were staying with us. This is a joke right?" Iris said as she turned to Sage, on the verge of hyperventilating.

"Soooo don't be mad, but I kinda told my brother he could stay with us just until he finds a decent airbnb. His apartment is already rented out because I called him back from his assignment early! And you know how crazy it can be the month of the Shelburne Harvest Festival. Every hotel on the block has been booked for over a month and don't even get me started on the house prices." Sage said calmly despite the storm that was brewing in Iris' eyes. "Besides, the festival only has a few weeks left and Ren said he would take the couch."

"Unless you would prefer I sleep with you, Riss? Happy to keep you safe and warm at night," Ren smirked. Like hell would she allow him to sleep in her room with her. Still glaring at her best friend, she startled as she realized something.

"Wait- so are you sharing a bathroom with me or your sister? Because MY bathroom is located in MY guest bedroom so don't even think about stealing the shower in the morning. I distinctly remember how long your morning showers were when we were growing up. Took a while to get all of the stink off."

"Awww, that's cute that you kept tabs on me Riss. Did you miss me while I was gone?"

"More like savoring the time away from you," Iris uttered under her breath.

She could not believe this was happening to her. In the span of one day she went from feeling giddy with excitement over finally getting to work with her best friend on a project they were both passionate about to being forced to not only work with her arch nemesis but apparently live with him too.

Fan-fucking-tastic.

They would surely kill each other before the week was done. The only thing stopping her from walking out right now and finding her own hotel was the look on her best friend's face, silently begging for forgiveness. She remembered the countless years they had walked through the store, back when it was a coffee shop, then a florist, and even a joke shop. Sage would practically glow talking about all her ideas for the antique shop, going so far as sketching a layout of the shop with all the antique pieces she planned to sell. So yes - she knew how important this was and she wouldn't ruin this over some petty feud.

"Just stay out of my way and we should be fine," Iris said, trying and failing to sound neutral about the situation for Sage's sake. "I'm actually feeling pretty tired. Guess the walk through sucked the energy right out of me. I'm going to head upstairs for the night."

Faking a yawn, Iris picked herself up from the couch and took the stairs two at a time before either of them could respond.

"See you tomorrow Sage! I have some great ideas I want to run by you for the shop after I get done with my meetings for the day."

"Don't forget to CC me, Riss! It would be a shame for you to go through all that trouble without getting my approval first." Ren yelled back. She swore she could hear Sage whispering disapproval, but didn't want to get her hopes up.

"Goodnight Riss, see you tomorrow!" Sage finally said back right as Iris closed her bedroom door for the night. She wished she still had some of that ice cream to cool her back down.

CHAPTER 6

Iris

Iris woke to the sound of the shower running. For a split second she allowed herself to forget that Ren was in the house, likely ready to torment her and ruin all her plans for the shop. After her second of bliss was up, she opened her eyes and peaked at the clock on her nightstand.

6:30 am! What kind of psychopath is up at this hour, she thought while grabbing the cream comforter aiming to pull it over her head.

Now both Anders siblings can harass me in the mornings.

She heard the shower stop just before the blanket reached her eyes and Ren stepped out into her room. Obviously Iris had lost the ability to think rationally because her eyes snapped up to meet Ren's. All air left her body because the man standing in front of her simply should not be real. Golden brown hair was sticking out in all directions- a sight that should have looked messy and untamed. Instead, she found herself wanting to run her fingers through it. His tan skin glistened with the remnants of his shower. Black stenciled ink trailed over one arm, clearly an outdoor theme, but she couldn't quite make out the detailed flowers within.

Oh you have got to be kidding me- is that a fucking eight pack?

Her eyes trailed down those chiseled abs down to the perfectly defined 'V' that was cut off by a towel. She found herself wondering what it would look like without the white cloth obstructing the view. Her thoughts were cut off by a loud cough. All at once she came out of the fantasy and remembered who it was that was standing in front of her. Her cheeks heated in embarrassment, heat pooling between her legs and rolling up to her chest.

"Good morning, sweetheart," Ren drawled, his eyes darkening at the flush so clear on her skin. She cursed her red hair and pale skin, but forced herself to keep eye contact, not allowing herself another glance at his perfectly defined body.

Of course - it's always the assholes that are the most attractive.

"One - not your sweetheart. Two - who the hell gets up at 6:30 in the morning to shower?" Iris said, relying on peripheral vision to check him out. The last thing she wanted was to be caught checking him out, but she couldn't stop herself from attempting to peek at the eye candy before her.

"Promised Sage I would get to the shop early today to get through the last of the inspections so we can get started on the construction phase." Ren said with a twinkle in his eyes. "And by all means Riss, keep checking me out. I don't mind. Has it been a while since you've seen a mostly naked man in front of you?"

"That just so happens to be none of your business."

Iris could feel her entire body heating, knowing her skin was close to matching her hair. She would die before she told Ren how long it had been for her. Sure, things have been a little slow in that department lately but everyone goes through dry spells. She had simply been too busy at work to go on countless online dates that always ended with her heading home alone and door dashing take out. Iris loved being in the city, the Boston nightlife was great and she was working her dream job but the men were the biggest downfall. All they could talk about was their stock portfolios and how much real estate their parents owned. Was it too much to ask to find a man that was able to have an intellectual conversation and blow her mind in bed? Apparently it was considering it had been far too long since she felt satisfied.

"Ouch, that long huh?" Ren said while lifting his arms and leaning both hands on top of the door frame. She could see his abs flexing but didn't allow herself to look fully. She tried to get a closer look at the detail in his sleeve tattoo, and he noticed, suddenly bringing his arms down to his side. He must have been able to read the look on her face if he figured out what she was thinking about.

"If you need any help knocking the dust off, just say the word," he gave her a shit-eating grin, muscles fully on display.

"I have plenty of ways to help me get the job done before I would ever ask you" Iris said, ignoring the feeling of her stomach clenching. He was obviously mocking her now. Iris wasn't lying, she had always had a difficult time with partners satisfying her. "You know the saying - if you want something done right you have to do it yourself."

Ren smirked, not at all phased by her insult and said confidently "Iris, I'm not sure about the boys you're used to being with. but I've never left a project unfinished. And come to think of it....wasn't I in your dreams? I seem to recall hearing my name on your lips this morning when I passed through here to get into the shower."

She felt herself get butterflies for the first time in years. How could one sentence get her so flustered? She must really need to get laid. Ren slowly walked over to her bed and leaned down. She held her breath and picked at the pilling on the comforter that had fallen to the side, unsure what he was about to do next.

"When did you get all of the ink?" she scrambled to change the subject.

He was the one caught off-guard for once.

Good.

"I've been working on this sleeve since mom died," he said, a little reserved. "I keep adding things that inspire me," his deep tone bringing her right back to the present.

He grabbed her chin lightly and lifted her face up to meet his.

"Let me know if *you* need any inspiration," Ren said as he let go of her chin.

She watched his eyes as they studied her body, lingering on her skimpy white pajama top. Iris studied Ren as his eyes trailed lightly over her body. His eyes darkened and hands clenched as he took in her exposed legs. She couldn't force herself to break contact, mesmerized by his reaction to her. Despite her feelings for the man in front of her, her body had other ideas. Goosebumps rose over her arms, her nipples pebbled, and her breath came quickly. Before she could process her body's reaction, Ren spun around and strolled into the guest bathroom.

"I'm headed to the store for the day. Make sure you CC me on any project plans so I can take a look," he said without looking back.

Iris felt like she was getting whiplash from the abrupt change in conversation. She was so busy thinking about what Ren had just offered that she forgot to respond. Surely, that was some cruel joke and he was trying to make fun of her right? There was simply no way Ren would actually offer himself to her like that. Besides, it's not like she would ever take him up on the offer. She could handle that problem just fine by herself, just like she did everything else. By herself. She tried getting a grip, just barely relinquishing the image of Ren leaning over her in nothing but his towel from her head. She pretended to fall back asleep as he left her room, so that they wouldn't have to interact again before her own shower.

Shower. Work. FOCUS.

After a quick cold shower of her own she headed downstairs to start work for the day. No sewer smell to wash off this time.

Both of the Ander siblings were gone by the time she got downstairs, and Sage left a note to let her know she ran out to get her latest antique find the next town over. Just like that, Iris was left to her own devices today. She quickly got to work answering emails and responding to vendors, letting them know she was officially in town.

Her primary focus was on Vintage Vixen Espresso's layout and design plans. She audibly scoffed to herself as she CC'd Ren on the planning email she sent over to Sage.

Sage had so many antique items saved up Iris knew she would have countless ideas for where she wanted all of them to go in the store. It had been her friend's idea to decorate the store with only antique furniture to allow customers to see how they would fit into spaces before they bought them. She had to admit it was genius. Most people have no vision when it comes to furniture and interior design. This layout will take the guesswork out of it and allow customers to fall in love with entire room designs, hopefully, leading to bigger sales.

She was officially done with her work for the day, so she decided on an afternoon run. Iris sprinted upstairs to change into workout gear and ran out the door. It was a crisp autumn day when she stepped outside. She lifted her head to the sky, enamored with the slight breeze and 60 degree weather. Fall had always been her favorite season to run, hearing the crunch of leaves under her feet soothed her and helped clear her thoughts.

Iris knew the area well so she set off on her usual path around town. The miles blended together as she allowed herself to reflect on her conversation with Ren this morning. He had to have been mocking her, she decided. It was just another one of Ren's tricks to humiliate her. Feeling resolved, she began scheming ways to get back at him.

Just like old times.

CHAPTER 7

Iris
10 years old

"Gosh Riss, I'm so hungry I could eat a freakin' cow," Sage whispered through braces. They always got chastised by Janice the lunch lady when they talked too loud in the line. With apple juice in hand, they moved forward at a snail's pace, desperate for a bite of the extra special Thanksgiving lunch the school put on before their Fall Break. They had second period lunch, which would have been fine if Sage's stinky older brother, Ren didn't have the same lunch period.

He's turning into a real jerk.

Iris' mom tried to explain hormones to them, and she didn't want to rock the boat. Soon, he'd be done at their town's small K-8 school, and move on to high school. Iris would only have to deal with him if she went to the Anders' house for sleepovers and hangouts for the next three years. They shuffled forward until they got to the entree options and said "yes" to the mashed potatoes simultaneously. They made it out of the line with only 15 minutes left in lunch, always the last ones to get their trays. They even got shorted a buttered roll.

Every day, Ren would come up to them and attempt to ruin their meal. Some days, he would "slip" and knock a fork out of Iris' hand or he would find a way to cough over their trays. *Boys are so gross,* Iris shuddered at the memories. When Iris would go over to the Anders' house after school, she'd move around things in his room, in retaliation. She once hid his deodorant under his bed, so he stunk like the hormonal boy he was until he found it.

Admitting he was losing belongings would be admitting to his parents he was messing with Iris, because who else would know how to get under his skin?

Today was no different, with Iris searching the crowd until she found him, stalking toward them with unruly legs and an attitude to match. She locked eyes with him from across the quad, wondering his intent for the day. Was he... smiling? And hurrying toward them? Well that was creepy. Sage was about to ask if he wanted a fry as he lurched forward holding a plate filled with mac and cheese, which was option number two for today. Everything happened in slow motion. All of that cheesy goodness slid immediately off of the plate, splattering Sage's lap, and Iris' entire head. Sage jumped up, red-faced, and ran to the bathroom.

"Oh no I am so so sorry you guys- Sage, please come back", Ren said.

"What do you want from me? Was all of this meant for the top of my head or was some of it for your sister too?", Iris questioned.

"No! No I came over to call a truce and see if you guys wanted to walk to ice cream after school", Ren replied.

"Oh really? There is no truce, I'll never trust you. So here's your lunch back", Iris said a little too calmly.

Iris reached into her own hair and smeared mac and cheese all over Ren's shirt, and stomped off.

Ren

14 years old

Ren spent a few weeks messing with the girls at the start of this year, but the guys he sat with at lunch started giving him a hard time about it. They would talk in P.E. about him leaving them to go "hang out" with his little sister and best friend. For some reason, he kept gravitating toward Iris. Honestly, he'd take any excuse to be near her. Even if the only one he could find was to get on her last nerve.

In the spirit of Thanksgiving, Ren walked over to the girls to share some of his lunch. He thought if he offered one of their favorite mutual cafeteria items, they'd forgive him immediately. Especially because the O'Connors were coming over to the Anders household for dinner the next day. He didn't factor in eating absolute shit and making everything worse. Sage started for the bathroom, and when he saw the look in Iris' eyes, he knew there was no going back. Standing as tall as he could, he accepted his mac and cheese related fate, and sulked to their lockers to pull out his musty P.E. clothes to wear for the rest of the day instead.

The juiciest-looking turkey created a scent so enticing that Ren floated into the kitchen from down the stairs. He got himself ready with the best maroon button up shirt he could find.

He looked around the kitchen to find glistening green beans with almond slices, a salad bigger than his head, and mashed potatoes practically dripping over a bowl. Looking at this spread made Ren wonder why he ever said that Christmas was his favorite holiday.

Ren always helped his mom around the kitchen for dinner, and Thanksgiving was no exception. Their dad really stepped up this year, though, because Mrs. Anders energy levels weren't where they used to be. The chemotherapy took a toll on her, and Ren was desperate to help out more and more. He wasn't old enough to be able to drive his sister around, so he figured after his homework he could help out around the house. His friends would ask him to go skateboarding or to the mall, but he always had to turn them down. Eddie, Michael, and Thomas kept calling him a "momma's boy", but he didn't understand why loving his mom when she was sick was such a bad thing. He wasn't sure how much longer he could last being tormented by them.

"Where do you need me?" Ren leaned in to give his mom a side-hug where she sat at their table, pre-folding dinner napkins into what was supposed to be a turkey.

"Actually, sweetheart, can you precut some of the pumpkin pie and put the cool whip in the fridge to thaw?" Ren's mom, Lily, called to him.

"Don't worry about it Ren, I already took care of it! Why don't you take the trash out?" his dad asked.

Ren recently started to lift weights and think about what sports he wanted to play, so taking out the trash was his latest chore specialty. Sage was too short to lift the bag up and out of the trashcan, anyway.

The doorbell rang and Sage ran from the dining room where she was setting the table for their guests. Ren thought she had great styling taste for a ten year old, or at least more than he had at his current age.

"I'll get it! I'll get it!"

She flung open the door and greeted the O'Connors with as much enthusiasm as getting a new puppy. Iris' mom wrapped Sage up in a tight hug, telling her that she "adored" her leaf-print dress, while looking up to evaluate Ren.

"Seriously, guys, what are you feeding this kid? He's as tall as me!"

Ren was proud of himself for always eating all of his protein and vegetables at dinner. He knew he had to eat in order to bulk up. His dad wasn't the best chef, but he got by with the basics when his mom got too tired to cook.

"How are you?" Dawn said, looking into his mom's eyes, assessing every micro movement she exhibited.

"It's Thanksgiving! I'm feeling okay, I guess," his mom trailed off, pulling her best friend further into the kitchen. Mrs. O'Connor worked long hours at the hospital as a doctor in the intensive care unit. She spent all day helping others, just to turn around and raise Iris by herself with limited time off.

This was part of the reason Ren offered to make Sage snacks still after school, just in case Iris was feeling hungry and didn't want to admit it. He wanted to ignore his own bullying tendencies and get to the part where they were all friends.

Their moms met in undergrad, and while his mom was getting a Communications degree and on the Pre-Law track, Dawn was getting a Biology degree and was Pre-Med. Both women turned out to be highly successful because they supported each other through it all. Break-ups, divorce, moving states together. There was absolutely no other way about it. His dad, Bud, always exhibited a mock jealousy of the women's relationship, joking about being their "third wheel".

Ren didn't know exactly why Iris didn't have any siblings outside of overhearing his mom talk about how "she couldn't have more kids even if she wanted to" one day. Iris was definitely enough to handle as it is, and Iris' mom never seemed to be too bothered by the fact that she only had one kid. Sage and Ren were basically adopted by them, just like his mom was another mom to Iris.

When Iris and her mom came over, he was determined to show her that he wasn't a complete jerk all of the time, planning to promise to never bug her again. There was just something that happened to him when he got a rise out of her.

"Hey Iris, I like your shirt."

Iris glanced down at the brown sweater with puffy sleeves, and mumbled a quick "thanks" before heading into the kitchen. Ren decided that in order to be friends again he'd have to continue to try and make some changes. So, after all of the pleasantries were over, he knew he'd have to play butler.

"Can I get you something to drink?" Ren said to Iris while she and Sage sat on the couch, watching a rerun of the Macy's Day Parade.

"Why would I want anything from you? Are you going to poison it?" Iris responded darkly.

"No I want to make it up to you. I'm sorry about lunch. I really wanted to eat that mac. I had to wear my PE clothes the rest of the day and Mrs. Matthews told me I stunk in my last period," Ren said more shyly than usual.

"Well, serves you right! We'll take two sparkling apple juices, then," Sage said assuredly.

"Coming right up!" Ren had a task and he knew he would carry it out perfectly.

"Where's my drink?" Dawn chimed in.

"I'll get one for you, too, Ms. O'Connor," Ren said from behind the refrigerator door.

"I'm about to carve the crap out of this turkey, you guys!" Bud called out to the group.

'Let me make your plate. A little bit of everything, right?" Ren offered.

"I'm a big girl, I can make my own plate thank you very much," Iris said, furrowing her brows.

"Listen, you're at our house as our guest and I want to build a bridge and get over this or whatever. Please just don't tell my parents what happened. I really want to play football or lacrosse or something, and I don't know if they'll say yes to my plans if they knew," Ren said pleading.

"As long as you don't spill all over everyone... fine. I'll take a little bit of everything," she said, crossing her arms.

Ren proceeded to make the biggest plate of food out of anyone at the table. He gently placed it in front of Iris after she sat down, and her eyes went wide.

"Oh thanks, this is..."

"Is it enough? I might have gone a little overboard..."

"Yeah this is plenty. I'll also take a box to go," Iris laughed a little as she sipped on her freshly-refilled sparkling drink.

The table grew quiet as they all prepared for Ren's least favorite part of the meal. It was an Anders family tradition to go around the table and say what they were grateful for. Ren dreaded it because he didn't want to say the wrong thing.

His Dad always went first. "I'm so grateful to be a part of a big, extended family. Dawn, Iris, we're always so happy to have you here," his dad said choking up. He knew Iris' mom was like a sister to him. They fought like siblings sometimes, but always came together when it came to his mom.

"I'm grateful to be here another year, looking at all of my favorite faces. Oh- and eating the best pumpkin pie Costco had to offer!" Lily cheered, raising a glass of red wine.

"I'm grateful for the kids being able to get together at school and hang out after. I'm so happy to have found a family we can both trust," Dawn reached across the table to squeeze Iris' hand. Iris returned it in kind, tilting her head at her mom lovingly.

"I'm grateful for crushing my last acrylic painting in art class. And food." Sage said mostly to herself, as she continued to drool over her plate.

"What she said," Iris said.

"Oh come on, you gotta have something a little different this year. You two can't always be grateful for the same thing," Dawn replied laughing.

"Okay. Fine. I'm grateful to be dry and not covered in food," Iris smirked at Ren.

His heart sank. She was totally going to tell on him. This was it for him.

"What do you mean?" Lily asked her goddaughter.

"Oh nothing much, I'm just surprised that all of my food ended up making it onto my plate instead of all over my head like it did yesterday at lunch. Remember, Ren?" Iris said scathingly.

Sage and Iris collectively brought down the house with stories of how Ren had been messing with them at lunch. He'd never get to hang out with his new friend Emmett after school again.

CHAPTER 8

Iris

The ringing of her phone alarm startled Iris awake the next morning. She had so much to do today, and talking to her mildly distant mother wasn't exactly on the agenda.

"Hey mom, what's up?" Iris said, trying to coax the frog out of her throat.

"You didn't tell me you were coming into town! I ran into Emmett at the diner grabbing a cup of coffee before my shift- lovely new barista there who sneaks to-go orders there now-but anyway, he tells me there's a hotshot event planner in town. It took me all of about 30 seconds to get him to spill. We could have had dinner or something when you got in, and I-"

"Yes, I know we could have, but Sage may have mentioned how busy you've been at the hospital lately with so many new respiratory cases. If you talked with Emmett, I'm assuming he told you I'm staying at the Anders'?"

A beat of silence passed, knowing her mom would never step foot in that house again. Her mom had just moved in with her new boyfriend, Steve. He was an administrator at the hospital she worked for and overall seemed like a good guy. Iris didn't want to disturb a good thing, and living with her mom made her feel suffocated.

"Yes, yes, he told me. There's plenty of room here for you though... if you change your mind." The offer was hollow and they both knew it.

"I know, Mom. Sage and I are co-conspirators when it comes to her new shop, and it's best if we're able to plot and plan together at all times."

This got a real laugh out of her mom.

"Okay, well. I love you. If you see Bud... tell him 'hey' from me. I'm not sure if he's still around," she trailed off knowing she didn't need to bring up how Mr. Anders practically abandoned Shelburne once his wife passed.

"He's in Cancun last I heard, but I'll let you know if he makes an appearance. We'll get dinner or something soon. I gotta run," Iris said, desperate to finish the conversation.

"Have a good day, Riss. I'm about to go toe-to-toe with an anti-vaxxer," Dawn ended the call before she could explain more. Having a highly-intelligent single mom growing up definitely had its ups and downs. The upside was being able to get diagnosed at a moment's notice, the downside was having to understand as an ICU physician, holidays and birthdays and free weekends didn't really exist.

Iris shook herself, knowing she had to get started reading through the ten page document Jordan had sent over late last night. This was not the first time something like this had happened to her. Contractors were constantly trying to take the reins from her and plan out spaces themselves despite the fact that they hired her to do that very thing. Typically, Iris didn't mind the revisions. She often felt their suggestions were a great way to get to see the primary client's interests, taste and, on some occasions, even helped her improve the events once they came to fruition. It was rare that an event planner started projects quite literally from scratch like this, but that's what made her the best.

Different.

Unique.

Her ability to maintain her composure with difficult clients was just another reason she moved up so quickly in her career. She had a natural ability to sway them in the right direction without coming off like she was forcing them, something she quickly noticed was not common with her other coworkers.

She knew Sage had been dreaming about the property for years. With Mr. Anders being in real estate, it was easy to see how she had a knack for understanding the market as an adult. With that being said, it wasn't until after she bought the storefront that she even told her dad. Iris recalled Sage chirping, "You know I had to do this for me and me alone."

What was not effortless, however, was understanding if all her ideas were going to be possible to complete so she found herself reaching out to the construction team often. For the last month she had been fixated on her emails with Jordan Poulter. He told her he was the lead construction manager for the project, putting him in charge of the entire planning process, so why was Ren even bothering to sign off on things? Jordan seemed to have things completely handled.

Iris hadn't expected much from their communication other than a simple yes/no on project ideas but over time, she noticed him start to get a little flirty when they talked. She didn't even know it was possible to flirt over email but somehow this man still had her on the edge of her seat waiting for his replies.

In the last email he sent to her before she left Boston, he had even asked if he could come meet her in person when she got into town. She surprised herself when she responded saying yes.

Honestly, she believed this final draft proposal had been some of her best work. So imagine her surprise when an email came through a few hours later with the title "Revisions".

Late last night, she had squared her shoulders, finally working up the courage to open the document. The suspense had kept her awake for two hours, wondering what it could possibly say. Did he love it? Was it a ten page document praising her good work?

All thoughts of praise vanished the second she had opened the document. She was immediately greeted with red markings, the pages were swimming with revisions. She couldn't find a single page without stupid remarks on the side. Annoyed, she slammed her laptop shut.

How could Jordan be sending this to me? Maybe my ideas aren't as great as I originally thought.

After ten minutes of screaming every curse word she knew in her head, she resigned herself to the fact that she had to at least try to maintain a professional relationship for Sage's sake. She could do this. She was the best at handling difficult clients.

Is he being difficult or is Ren getting in his head?

Feeling better this morning after her pep talk to herself, Iris grabbed her running shoes after slipping into a dark blue tank top and black leggings. She needed to get a quick run in to clear her head before going through the commentary. Not wanting to wake anyone up, she silently tiptoed down the stairs aiming for the back door. Just as she was rounding the couch something caught her attention. In her rush to get up this morning she hadn't allowed herself to think about who was sleeping downstairs.

She stopped in her tracks, almost knocking over an antique end table from the 1920s that Sage had beautifully restored. Despite the new squeaking noise emanating from the end table, Iris's mouth dried. Ren was stretched out completely on the couch giving her an uninterrupted view of his entire body. He wasn't even sleeping with a blanket, so everything was in view. She allowed her eyes to roam, noticing how toned his arms were even in his sleep and once again getting a view of his abs.

She was still too far to see the individual images on his sleeve, and she had the urge to get a better look one day. The only thing he had on was dark gray sweatpants, but even those weren't leaving anything to the imagination, with his morning wood in full effect. Iris finally forced her eyes back up to his face. Thankfully, he was still sleeping. What she didn't expect to see was that he was also smiling. Iris rolled her eyes, what he could possibly have to smile about in his sleep?

He's probably thinking about all the ways he can ruin my project. Should I smack him?

Just then, an idea came to her. If Ren was going to fuck with her, she was going to fuck with him. They had constantly been at war with each other while growing up. For a while, there hadn't been a week that went by without Ren doing something to humiliate her.

Iris remembered one particularly cruel thing that Ren had done when she was about fifteen. She had just started to wear makeup, hoping it would look nice for her first-ever movie date. He was a senior that Iris had been pining for since she started her freshman year. His only downside was that he was another lacrosse player who knew Ren and Emmett. Iris had been so excited she remembered how big her smile was when he asked her out. When her doorbell rang, she thought it was her date. But no. It was Ren Anders.

He took one look at her smiling face and told her very plainly, that her date was no longer interested in her. Iris had been devastated that the boy she liked had to send a messenger to let her down. She could feel the mascara running down her face along with her tears. Years later, she found out that her date hadn't planned to stand her up at all. Emmett ended up confessing to Sage about Ren's plan to sabotage the date one night at the local bar.

Iris dragged herself out of that painful memory and focused on the opportunity in front of her. When was the last time she had the chance to get back at him? The annoying angel on her shoulder tried to remind her that she was in fact an adult now who didn't need to "get back at him". She ignored it.

She tiptoed to the kitchen on silent feet and gently twisted the cold nozzle on the sink while grabbing a bowl and filling it up. Once it was completely filled, she moved to the back of the couch directly over Ren's head. Smirking to herself, Iris tried to contain her laughter.

Payback really is a bitch, she thought as she dumped the water directly onto Ren's face.

"WHAT THE HELL!" Ren yelled as she ran toward the front door.

"Figured you'd want to know what the water from those faulty pipes felt like." Iris said over her shoulder as she slammed the door and headed out for her run.

CHAPTER 9

Iris

Everyone in the house was gone by the time Iris got back from her run. She snickered when she noticed there was still a wet spot on the couch right where Ren's head had been just an hour earlier. It was just water, and she knew Sage wouldn't notice before it dried. *Hope he enjoyed his wake up call.*

Iris showered and made herself presentable for the day. Her copper hair was lightly curled around her face, and she had taken the time to put on a little mascara and dusted some concealer over her freckles. Walking over to the coffee, she expected to see an empty pot. Sage was notorious for drinking an entire pot of coffee by herself, so she was surprised to come across it completely full.

Sage must have made me a new pot before she left for the day. Now that was a great way to start her day of revisions.

With a fresh cup of dark roast in hand, Iris opened her laptop to get to work. Deciding to bite the bullet and start on the first page of revisions she centered herself. The first page of her draft started with the renovation and construction plan. It was supposed to be a fairly straightforward document that started with the current layout of the store and then went into the proposed new layout focusing on which walls would need to be torn down or altered. Iris had become giddy when she realized the store could have the most perfect open layout by knocking down only two walls in the shop. It was a no-brainer once she saw it. The new layout would allow for a seamless flow for customers to browse the shop. So imagine her surprise when the first revision she saw was a giant red "X" over both walls along with a comment stating the construction crew couldn't take out those walls.

"LOAD BEARING? YOU HAVE GOT TO BE KIDDING ME!" Iris screamed to herself while throwing her hands in the air.

This was unacceptable. In all her years working with clients she had never had someone completely dismiss her ideas without the addition of a realistic solution. What kind of solution was "load bearing", "Need to keep both walls", or "will see if able to tear down half of the wall but need some structure for building support."

Iris had watched plenty of HGTV renovation shows. There always seemed to be a work around for load bearing walls. Couldn't they just add some sort of structural beam thing? She thought she remembered seeing that once.

Even though her contact at the company hadn't been the one to send the proposal back, Iris decided to email Jordan. If anything, he could tell her more about whatever the hell a structural wall was.

To her surprise, he responded right away.

From: Iris O'Connor
Subject: What is a load bearing wall?
Date: October 8th
To: Jordan Poulter

Hi there!

Hoping you can help me with a question - what is a load bearing wall and *please* tell me there is some way around it to still tear it down?

Also, I know Ren is signing off at the end, but you're still the one working with me on leading this, right? If so, we should set up a meeting at the diner like you mentioned in a previous email. It would be easier to understand your edits in person, those giant X's you put all over the last document made it difficult to read.

Regards,

Iris

From: Jordan Poulter

Subject: What is a load bearing wall?

Date: October 8th

To: Iris O'Connor

Happy to hear from you Iris, hope you're having fun being back home in Shelburne.

The simple answer is - a load bearing wall is a wall that is actively holding the weight of the elements above it. How much of the wall you can remove depends on what is inside the wall and what it's currently supporting. Most contractors need to see the inside of the wall before they can tell you how much needs to stay.

I know the man who is now in charge of your project quite well. He's a little rough around the edges, but he means well. I'll talk to him about it as he's your current in-person contact.

I'm out of town right now, but will still be working with the construction team on your project remotely. I look forward to seeing you around the site as soon as I'm back.

Happy Fall,
Jordan

"Ugh! Stupid walls with stupid structural integrity. Wait. What does that last line mean? Where is he?" Iris questioned out loud despite the fact she was still alone. She leaned forward, squinting, at that last line.

Giving up on that fight for the day, Iris continued reading through the pages of revisions. She was reluctant to admit that they were actually quite good. There were definitely still things she didn't agree with, so she'd just have to put on her big girl panties and ask Ren if he knew about Jordan's edits. The revisions may have been written in a rude way but at least they made sense. She couldn't believe she was even thinking this but some of the ideas were better than hers. They even suggested an oval coffee bar instead of the simpler rectangular style so Sage's custom antique bar stools could be the focal point of the shop.

Iris made it to the end of the revised document, jotting down notes and her own revisions as she went. When she was finished, she sent it to Ren instead of Jordan to get ahead of things.

Iris decided to take a break in the late afternoon, briskly walking to the hardware shop downtown to grab a new screwdriver to fix the end table she nearly broke earlier. She was sure there were plenty of screwdrivers at the house, but she couldn't even begin to sift through Sage's workspace supplies since they were scattered across the entire garage.

Jim, the crotchety hardware store owner, gave her a half-hearted welcome when she entered the shop.

"Oh so are you finally here to tell me what all of the commotion across the street is about, young lady?" Jim asked.

Jim had a reputation for hating change, and hating the fact that the store had such significant turnover even more. Luckily she and Sage had won over Jim years ago, because they always went to his wife, Dolly, for haircuts in her salon across the street. Whether he admitted it or not, he looked out for the girls.

"I know it's a lot of noise, JimBo, but you have to trust Sage and I on this one. This time, it's going to stick."

"Well, are you sure those two goons know what they're doing? I see them running around town at all times of the night, I barely believe they're involved in this!"

"Listen, you know I only love some people in the Anders family, but Ren and Emmett mean well...I think," she said with only partial certainty after picking out a basic toolkit.

"Okay, okay fine. Well make sure to see my Dolly when you're in town. She really misses you being in the big city and all," he said, checking her out at the register.

"Don't you worry, I already have an appointment with her!", she said, throwing a wink over her shoulder at him.

Looking down at her watch, she realized it was only 3:00 PM. Having nothing else to do for the day, Iris decided to make a quick pitstop into the salon. Hearing Jim mention Dolly had opened a hole in her heart. Dolly was the town hairstylist first and foremost but she was also the town gossip. Nothing, and I mean nothing, got past her. Once, when Iris was 17, she stopped in to get a quick trim and ended up spilling her entire failed high school dating history to Dolly all in the span of one hour. She left feeling a tad violated but also very liberated after getting it all off her chest. Over the years, she came to realize Dolly just had a way of getting information out of everyone. Something about the way she silently stared at you through the salon mirror had everyone in town confessing their sins to her like they were kneeling in a confessional.

The bell chimed as Iris walked into the store announcing her arrival. Thankfully, Dolly didn't have any customers lined up. The worn black leather chair was outdated, but the pink-and-white checkered flooring reminded Iris of all of the times she made impulsive hair decisions. There was the bang phase, the purple tips phase, and she couldn't forget the "do whatever you want so I don't have to think about it" phase.

"Hi honey! Wait, did I get the date wrong? I could have sworn you weren't scheduled for another few weeks... but these days my memory isn't all that great." Dolly said while practically skipping over to her schedule book. Even at the age of sixty, Dolly had the best style in town. Today she wore skin tight black leather pants and a bright red top making her look just like a 80's biker chick. She was rocking her signature hairstyle. Half of her long curly white hair was clipped behind her head achieving that perfect "messy" look that all women know actually takes hours to achieve.

"No you didn't get the date wrong! I was just on the main drag and needed to see my favorite salon owner. Any hot gossip to share?"

"Always, honey. But I am afraid to say the majority is about you and your group of misfits. What's this I hear about Sage opening an antique shop?"

Iris couldn't believe news had traveled this fast around town but she hoped the saying "any publicity is good publicity" rang true. She spent the next few minutes explaining the antique shop and her and Sage's vision to Dolly. She even went through some of the anticipated event ideas she had been planning, hoping Dolly might get so excited that she "accidently" shares the plans with others in town.

"What a fantastic idea! I've always said this town could use some fresh business, and you know how much I love Sage's furniture. Hell, she probably restored half the stuff in this salon."

Iris felt her shoulders drop slightly hearing Dolly approve her ideas. She hadn't realized until that moment how important her opinion was. She could only hope the rest of the town shared Dolly's excitement.

"That means so much, especially coming from you. Maybe your opinion will start to rub off on the rest of the town." Iris said with a self deprecating laugh. Hearing Jim talk about the shop had gotten to her head. He wasn't the only one in town who hated change and it was well known that all the previous businesses in the shop's location had failed within the first year.

"Don't you worry about the rest of the town. They will have me to answer to if they give you any trouble."

Dolly spoke with such conviction Iris had no choice but to believe her. She spent the next hour on the edge of her seat listening to Dolly spill the town's gossip. As it turns out, Cherie, the town grocery store owner, had broken her leg a few months back while trying to unload a shipment of apples. Iris found herself falling off her seat laughing at one particularly funny story when the town's only boutique owners had run a couple out of town for wearing "last year's colors" to their fashion show. Even though it had been years since she last visited home, not much had changed at all.

CHAPTER 10

Iris

Iris took her time running errands and making conversation with some stakeholders around town. The girls needed buy-in from the rest of the shop owners to make this store a true success, so Iris started rekindling old friendships on her third day back in Shelburne. By the time the Fall Festival rolls around in a few weeks, everyone will have heard about the store, and there should be a massive line out the door when they open New Years Day.

Iris finally got back to the house, tools in hand. She was grateful to have some time to bop around town to clear her head. She even stuck true to her word, catching an Uber to stop by the hospital to say hi to her mom on the way home to drop off some afternoon iced coffee for her and some of her favorite nurses.

"Oh my god, Sage, when did you learn how to cook? This smells phenomenal." Iris yelled as she walked in, getting no response in return over the music playing.

She was overwhelmed by what she hoped was the smell of dinner. Sniffing dramatically, she noticed hints of chicken, lemon, butter, and garlic. Just then, her stomach decided to make itself known and growled loud enough for the neighbors to hear. She walked into the kitchen ready to devour whatever she was smelling but frowned when she noticed it was completely empty, even going so far as to check the refrigerator for leftovers. She wasn't ready to give up, so she walked down the hall to the dining room even though she couldn't remember the last time Sage ate so formally. Iris watched Sage scoop the last bite of chicken piccata from her plate into her mouth as she walked in. She also had time to observe Ren's very empty plate before either of them noticed she had walked in.

"Oh my god! Riss, thank god you're finally home!" Sage squealed as she jumped up from the table to tackle her. "We were just about to call you, Ren here hasn't shut up asking where you were- you smell like bleach," Sage said, sniffing her.

"Dolly," they said in unison, and Sage sat back down.

Her salon was nothing if not traditional when it came to the blondest blondes.

"I got done a little early so I stopped in town to grab a screwdriver and see Dolly. Then I drove by the hospital to see my mom."

Iris held up the wrong end of the screwdriver awkwardly to show Sage and Ren. She didn't know why she felt so left out. There wasn't any reason they needed to wait and eat dinner with her and she was perfectly capable of making a meal for herself. She should be more used to this feeling by now. She had been eating meals alone since she was a kid. Her mom was there for the important things, but getting stuck late at the hospital meant fending for herself for dinner. Even as she tried to reason with herself she felt tears prick the back of her eyes.

"I see I missed dinner?" Iris said and coughed to try to hide the crack in her voice.

"I figured you'd be out on a date tonight or something so I altered the recipe so it only made two servings." Ren said. If he heard the crack in her voice, he ignored it.

"You made that? Since when do you cook?" Iris said, failing to hide her shock.

Most men she knew could barely reheat pizza let alone make a full meal. Come to think of it, she couldn't remember the last date she went on where they even paid for her meal. Most of the men she dated insisted on meeting later for "drinks only". Things hadn't been much different during her last serious relationship in Boston. She dated Bennett for almost 2 years, at one point even thinking maybe he could have been the one for her. Looking back, things hadn't been as serious for him as they had been for her. Bennett never seemed to make time for her, saying he was "working late" or "meeting up with friends".

In reality, he had been seeing someone else the entire time they had been dating. Iris had known the breakup was coming in the end, it wasn't too hard to notice that his priorities were elsewhere. Eventually she caught him texting the other women and broke it off. The conversation lasted a total of five minutes. She hadn't been all that heartbroken considering they barely saw each other most months but it stung all the same. The group chat she maintained with her girlfriends from Boston remained relentless in their questions about her dating life-even while in Shelburne. Iris was almost sad to be so lackluster in that arena.

"I'm not fifteen anymore Riss. I can cook just about anything. You don't get this far without getting in your protein," Ren said, bringing her out of her memories of the past. "And I would learn to make anything, but you have to ask. Maybe even beg."

Iris felt like this was a challenge, and her empty stomach couldn't handle it.

"Right. Those lunchables you'd make from scratch after school weren't always too bad... Well, I won't get in the way here. I guess I'll just order some takeout tonight."

"I'm sorry we didn't ask if you wanted to eat with us! I just smelled that aroma and couldn't resist when he put a plate in front of me!" Sage responded in honest innocence.

"Did your date not buy you dinner? That's just tacky if you ask me." Ren cocked his head to the side like he was about to ask more questions about her non-existent date.

Iris couldn't take the emotional sparring between them tonight, not when she was already feeling so raw. She found she didn't even have the energy to come up with a sarcastic reply.

"I didn't have a date tonight. Not unless you count Jim from the hardware store. I haven't had a proper date in a while actually. I'm going to head upstairs for the night. Sage, I'll see you tomorrow morning to go over the plans for our stand at the fall festival."

Iris was careful not to run upstairs too fast, Sage would surely know something was wrong if she did. She closed the door softly and slid down until she was sitting with her knees to her chest. Tears silently started falling down her cheeks. She let herself ruminate in old abandonment issues, just for the night. Being back home was still harder than expected, coming at her like an insurmountable wave. Despite years of therapy and constantly repeating "I am enough" she still had days that she felt so useless... so weak. Memories flooded to the surface. Iris, alone at school with no friends. Countless times where she was the last student picked for sports while the other kids whined about having to play with her. Her dad leaving one night and never looking back. Eating alone at home on nights that she couldn't stay over at Sage's house. Ren making fun of her on the nights she was able to stay at their house for dinner. Bennett standing her up on all the dates they had planned. No one wanted her around.

It's fine. I've always been better off alone.

Wiping the tears from her eyes, Iris tried to slow her breathing. Maybe she shouldn't be here. Sage definitely knows what she's doing and it's obvious now that her and Ren were incapable of getting along. He was probably downstairs right now thinking up new ways to sabotage her plans.

They would likely just end up ruining Sage's dream.

They didn't need her.

Things would be better without her here.

Iris squared her shoulders and got up from the ground. There was no need for her to be dramatic about this. She would never forgive herself for ruining Sage's dream just because she and Ren couldn't stand one another.

Iris went into the guest room closet, grabbed her suitcase, and threw it on the bed to start packing. Sage would understand once she explained it to her. Ren was her brother. The company he worked for was even giving her a huge discounted price on the construction. Sage needed Ren more than she needed her. Besides, they would have made a third portion if they wanted her around right? Or had being away from her hometown chipped away at her ties more than she wanted to admit?

All she had to do was make it to the fall festival in two short weeks. She had already signed her and Sage up for the caramel apple making booth so they could start to get the word out about the antique shop. Then she would head home to Boston.

CHAPTER 11

Ren

"I cannot believe Sage talked her way out of running the caramel apple stand again this year. You do know she comes up with a different excuse every year right? What was it last year....her nails were too pretty? Or was it that she just got a massage and 'couldn't give up the zen vibes'? Oh wait I know! She wouldn't allow her blowout to get ruined by the wind."

Emmett had been rambling on and on about Sage all morning. So yeah, she had definitely cornered Ren this morning and guilted him into taking over the stand with Iris but what was he supposed to do? He had never been able to say no to her even when they were kids. All she had to do was stare up at him, eyes wide, like he hung the moon and he was done for.

Today was no different. One big eyed puppy dog like look from Sage and he found himself running the caramel apple stand at the fall festival tonight. Sage had also taken it upon herself to sign up Emmett to be the volunteer in the dunk tank, hence why his oldest friend hadn't shut up about how terrible his little sister is for the last hour. He was sick of hearing him talk about his sister. They saw each other almost every day, so what was there to talk about?

Ren couldn't piece together if it was odd or just considerate. The foursome had been working together on Vintage Vixen over the past two weeks, with Iris growing quieter by the day. He attempted to probe Sage, but she refused to give details. Ever since they made plans without her for dinner, she's been closed off. She even dropped most of her battles with him, and he missed the fire coming from her directly. Iris was a powerhouse when she was on a project, even if she was keeping her head down. It was amazing to see her work through the most miniscule detail, bringing every one of Sage's visions to life on the drawing boards and for the opening day timeline. Had either of them said 'thank you'? He wasn't so sure. Ren needed to do something-and fast- to grab her attention once more.

"Oh come on man, like you aren't a little bit excited to see all the women at the fair drooling over you once they see you soaking wet. I bet you even bought yourself a white shirt didn't you?"

"That is besides the point."

Judging by the fact Emmett wouldn't look him in the eye, he assumed he had been right.

He would never admit it, but he was actually looking forward to running the stand with Iris. She had been unusually quiet this morning. He thought they had been back to their old ways when she dumped water on him two weeks ago. Truth be told, he had been impressed when she pulled it off. It had been years since they messed with one another and he hadn't thought they would ever get close enough to start again. He had expected her to be smug the next time he saw her after her perfectly executed water dump, but he noticed something had changed over the last two weeks.

Ren honestly hadn't expected Iris to come home. He had assumed she would be on a date, I mean it had been friday night and Iris was - well fine he could admit it... gorgeous. She had always been beautiful growing up but since she got back into town he couldn't stop himself from staring at her. And apparently, neither could the other men in town. In a weak moment he had even told a group of men at the bar that she was married just to shut them up. In his defense, they were hockey players so she could do much better.

Not that he cared.

He had definitely been surprised to see her show up at the house when he made dinner for Sage and himself. She seemed so quiet and defeated when she entered. In all the years he'd known Iris, he had never seen that look in her eyes. The usual defiant gleam was gone, replaced by a lonely, lifeless gaze.

Sage had noticed it as well, and told him to "make it right or else". Which, for his sister, was basically a death threat.

The problem was, he had no idea what he'd done or how to make it right. He just knew he would do just about anything to never see that look in her eye again. If that started with helping her at the caramel apple stand, so be it.

"By the way - the boys at the office looked over Iris's proposal for the shop. It's very good. Can't say I was surprised though, she's always been incredible at what she does," Emmett said with brother-ly affection.

"Yeah, she has. Glad you all approve. I heard Jordan was doing a good job of running point. Why do you bring it up?" Ren side-eyed Emmett. He pretended not to care, even though his heart was pounding out of his chest.

"Sure, well, right. It's just when I looked over the contract, I noticed an email address that was strange. Jordan's name was attached to the correspondence, but when I went to his office, he wasn't in. I know he's been doing some work from home days, so I called him to touch base. He's so self-sufficient I hadn't bothered before. I'd like to know why he was in fucking Texas, telling me you sent him there," Emmett shot him a piercing look. "And even more, it looks like Iris has been corresponding with this... Jordan imposter for over a month. Jordan said you held a private 'emergency meeting', and told him to take over the office building project in Austin. I heard you even labeled it a pro-motion. You wouldn't happen to know anything about this would you?"

Emmett wasn't always the most serious guy, but he had definitely been collecting evidence. Ren was allowed to be autonomous in his own company, but it was a miracle it took this long for Emmett to notice Jordan was MIA from the office.

Shit.

Busted.

How was he supposed to tell his best friend, and coworker, that he was the one behind that email address? It had started out harmless. He had just needed a way to hear about Iris's plans for his sister's shop before she came back to Shelburne, and there was no way in hell she would have responded if she knew it was him. Ren intercepted the communication after Jordan's first email exchange with Iris. He convinced himself he simply believed in Jordan as an employee, so he sent him away with a promotion. It wasn't out of jealousy or anything. He needed a pulse on Sage's project from the start, so Ren used a generic company email that was usually used for log-ins and spam.

Besides, her ideas had been incredible. He had been so mesmerized by her work and reviewing her recent portfolio, he couldn't stop himself from keeping up the facade while they messaged back and forth. He often found himself staring at his phone waiting for her replies to come through just to see what else that beautiful mind of hers had come up with.

He only sent back massive revisions when it made sense for the structural integrity of the store. He attempted to set up a meeting with her to explain the revisions, but after the dinner she felt rejected from, she just accepted them and moved on without a fight.

Iris's ideas from August jump started the project and allowed him to approve the demo a month early. He should have known he could never keep things strictly professional between them though.

Soon it became less about business and more personal. Iris was witty, sassy, and downright adorable even through emails. He had been finding new ways to spark up conversations with her everyday.

Yes - it was wrong. He knew deep down that it was wrong. There was a part of his brain that tried to tell him to stop every time he hit send, but the demon on his shoulder was louder.

"That's weird. I'll check it out. Maybe it was a scammer or something." Ren tried to keep his voice even. Emmett could always tell when he was lying.

"That's the thing - I already did. Do you think a scammer would give demo approval and have that slip by you? Turns out it is coming from one of the computers in our office. Yours."

Ren looked up, cringing. Damn. He really couldn't lie his way through this one. "Fuck. Me," he responded in exasperation.

"Look, man. It's not my place to get involved in whatever the hell is going on here. I just hope you know what you're doing for Sage's sake. That's her best friend and we all know Iris has been through enough. Just please tell me this isn't another one of your pranks you used to pull on her."

"It's not. I swear it's nothing like that. I just knew she wouldn't have responded if it had been me asking about the project. I needed a way in. Plus - you're right, that's my sister and it should be none of your business." Ren attempted to joke to lighten the mood.

"Do not hurt her, Ren." Emmett was shockingly serious as he responded. Staring down at Ren despite the fact that they were basically the same height. As intimidating as this was, Ren couldn't help but feel proud of how protective his friend was over Iris.

"I will never hurt her again," he said, making a promise he wasn't sure he could keep.

"Good. Let's finish loading this shit up and get to the damn Fall Festival." Emmett said, hauling a crate full of apples into the back of the truck. "Don't say shit about what I have to change into."

CHAPTER 12

Iris

"Yeah buddy right... over... there" the Bride of Frankenstein said to the Count as he hauled five dozen apples out of the back of the truck. Iris couldn't help herself but stare at Ren's triceps as he did all of the heavy lifting. The vampire costume was way too tight for him and she could clearly see the tag still on the coat. Leave it to Ren to purchase a costume the day of the event. Iris was happy that he was uncomfortable, but also that the eye candy was stronger than the sugar rush she'd get from the caramel apples.

I think this guy is going to be the death of me, Iris mused. *The least he could do is suck me dry with the fake teeth he was struggling to put in.*

"Where can I put these down, Bride?" Ren said in a shitty Transylvanian accent, trying to flip his cape out of the way. The lisping on the "s's" from his fake fangs made it hard for Iris to stay mad consistently. She was sour over the past two weeks, but her friends and singular enemy were wearing her down without trying. Iris had been working in overdrive so she could manage everything else from her cozy apartment back in Beacon Hill. She just hadn't mustered the courage to tell anyone of the plan yet.

Iris pointed out a spot underneath their booth that had room for all of the apples and supplies until they were ready. They seemed to be falling into an appreciable rhythm. Especially considering he and

Emmett washed and stuck the stick through all 200 apples. Since the local bakery, Batter Together, decided to go a different route this year with a bake sale-styled table, Sage sweet-talked her way into getting vats of caramel and toppings for customers.

Iris' marketing strategy would go perfectly tonight. Sage couldn't caramel an apple to save her life and because Ren was the self-proclaimed chef of the family, it was decided Sage would walk around passing out fliers instead as Stevie Nicks. Iris worked on the graphics for them so late the other night, she could hear Ren making the couch squeak with his tossing and turning. They included the date of the shop's grand opening and the activities they would have to really get some buzz going.

Sage had also managed to rope Emmett into tonight's festivities, apparently he was her official flier-holder, because she "simply couldn't be bothered with holding all of them herself". Emmett made a joke about being her personal security for the first 2 hours of the event, up until his shift at the Dunk Tank. Iris had definitely caught her best friend's eyes twinkling for a moment, but who wouldn't with the mental image of Emmett in an all black fitted suit holding back the crowd with one hand while protectively holding onto you with the other.

While the burly lumberjack wasn't her type, she could still appreciate the appeal.

The festival was now in full swing. Children and adults alike rushed in at exactly 4:00 PM when it opened and the lines hadn't stopped since. As she and Ren worked side by side for the next hour organizing supplies, she noticed his hips and hands found reasons to brush up against her on more than one occasion.

Do I like this? Why do I like this? Is it okay to even like this?

Shaking her head at her own confusion, she felt herself looking around for her Frankenstein. Jordan was the one who brought up the idea of meeting with couples costumes, and although he didn't explicitly say he would be showing up tonight, she thought the most romantic gesture would be to show up as her counterpart. Once again, she was disappointed by the lack of stitches she found on passerby face paint.

Just another sign that she wasn't meant to be here.

Iris hoped Ren didn't notice her growing unease. He started heating up the caramel in the contraption provided by the bakery. After a few weird noises, the warmer roared to life. Ren dumped in the chunks of caramel and started stirring with his sleeves pulled up. Iris watched as the tendons in his forearms strained against the resistance.

Ren swiped his finger on the inside of the bowl and held it out to Iris.

"Can you give this a go for me? Wanna make sure it tastes right," Ren coaxed.

As if she were under a spell, Iris took a small step toward him and wrapped her mouth around the tip of his finger. She closed her eyes for one brief second, smelling his skin and the taste of gooey caramel wrapped around it. She sucked the drop off, using her bottom row of teeth to scrape off what was left.

"It's perfect," she nearly whispered in response. Her voice was unintentionally breathy and her cheeks flushed.

"Hmmm... Such a good girl, thanks for the help," Ren said as he continued to stir the pot.

If she thought her cheeks were flushed before, now they were on fire. Clearing her throat, Iris spun around to avoid looking at Ren's stupid handsome face. As she did, her thighs rubbed together creating the perfect friction and getting her even more worked up. She could feel how wet she was. Her mind wandered, imagining all the other scenarios Ren might call her a good girl.

God, what the fuck is wrong with me? Did I just willingly suck Ren's finger? That's not the only thing I'd mind putting my mouth around.

Iris's thoughts remained in the gutter as she remembered him that night on the couch with no blanket in sight.

With a deep breath, Iris forced her mind out of the gutter. Daydreaming about undressing her arch nemesis wasn't on the to-do list around toddlers and folks from out of town.

Sunset came almost as quickly as the hundreds of festival-goers came onto the grounds.

Iris couldn't believe how many people showed up compared to the last time she was an attendee.

"You ready for this, Riss?" Ren said.

"You bet," Iris said, still shaking off what just happened.

She'd rather deal with hundreds of 10-year-olds than confront her heart racing and the dampness between her thighs.

She and Ren worked together like they never had before. She would hand him the blank caramel apples, and he would create caramel apple masterpieces for each person. He sprinkled chocolate chips and sprinkles on one for Michael Meyers and dusted some cinnamon on another for Barbie on rollerblades. When a teenage "Say Anything" John Cusack approached, Iris noticed Ren doused more than enough crushed up Oreo bits onto the apple. Iris started laughing at the site of these two talking about their favorite store bought cookie, and the 80s flick.

When the young actor walked away with what appeared to be Molly Ringwald, Ren turned to slide his arm around Iris' waist.

"I love when you do that," he said.

"Do what?" she said, trying to refocus on the task at hand.

She was momentarily distracted as he rubbed his thumb on the side of her waist and said, "Laugh. I love hearing it. I'm sorry for not making it happen more often when we were younger."

In near disbelief, Iris took off her apron to walk away.

What the fuck was she doing? It was one thing to mentally undress him in the safety of her mind, but to actually lean into him while his skillful hands danced over her waist was completely unacceptable. Frankly, she was too turned on to handle it.

At this point, she couldn't figure out who she would be disappointing the most.

"Just need to see how Sage is doing while Emmett's getting dunked," Iris nodded near the massive dunk tank. She wanted to know why a huge crowd of grown women started corralling.

Wasn't this usually the chance for elementary school kids to laugh at whatever willing victim the dunk tank claimed for charity?

Iris noticed Sage at the edge of the crowd going over the flier with Jim and Dolly. Dolly must have gossip to offer from tonight's festivities. She looked up just in time to see a small Peter Pan nailing the bullseye, sending what appeared to be AquaMan into the depths below. She jogged over to the small group to see what was happening.

"Oh god-I didn't know there was a costume involved," Iris clutched her chest in mock horror.

"Let's just say he's getting something in return," Sage replied quickly.

Ah, so she caved on getting a barn door on the back office. Emmett kept bugging her the past week about it, saying how much nicer it would look.

Just then with a roar, a soaking-wet Emmett, leaned out the side donning a green and blue sparkly merman tail, and with no surprise to anyone, zero shirt.

"Hey Riss, only $1 to see me get wet," Emmett winked playfully.

"I think you have enough offers from the looks of it," she replied while pointing to the line of twenty or so women of all ages lining up for their turn.

Iris heard Ren calling her name as the line for their own booth was starting to form again, and she departed from her all-too-brief break.

As the hours went by, they settled back into an easy rhythm. The smell of kettle corn started to make her stomach growl.

"Hey there, I can't let you get hangry. That'll end badly for everyone involved. We only have a few apples left, so let's pack up a little early to see if we can snag some shitty fair food that we'll regret in the morning," Ren said.

Iris was too hungry to argue or scold herself for spending any more time with Ren tonight.

"Honestly you read my mind! Let's do it!"

"Two nachos, one churro, a large pretzel, and a Coke please," Ren said approaching a concessions stand.

"Damn how'd you know what I wanted?"

"Oh you think I've never been privy to your sleep over messes? Who do you think cleaned up melted cheese in the mornings during your 8th grade summer?" Ren laughed.

"Come to think of it, we did think it was weird that things were always cleaned up when we woke up in the morning. Guess we just assumed it was your parents or some magical fairy that came in overnight."

"Magical fairy, at your service." Ren smirked.

They finished the rest of their food in silence. Just as Iris was about to suggest they head back to the apple stand something caught her eye.

"OH MY GOD. How did I not know this was here?"

"...The ferris wheel? Not sure Riss, it's here every year, remember?"

"I cannot believe I forgot about this!" Checking her watch, she realized the festival was about to close. "Shit. Looks like I missed my chance. Bummer, that was my favorite ride growing up." Iris had never told anyone why she went on the ferris wheel every year but she found herself continuing.

"My favorite part was always when they would stop you at the very top. You could see the whole town from up there, you know? I remember seeing it for the first time and realizing how small and insignificant our town looked. Back then, everyone had an opinion about me." Her eyes were still trailing over the giant ferris wheel in front of her but she could feel Ren looking her way. Something about having his attention gave her the strength to continue.

"I was the strange kid who only had two friends, one being a stuffed animal. Or the little girl whose dad up and left one day without saying goodbye. Everyone had made up their mind about me in town. But up there - I could be anyone I wanted. I was actually on that ferris wheel when I decided to leave Shelburne and go to college in Boston."

She was still staring up at the ferris wheel deep in thought when she realized Ren had left.

So much for us sharing things with each other.

She tore her eyes away from the top of the ferris wheel to find where Ren had run off to. Knowing him, he probably just couldn't stand to hear the reminder of how weird she was as a kid.

After a minute of scanning the crowd, she found him. To her surprise, he was in front of the ferris wheel talking to the guy in charge of running it. She watched him reach into his pocket and pulled out what looked to be a twenty dollar bill. Next thing she knew, he was waving her over with a smile on his face.

"Hurry up! We only have five minutes but he said he would keep it open for one last ride." Ren said when she walked up.

"Wow. I can't believe you made this happen. Really, Ren, thank you," She said as they climbed into the cabin seat. It was just the two of them on the ride so the boarding process took seconds and then they were being swept up into the air. She felt her eyes blur when the ride stopped as they were exactly at the top.

"So you were listening," she said in disbelief.

"I've always listened. Now shhhh... I am trying to enjoy the view." Ren said with an amused grin and winked. Iris flushed and tore her eyes away trying to shift her focus back on the stars.

They spent the rest of the ride in comfortable silence, Iris only glancing over to scan the crowd for her Frankenstein. More than once, she felt Ren staring at her rather than the sky. The attention was making her squirm but she refused to give in and look at him no matter how badly she wanted to turn around to meet his gaze.

"Looking for someone?" Ren asked casually.

"Oh, um, no. I guess not anymore," Iris trailed off, trying to hide disappointment.

The air at the top of the ferris wheel was crisp and clean. Iris felt lighter than she did in months. For a moment, she could forget about the sting of rejection from Jordan and every other guy from before. Up above, she was too elevated to be bogged down with real life down below. As the ride stopped and her feet touched solid ground, she found it even harder to look at Ren to acknowledge that they had to drive back home together. They were about to look for Emmett and Sage until Iris got a text from Sage saying "Might crash at Emmett's, we have a lot of ideas to talk over after everyone we ran into tonight" and immediately after "BTW-Ren isn't allowed to stay in my bed tonight just because I'm gone- I literally just changed the sheets". Ren got a text from Emmett that he wouldn't reveal to Iris.

She wondered if he sensed something was off in the short drive back to the Anders residence, when Ren switched on a playlist that was a suspicious blend of her favorites- 90s pop and what sounded like tracks from the 10 Things I Hate About You soundtrack. She never thought she'd hear every lyric of "I Want You To Want Me" perfectly sung by Ren Anders.

"I knew I could make you smile," he said, sounding lighter than ever.

Iris and Ren walked up the porch steps and simultaneously went for the front door handle. The porch light wasn't working, making it darker than usual. There was a glow from the light on in the kitchen, so they worked together in order to get the door open. Ren kept bumping Iris' hip out of the way, making a mockery of being a gentleman. She laughed again despite herself, so tired she was delusional enough to imagine herself being bridal carried across the threshold.

Once inside, Ren went to the cabinet near the TV stand where the extra linen was held to make up his bed. He bent over to pull the sheet to one of the sides and groaned loudly.

"Hey are you okay? You look... creaky?"

"Yeah," he grunted, "My back has actually been killing me sleeping out here but it's okay"

"I mean you're Mr. Owner, why don't you just get a hotel or a long term airbnb while your house is being rented out?"

"That adds up and I like being close, knowing my sister is safe if I'm down here by the door... Well both of you guys," he added quickly.

"Oh... Um... well can I bring you some extra pillows?"

"Sure, I'd like that actually thank you," he said, the tips of his ears reddening.

Since when does Ren Anders give a shit about my safety? I woke up to a dead bird in my bed on Christmas morning when I was in 6th grade. I told him I was going to ask for a pair of binoculars to go birding because I saw a documentary, and there was a note attached that said "FOUND ONE FOR YA".

Iris winced at the memory of the prank, and quickly went up the stairs to see what extra pillows and blankets she had to attempt to cushion the couch more. As if on cue, the extras she never used were down pillows filled to the brim with plush feathers. Because of him, whenever she saw a luxurious pillow, she dreamt of dead fowl. She ran back down the stairs with the extras in hand, shaking her head at what a sorry sleeping state it really was.

She caught Ren sitting with his face in his hands. He had managed to de-fang himself, but the rest of the outfit remained.

She was a few steps above him on the stairs still so they were eye-to-eye.

Iris huffed, "Can we just call a truce?"

"What do you mean?" he asked blankly.

"Maybe I'm tired of being mad. I had a really nice night with you and I want to keep working toward having a better relationship... for Sage," Iris said, wringing her hands together.

Ren lit up "Yes of course I want that too, thank you, Riss. I need this chance. The chance to show you who I really am."

CHAPTER 13

Ren

Standing this close to her was dangerous for his health. How had he never before noticed her eyes could glow with want? No- not just an olive color like he originally thought, he found a ring of hazel at the very edge with scattered specks of gold.

Beautiful.

He allowed himself one second to let his eyes travel down Iris's body. He hadn't been able to keep his eyes off of her on the ferris wheel. Up there, it felt like they were the only two people in the world. But every time she looked down at the crowd, he knew who she was searching for. His cock strained with jealousy against his black slacks.

Why did I have to make myself more appealing on paper?

From this angle, Ren was finally going to get Iris to look him in the eye. They had been dancing around each other all night. Everytime he thought he was close to getting a moment alone with her, someone ruined it by coming over to their stand to buy a caramel apple. And on the off chance no one was at the stand, Iris had run away to find Sage. Even now, she wasn't looking at him.

Instead, she was staring down at her ridiculous high heeled boots she insisted on wearing to complete her Bride of Frankenstein look tonight. He had been about to make fun of her earlier when she had walked down wearing a jet black beehive wig, but then he got a full view of how incredible that outfit made her breasts look. He was pretty sure half of the customers tonight only came to the stand to get a glimpse of Iris in that corset top. Even with heels, he towered over her, walking the line between respectfully looking down her cleavage and throwing her over his shoulder all night.

"Iris, look at me." Ren grabbed her chin lightly, his eyes darkening. "I am not the same asshole you knew years ago. I need you to know that."

Tightening his hold on her chin, he stared into Iris' eyes. He needed her to understand how serious he was at this moment. This wasn't just some lame truce, it was a promise. He would never hurt her again.

"Okay," she said, giving into him.

Ren thought he heard a slight tremble in her voice as she responded but he made sure her eyes never left his.

"Good." Ren responded.

The air shifted. He realized they were still staring at one another after a few moments and started walking up the steps, needing to be closer to her more than he needed air. Every step he advanced, Iris responded by backing up one.

Lucky for her, he loved this game.

He untied his cape, and tossed it down the steps.

She tossed her wig, and shook out her hair.

He slowly unbuttoned his white shirt.

She pulled off her satin white gloves.

They met each other's challenge until they were fully upstairs and she was flush against the guest bedroom door. His posture was predatory, and he needed her. Now.

It was as if he was under a spell. Her striking green eyes bore into him. For once, they weren't full of mistrust and fear. Iris was staring up, almost pleading, with a need matching his own. His cock was so hard it was pressing painfully against his zipper. He resisted the urge to reach down and start stroking it.

This close to her, he was immediately hit with a floral scent. Hints of lavender and jasmine, making it feel like you were waking up on the first spring morning,

Ren placed his left hand on the door frame, caging her in and angled his body closer. He snaked his right hand around her slender waist, and pulled her tightly to him. Ren started to gently tug at the tie holding her corset together. Before he could register what was happening, he was leaning in further and placing his forehead on hers.

Just this once. I can give in, just this one time.

His fingers traced the side of her face, outlining her jaw up around her ears to the back of her neck. Grabbing a fist full of her hair, he tugged just hard enough to hear her gasp as he forced her head where he wanted it.

Her plush lips were inches from his. He could almost taste the sweet sounds she was making. His cock strained as he imagined how perfect they would look wrapped around him, choking on it as he fucked her mouth.

"Iris."

Her breath grazed his lips ever so lightly as she shakily responded, "Ren."

"Are you going to be a good girl and close this gap? Or am I going to be fucking my hand to the thought of those perfect lips all night?"

He could see the internal war going on in her head. Iris was never one to give up on a challenge.

Seconds ticked by with only the sounds of their heavy breathing.

Finally, Iris tipped her chin slightly, their lips now centimeters apart. Ren fought the urge to say fuck it and take control. This needed to be her choice.

He watched in utter fascination as Iris blew out a shaky breath, her mouth making the perfect "o" and he was once again imagining how perfect she would look on her knees for him.

But when his eyes traveled back up to hers, he knew she had made her choice.

"Wow! Look at the time, I need to get to bed!"

She immediately dipped out from under him, twisted the door handle, and ran inside the room.

Shit. Is that her suitcase? Why is it packed?

Did he just try to kiss her? What was wrong with him, they had just called a truce two seconds ago and he was already messing things up.

Way to ruin the best night you two have ever had together. Dick.

Running his hands through his hair, he took a moment to collect himself before walking back down the steps and into the living room. He had to physically stop himself from banging his head against the wall in embarrassment. He looked at the tossed garments scattering the living room floor and felt embarrassed by the animal that took over. Although, the more he thought about it, didn't Iris angle her head up to him? Didn't she squeeze her thighs together when he called her a good girl? Could she have been feeling the same way? Was she as into that moment as he was even though she apparently had one foot out of the door?

It was too much to hope for. He had ruined his chances with her years ago.

Even as he tried to convince himself, a plan was forming in his mind.

I'm going to make sure she stays.

CHAPTER 14

Iris

Come on Iris, don't be a pussy, Iris pointed at herself in the mirror. Iris worked off all of the Franken-makeup with her trusty micellar water, scolding herself.

She was an adult. Adults do adult things. She will not be embarrassed by how wet she was getting while Ren advanced on her. Or how she had almost moaned when the words good girl left his lips. Besides, she guessed he had to have been sleeping poorly on that old couch. Good girls share. Iris paced back and forth in her room for the next hour, her mind spiraling over the possibilities. She took out her clothes from her suitcase, hung them back up, and then put some of it back in all within the hour.

She could either be a good friend, and not want to make out with her best friend's brother, or she could be a bad friend and give in to what she'd been feeling since they got home.

How was she still turned on hours later?

By the time she worked up the courage to resume what they had started, when she creaked open the door, all of the lights were off downstairs.

Fuck. Too late. Maybe this is for the best.

Three hours went by, and Iris continued to toss and turn, not fully entering REM. She decided to start her nighttime routine which usu ally included getting a glass of water. Too tired to think, she opened her door and was shocked to find Ren already at her door.

"Jesus, Ren! It's 3AM, why are you at my door?"

"It's 3AM, why are you still awake?"

"Why are YOU still awake?"

Iris knew they were dancing around why insomnia took them away for the night. There's no way she would give in first.

"Well, I was just going to try to get another pillow," he said, rubbing his lower back dramatically wincing in pain.

"Oh really? Because I gave you all I had to spare."

Ren looked behind the fussed up bed, noticing only one small pillow left for herself. He kept glancing between her and the bed, and she couldn't tell if he was interested in her or the mattress. Maybe both. Unable to bear his pathetic glances, Iris caved quicker than anticipated.

"Fine. You're invited in, Dracula," she swept her hand behind her, too tired to argue.

Ren took a dramatic step inside, getting close enough to her face to catch early-morning breath. She noticed him glancing around, his eyes landing on her now-empty purple hardshell suitcase shoved in the corner.

"I'll grab my stuff and be right back," Ren said confidently before backing up and racing down the steps.

She was still standing in the same spot when he came sprinting back up the stairs, so fast it was like he thought she would take back the offer if he took too long.

"I swear I will never take you for granted ever again, baby" Ren said, petting the mattress.

"Do you two need a moment alone?"

"Nope, all done. Just giving her the love she deserves."

"Okay well take those pillows and line them up between us so we don't fight in our sleep," she said.

"Is that what you think we'd do in our sleep? Interesting," he said, patting her side of the bed, encouraging her to get in. "I'll sneak up here at night after Sage goes to bed, and leave early in the morning. She won't notice a thing," he yawned.

Before Iris could agree or disagree with his idea for a new sleeping arrangement, Ren was snoring like the baby he was right next to her. Too delirious to care, Iris pretended it was a white noise machine and drifted off to sleep.

CHAPTER 15

Iris

Iris woke up with her best friend's brother next to her.

First, she thought, *I can't believe this is happening to me.*

Next, came *Is he inching closer in his sleep or am I making this up?*

Even sleep deprived, she knew Ren would fight her for the bathroom. She griped under her breath "There is no fucking way this is happening, especially when it's my turn for first shower". Just as she attempted to slink away, a warm and toned arm came across her chest and pulled her to him.

Ohhh so this is it. This is how he takes me out. At least death by suffocation is kind of kinky. And his smell, oh god how does his cologne from the day before get to mix with his natural body odor? So unfair.

Iris was stuck. Stuck between wanting to actually feel the warmth of a man in the morning and desperately needing to get away to shower and brush away her morning breath. She gave herself a small countdown in her head to allow herself a few more seconds of peace before they were at each other's throats again.

Ten... Nine... Eight... Seven... Six... Five... Four... Three... Two... Deep breath... One.

In a flash she tossed the arm off of her and looked back just in time to see him wake up confused and searching for her, only to find a pillow in her place.

She turned the shower to the hottest possible setting, and started to shirk off the oversized tee and jersey shorts she slept in, leaving the sports bra and underwear on while she brushed her teeth. She thought the extra layer of protection was overkill until she turned around to see him leering at her in the bathroom doorway in only his gray boxers.

"Jesus Christ, Ren, you scared me! I thought you were still asleep, and it's my turn for the first shower anyway".

"Are you sure about that?"

"Well yeah I'm sure that you were asleep a minute ago and I'm sure you need to get out of this bathroom."

"If I recall, you took two showers yesterday, one in the morning and one after your midday run that you go on and tell no one about."

"How did you know I took a shower then? You weren't even home."

"Sage isn't the only one who has access to her security system."

"Okay whatever, stalker. I hate that you're trying to check up on me, but if you would kindly back up so I can let the steam actually build, that would be great," Iris went to grab the door in the hopes of hitting his pinky toe.

"You just left me in bed," he interrupted the door shutting with the palm of his hand and a frown on his face. Not the kind of frown a child gives you when they dropped their ice cream, the kind of sleepy disappointment that only comes with being blue-balled in the morning.

"Yeah well you tried to trap me and suffocate me, which is creative, but I'm still here sorry to say," Iris made her best effort at shoving him back until he grabbed both of her hands in one of his.

"There are plenty of ways I can suffocate you, holding you in bed is not one of them," Ren said as he backed her into the bathroom and closed the door behind him. He slowly turned her around by her shoulders so her back was to the door, and he slid his hand up her chest, ever so gently under her neck. They locked eyes as he gently squeezed, not quite cutting off airflow.

He tilted her chin upwards and she felt speechless for the first time in her life.

She watched, completely shocked, as he slowly descended on her like he had all the time in the world. Heart rate spiking dangerously high as he touched his lips to hers. Her breath caught. She was at war with herself, wanting to pull away but instead found her hands traveling to the waistband of his boxers. That thin elastic band was the only barrier, she fought the urge to pull them down with her teeth. He added the most perfect pressure sensing her decision to not back down from this, and his tongue coaxing the slit of her mouth open. Forcing his way into her with need. She felt his anger, his frustration. It was her fuel.

This has to be what an out of body experience feels like. Did he kill me? Am I actually dead?

The kiss turned from kind and tentative to outright aggressive when he lifted her onto the bathroom counter wrapping one hand around the back of her neck to hold her in place. The other gripped her thigh to angle her hips so her core was directly against his quickly growing bulge. Ren's kiss was brutal, forcing her to follow his lead in every way. His grip on her thigh was bruising. His hand on her neck controlling her movements, completely in control.

Feverishly, she increased their tempo, desperate to keep up with him.

Was this what a kiss was supposed to feel like?

She forced her lips off his for a second to catch her breath and then bit his lip before meeting his waiting mouth again. Needing to feel closer, she dug her hands into his hair and pulled hard. He moaned and responded by grabbing her waist and pulling her flush to his chest. Her hardened nipples brushed against his solid chest through her bra, creating the perfect amount of friction. She whimpered, pressing herself even closer and clawing her nails down his down his back as he moaned into her mouth.

Had she ever even heard a man moan before? She didn't think she had been more turned on in her life. Instinctively, she wrapped her legs around his waist, pulling him in. That was a mistake. She could feel his abs pressed up against her, and she fought the desire to lean down and lick them. She needed.... Something. Anything. More. Yes, she needed more. A breathy whimper escaped when started to grind her hips against him, feeling a rather impressive bulge against her core.

Conflicting visions of years of her talking shit about him directly to Sage, him laughing at her on the ground, and the idea of him coming to help his sister for nearly no money flooded her thoughts as he pulled away first.

"So greedy, Iris. Just like you are with this shower," Ren breathed a laugh, cutting off the moment. The steam from the shower coated their skin, and Iris remembered where she was. In one swift movement he took her off of the counter, and shoved her out of the door with a pat on her ass to send her on her way.

Iris couldn't tell whether she should be offended or laugh. Staring into the abyss at the incredulity, she chuckled to herself, and hid in the bed, sheets pulled over her face until he left for the day.

CHAPTER 16

Iris

Iris took a long-awaited sip of the coffee that was left for her on the counter. She crept down the steps tentatively, after her nose caught a whiff of the freshly ground beans.

Sage must have slipped in and out this morning.

Iris was instantly grateful Sage didn't catch her with her brother this morning. She wasn't caffeinated enough for a conversation like that, and she didn't have any answers anyway.

Wait, where is Sage now? Did she even come home last night?

In a quick panic, she checked her friend's location and it looked like she was getting some morning grub from the diner. Anytime Sage drank too much hard cider, she'd make fast friends with whomever she was partying with, capping out the night at the diner. Nothing cured the girls' hangovers faster over the years than greasy potatoes and bacon.

Iris shot her a quick text goading,

> Stay out with Emmett for too long last night? Don't you remember how he drank you under the table with those apple-cider-tinis?

> Ugh please don't remind me. But yeah we got a lot of work done!

Sage responded a few minutes later.

Did you get enough sleep last night? I hope Ren wasn't too much of an ass about sticking with the couch still. I hate having to leave you two alone for too long

Oh fuck, her heart skipped a beat, *I didn't realize we were seen leaving together.*

Yeah he didn't try to come upstairs and kill me in my sleep, so that's a win.

I know you're working from home today, but you'll see me pop by to make coffee before heading back out into the world today. If you say one nice thing about my brother, maybe I'll make you a cup.

Iris stared at the mug in front of her and snapped a pic,

Didn't you make this?

I haven't been back to the house yet, goon. Besides, I never use whip, you know that. I'm still in my Stevie apparel from last night and I think I smell like incense? Emmett's was closer to the bar we all went to so I crashed there.

Iris had always figured if she pretended to not know how to use the coffee maker, Sage would inevitably brew a pot, and she would be the benefactor by an extra cup or two. She had only ever told a select few in her life that her guilty pleasure was a little whip to top it off...

Iris silently accepted Ren's olive branch, wondering if he had noticed her add the whip sometime since she's been back home.

Iris was caffeine-buzzed and out the door, taking off toward her favorite running route. She maintained her warm-up pace, shuffling through her running playlist and landing on Applause by Lady Gaga, needing to lean into some bad bitch energy. It was a pain to distract herself from her own thoughts after last night... and this morning. Getting her adrenaline up in other ways always proved to be effective. Between workouts and throwing herself into planning events, there was nothing Iris couldn't distract herself from.

She loved living in the northeast. Running outdoors through each season was one of the reasons she got into exercise to begin with. That and Sage would be the only person to show up to her track meets in high school. After her dirtbag of a father left because her mom's career had been "too much to handle", Sage would be in the stands holding signs that would say anything from "GO IRIS!" to "KICK ASS FIRST, ICE CREAM SECOND". She even walked with Sage on Senior Night because her mom had been working on a case she "had to see through".

The leaves changing with the seasons never got dull. Her hometown smelled like homemade apple cider and kettle corn in the festival aftermath. Boston was a clean city for being such a massive metropolitan area, but it never had the same level of charm as Shelburne. She hooked a left at the edge of the park to take her to Main Street. Iris jogged by the moms and dads running around in the park, looking tired but hopeful for their little ones. Iris mused that if she had to raise a child it wouldn't be here. Not enough opportunity. Besides, having a child meant having sex.

And having sex would involve having someone to have sex with, which was lacking as of late.

Iris tried to convince herself that the sweat started dripping off of her from the run, but she'd only been jogging at a moderate pace. Her legs pumped, rubbing together with every step needing to get back home.

CHAPTER 17

Iris

Iris walked through the door panting, needing to find a distraction. Or a release. She trudged up the steps on sore legs. Leaning onto the bathroom counter, she studied herself in the mirror, making sure nothing had outwardly changed. She felt different. Iris reached her hand into the shower and turned the water on high, excited for the cleanliness that she was denied by Ren. Stripping off her sports bra, leggings, and yoga thong, she hopped into the steaming hot water. Unable to tell if the heat was from the water or looking at where she was propped up on the sink too long, heat started to pool in her core.

Like a ghost, she felt his hand slide up her stomach, under her breast, taking time to softly scrape over both her nipples as he passed, and finally finding its place at her neck. Staring into his ocean blue eyes, she took two of his fingers and started to suck, needing to get them wet for what he was about to do. Not that he would need it. She started to drip by the time she crossed the entryway, pants about to soak through. She sucked for a second longer and pulled his hand down, down, down, to her sweet bundle of nerves.

Oh baby, I've been watching you. I know what you need. You can't begin to imagine what I've been wanting to do to you.

Her backside pressed up against that bulge, and he started to slide his fingers up and down firmly in between her folds. Her hips began to buck against his hand, silently pleading him to slide two fingers inside of her.

So greedy, Iris.

She snapped out of the fantasy to find her own fingers in between her legs. Alone but ashamed, she stopped her own pleasure.

Oh, this is so wrong. I will not masturbate to thoughts of Ren Anders.

She used her body scrub to attempt to wipe away the memory and mentally prepare for the meetings she had for the rest of the day.

Iris set out business casual clothes for her day. A pair of trusty jeans and a cream mock neck top. She didn't have enough time for an at-home blowout, so threw her hair back in a quick braid. Iris decided to take her calls from home today, instead of the busy park. After noticing how busy it was getting this morning, she knew she had no room to fuck around on her agenda.

She set up shop at the counter, just in time for Sage/Stevie Nicks to walk in the front door.

Too tired to make a "walk of shame" joke, Iris simply held out her cup of coffee saying "more please" with her bottom lip out as far as it would go.

"You're lucky you're so damn cute," Sage responded, making a fresh pot.

In her first hour, she finally managed to wrangle a caterer for the grand opening. She phoned in a favor to her favorite Boston catering company, and decided on an array of pastries and mini quiche. Iris wanted the fare to be served to be similar to what small menu items the coffee shop inside would carry. Eventually, Sage would find a more local vendor to support, but a former trusty vendor would have to work, as she knew the family who owned Batter Together would still be on winter vacation at the start of the year.

By the time that call concluded, Sage kissed her on the cheek on her way out saying "I'm off to help the Watersons refurbish that dresser! It's a massive sanding and staining effort so I'll be gone until dinner! I'll grab lobster rolls on the way home".

"Get three this time!" she half-joked to make sure she wasn't left out of dinner plans again, even though that had happened only once.

Iris loved how they took care of each other. Sage fed them, and Iris tidied up after her. It's a miracle either of them could do either, with only one semi-present mother between the two of them.

Iris refilled her reusable water bottle and stretched before her next call, still pent up. *Drinking more water will cool me down and keep me hydrated. Best of both worlds,* Iris attempted to convince herself. Before the call, she shot off an update to her group chat from Boston in an effort to offload the work-related side of her recent frustrations. She got messages of support, reminding her of her purpose here and powered through to the next call. She checked the time, and started the Zoom call turning on her audio and visual features. She didn't love doing things online, but sometimes it worked out better that way for both parties.

"Hi Joey, it's Iris," she chimed at the DJ she found on Instagram.

"Hey girl! Did you lock in a date?" he responded, his video already coming across with a short lag.

"Yes we did! January 1st, are you still free?" Iris was hoping to get through this call as quickly as possible. Not because she was anti-DJ, but because she had a new plan for her morning.

"Absolutely! Book it officially through my site, but I'll put it on the calendar. A mix of oldies and Top 40, right?"

"You got it! The crowd will be filled with people of all ages so we're going for generational appeasement with a hint of something we can shake our asses to," Iris chuckled, finding herself sitting forward in her chair more and more. The split seam of her jeans was hitting her clit just right.

"I hear you! I'll put together a suggested playlist and we can go from there. I'll send it to the email when you submit the form," he said jovially.

Not enough friction.

"Sounds good, thanks DJ Spinna," Iris concluded.

Finally.

If you had shitty music at an event, people would leave early. Or even worse, they wouldn't be enticed to walk in in the first place. After making a short list of personal requests to DJ Spinna, she slammed her laptop shut and moved to the couch. The next call wasn't for 30 minutes, which was plenty of time to finish what she started. The last call before lunch happened to be Ren and the paint team, and she'd be damned if she saw him, albeit over a video chat, without a clear head.

If I just give in to the fantasy one time, I'll be completely over it. One good fuck-or rather a good time with just me, myself, and I- and all of my problems will be solved. I'm a grown woman. One quick lapse of judgment will be okay. It's not like anyone is around to bother me.

Iris shrugged off her jeans, missing the tightness they caused while she was seated at the island barstool. She could already feel the pulse of her need. Iris had recently grown used to the cold silicone of her toy, but was too impatient to run upstairs to grab it from the bedside table.

Iris let her mind run free and mimicked what she wanted Ren to do to her this morning. She sucked the middle two fingers on her right hand, slipping them under her underwear, and in between slick folds. She pushed open her wetness using a "v" shape, pushing her clit between her fingers. Iris explored her body with her free hand by grazing her own breasts and pulling at her hair from the top. Iris wished Ren was here to put his massive hands all over, controlling her, taking what he wanted. She elicited a whimper from herself, knowing that making sound always turned her on.

Nothing fun about a shy girl unwilling to speak on her own pleasure.

Iris missed the feeling of his skin, the smell of him. She was in heat. No one would be home anytime soon, so she withdrew her fingers and pulled down her silky green panties. She was glad to be near his scent again. He was only in her bed one night, and it didn't linger like it did on the couch. The thrill of fucking herself in the middle of the living room wasn't lost on her, and she realized she needed this time to herself badly.

She could never let him know she was touching herself to the sheer thought of the tattoos showing through one of his white work shirts he'd always come home in.

A little sweaty, a little dirty. Iris kicked her left leg over the back of the couch, ready to give herself as much access as she needed. Why hurry up when all of this felt so fucking good? She was hungry for an orgasm, but was determined to draw it out as long as she could. She felt her ridges from the inside and curled her fingers on impulse, dragging them through her sex over and over. Panting and smiling alone, she would get close to pleasure and then deny herself. Close, and then deny.

"God Ren, what are you doing to me," she said out loud to no one in particular.

CHAPTER 18

Ren

"God, Riss, answer the phone, it's 11:30," Ren said under his breath.

He had an entire team of guys around him at the table, ready to finalize colors. He thought maybe she was regretting this morning, choosing to be petty and not answer the call instead of being a professional.

Now is not the time, baby. Be mad later. Answer me now. I'm getting worried.

"You know what boys, I'm going to give the shop owner a chat to see if she can get a hold of the Creative Director," Ren said nervously.

This crew was a massive client and Ren didn't want to fuck up the relationship because of one bad call. What they didn't know was that he already texted his sister, and she mentioned she was about to call the DJ when she left not too long ago. Sage had Iris's location placed inside of the house, so there was no reason to not answer unless she was sick in the bathroom or taking her call outside.

What he actually wanted to do was be a creep and check the security because it wasn't like her to not respond to anyone. Work was so important to her that she would go "camera off" on the toilet before declining a call.

He excused himself to figure out how to ensure her safety, but also maintain his own professional dignity. Fighting his own instinct to be a gentleman, Ren decided to be a dick and yell over the security camera to get her attention. Pulling up the app, he toggled to the one camera in the house which was in the kitchen.

He turned the sound on, prepared to whisper-yell "Answer the fucking phone before I spank you". Instead he heard... panting. And... his name.

What the fuck. Is she trying to call me while I'm trying to call her?

"God Ren, what are you doing to me," Ren heard faintly over the security camera.

Then, "Yes, just like that", and "Please more, just this once. Just this one time."

He could have sworn a minute went by before he heard "SHIT".

CHAPTER 19

Iris

Iris was writhing against her own fingers, making herself come harder than she ever had before. Desperately pumping them in and out, wanting the orgasm to last as long as possible, she started revving up for a second one. Grabbing her phone to pull up some erotica as outside source material, she screamed "SHIT!" as she looked at the time. 11:40. Ten entire minutes late to her meeting with Ren. 12 missed texts and 7 missed calls between Ren and Sage.

Ren:

These colors look great, thanks for putting this together, Riss   11:10 AM

Yo, you ready for this meeting or what?   11:10 AM

I want to talk about this morning, but I wanted to check in before our call...   11:15 AM

I need you to know I don't have any regrets... In fact... 11:20 AM

Okay. Talk soon, then.   11:25 AM

Hey, waiting on ya.   11:32 AM

Hang up with the DJ, he can't spin beats like me!   11:33 AM

Respectfully, where the fuck are you? Sage told me you were home!   11:37 AM

OH. I see you're busy. ;) No problem, I'll take care of this.   11:40 AM

Sage:

Ren asked where you were but I saw you were at the house.   11:32 AM

You good?   11:33 AM

Shit. Shit.

"SHIT!" Iris yelled again. She yanked on her clothes, and quickly tightened the braid that had gotten a little too loose for her liking. She was coming down from an orgasm of her own creation and Ren had been sending her messages the entire time, attempting to get her on the line.

"Hey Ren, sorry I'm late," she said, holding up a mug to her computer camera as if she had just brewed a fresh pot, reaching for any excuse possible.

"Oh no worries, I'm glad you came," She watched him give her a knowing smirk from her view of him on her phone.

"I was just telling the guys how you lost your internet connection. All of your messages back just got through to me," he said casually.

Smugness was dripping from his face and in her crashing down from the high she was on it took a little too long to register what he said.

I'm glad you came.

FUCK! He knew I was busy because

Iris looked up from her computer at the camera above the fridge, pointing directly at the living room, with a perfect view of the couch.

The rest of the call went by uneventfully, but she felt just as pent up as she did before it started.

CHAPTER 20

Iris

"God this thing is fucking heavy," Emmett said grunting, "Can I have candy now? It's Halloween and I deserve it after today!"

"You're here to lift heavy things, and if you're good we can even watch a movie tonight," Sage replied, clapping her hands in a "time to get a move on" sort of way.

"What movie?" He momentarily put down the side table to put his hands on his hips to address her, "I want to make sure the three of us have plans, because everyone else will be out."

"Scream- the first one. Billy is kind of hot," Sage giggled.

"That works! The original is the best. And make that candy a king size snickers bar!" Emmett lifted the side table once again.

Iris had yet to determine what pull Sage had over Emmett, but she suspected something was going on between the two of them. Emmett was a classic playboy, who was never tied down. And yet, he dropped everything to help the girls pick up and transport side tables.

"So these are actually going to go with that dresser for the Watersons I told you about a few days ago, Riss. They were incredibly hard to find, so I'm going to flip these for a massive profit. I'm going to use the extra cash to pay the rent a few months in advance, or put it in my savings. Haven't decided yet"

"You have a savings account? Imagine that," Iris snarked.

"Well there wasn't much in there... but now there will be!"

"Okay, as long as you don't spend it on that massive mirror I saw you eye last week," Iris chided. She threw herself into working with Sage on the store, avoiding Ren at all costs. He went back to sleeping on the couch the past two weeks after their encounter, and she wasn't sure if it was because of what she did on that couch, or if he silently agreed what happened was too weird. As always, there was more important work to be done, and worrying about Ren Anders was back on the bottom of her priority list.

"That mirror would look great behind the coffee bar, obviously." Sage gave her a mischievous smile as she added, "Or on my bedroom ceiling."

The girls sat and went back and forth like this for some time, watching Emmett quite literally do all of the heavy lifting into Sage's Jeep. There wasn't much they could do except admire his physique and say "a little to the left" and "here's a blanket so the corner doesn't get scratched up".

"Hey where's that annoying best friend of yours to help out?" Iris inquired.

"That asshole went back to Austin for a week to chat with Jordan Poulter," Emmett said quickly.

"Oh that's... interesting," Iris probed, "I thought Jordan was here? I just sent him the final paint colors that we're using."

"I mean, yeah, sure of course. He still is. It's just that... Ren is following up on a project he's heading out in Austin," Emmett said.

"In person? He flew all the way to Texas to... follow up? Wait- when will Jordan be back?"

She was growing incredulous that her main contact up and left in the middle of a project. And even more so that he stood her up at the fair because of it.

"Yup!" Emmett said dusting off his hands. "Where to, little Miss" he peered past Iris and asked Sage. He avoided Iris' second question like the plague. Iris threw up hands toward Sage, and Sage just shrugged and widened her eyes saying "Don't worry about it" without even speaking.

A few minutes later, they had finished harnessing the two side tables in the back of the Jeep. Sweaty, and a little hungry, they set off back to Sage's house to unload everything. She was surprised to hear that Sage had gone and picked him up this morning, seeing as now one of them would need to drop him at his apartment after he helped unload the monstrosities in Sage's car. For two little cute and dainty end tables, they sure were heavy. Or maybe she just really needed to start a lifting routine beyond her running regimen.

Iris resigned herself to listen to Sage and Emmett bicker back and forth for the next hour. Unsurprising, because he was basically a 6'5 real life mammoth, Emmett couldn't fit his legs into the back seat of the Jeep so Iris was stuck riding in the back.

"All I'm saying is you were lookin' a little out of breath today. Maybe you need to hit the gym more?" From this angle, she could see Sage smirking as she said it. She loved trying to get a rise out of him.

"Oh please. That was like lifting a toothpick."

Iris tuned them out and let her eyes wander. They were just passing through town, driving straight through main street. There was something that felt so right about small town main streets. Everything you could ever need, all on the same street, sold to you by people who undoubtedly knew you since you were a little kid. Lost in memories, a soft smile graced her face as they passed by Jim's Hardware store, Dolly's salon, the local grocery store, Cafe, bank, and finally the boutique clothing store run by Jared and Ulysses. All the buildings on main street looked the same on the outside but had their own uniqueness about them. Tall, two-story brick buildings, with large glass windows covering the entire front of the building, lined up one by one inviting you in.

The hardware store had a beautiful white awning with the store name on it. She chuckled, thinking that had to have been Dolly's idea, Jim would never want to make the store look more inviting. Dolly's salon was the only building on the street with any color, she had decided to paint the salons name right in front in huge pink letters. The local grocery store had tables set up outside showcasing the mouth watering produce for sale that day. Squinting, she could just see the boutique sign.

The boutique was the newest successful business on the block, having opened four years ago by Jared and his partner Ulysses. They had moved to town from New York City, saying they needed to get away from the vultures in the city but refused to give up on "proper clothing". She had to admit, even living in Boston for a few years hadn't prepared her for the clothing they sell. Beautiful designs of all sizes and styles line the store's walls. The boutique only sells unique, up and coming clothing designers so everything feels fresh and new. So far, they've been true to their word. The town's style had definitely stepped into the twenty-first century since the store opened.

As the drive through main street came to an end, Iris found her mind drifting back to Ren. That kiss had been life shattering. Iris had never, in all her years, been kissed like that. Ren had been in complete control, lifting her like she weighed next to nothing, keeping a tight hold on her neck like she would dare try to run away from that moment. What had surprised her the most was the passion. She had been kissed by plenty of men but she couldn't remember a single one that made her feel as connected to someone. She felt her cheeks heat when she thought about what she did after the kiss. She had mixed guilt, a combination of how she did it and the fact that she still had such a strong online connection with Jordan.

But had she ever had to stop work before because she was too distracted? She didn't think so. She definitely had never been late to a meeting before that moment. She felt humiliated.

I'm glad you came.

That statement had been replaying in her head for days. How could she have forgotten that Ren had access to the security camera? Her only hope was that he didn't hear her calling out his name when she came. She would never be able to live that down and he definitely did not need that boost to his ego.

Satan? Me here. I thought we agreed that it was supposed to be a one time thing? Despite how embarrassed she was, she still felt her nipples peak and her clit begin to pulse.

The whole point of the most embarrassing moment of her life had been to get it out of her system. One life-changing self induced climax, and she was supposed to be cured. Instead, it seems her mind latched onto the fantasy and now it was all she could think about two weeks later.

Her mind was running in overdrive creating new versions of her usual fantasies.

This morning, she had even woken up at the end of one. This time, Ren was on his knees in front of her, licking her clit while pumping two fingers in and out. He used his other hand to palm her ass for support, lapping at her juices. He only stopped to whisper "good girl" while she came. She was so turned on by the creativity that she had to finish the job in real life.

The fantasy was ridiculous for many reasons, the most important being that she had never even liked when men tried to eat her out. She was always so preoccupied with the things they were doing wrong down there to even finish. Yet, that devil in the back of her mind kept wondering if maybe Ren would be different. He had seemed to know exactly what he was doing during that kiss.

Down girl, she scolded herself.

Obviously, she just needed to get laid. By a stranger. Definitely not Ren. Or an online admirer.

She found herself thinking about her mysterious email admirer next. She had been sad to hear that Jordan was still in Austin. Part of her had hoped for a little short term romance while she was in town, and Jordan had seemed pretty into it when they last talked.

Being single the last six months was her choice. She had needed to clear her head and do some soul searching after her last train wreck of a breakup, but lately she had started to feel ready to get back out there in the dating world. Or at the very least get some action. She even wore the ridiculous bride of Frankenstein costume to the fall festival in hopes he would show up and sweep her off her feet. Maybe she misinterpreted? It is hard to tell what someone is thinking through emails. Come to think of it, she hadn't heard from him in a while.

Guess I'll just have to stick to my fantasies for a bit longer.

She was forced out of her own thoughts when they pulled up to the house. Unsurprisingly, Sage and Emmett were still bickering in the front seat. Emmett was saying something about how he could flip furniture faster and better than Sage. Sage had completely turned to the side in her seat so she was eye level with Emmett, talking animatedly with her hands about the "delicate process of furniture flipping" and "Emmett's massive hands couldn't possibly handle it". Emmett shocked everyone when he responded, "You have no idea what my massive hands can handle."

When was the last time she saw her best friend that worked up?

Interesting.

Deciding to leave them to their lovers quarrel, Iris hopped out of the jeep and walked inside the house to check some work emails. She hadn't lifted a finger when they went to pick up the tables so she doubted they would miss her for now.

Later that night, the threesome cozied up on the large living room couch at the Anders residence, watched Skeet Ulrich lick blood off of his fingers, and ate candy until Emmett got sugar drunk. The girls tossed a worn blanket over him as he fell asleep. The girls tiptoed up the stairs, and Iris hoped her own dreams wouldn't be haunted by the ghosts of bad decisions.

CHAPTER 21

Iris

One week later, the town of Shelburne was out of the Halloween hustle and bustle, and deep in the throes of Fall weather. Iris wrapped herself in a cozy cream sweater borrowed from Sage, and briefly made eye contact with Ren as he left the house for work. He hadn't given her more than a cursory glance since getting back from Austin, and she wasn't sure if she was grateful or pissed off.

She ignored the door shutting and scanned through a few emails from various businesses she had reached out to for the shop opening. After securing the DJ and bakery, she only had a few more vendors to secure. Luckily, her favorite bartender was available and willing to come from Boston for the event. Iris planned on having espresso martinis as a featured drink, so Sage requested both liquor and coffee. Beyond the specialty items, they planned to serve wine, champagne, and some local craft beers. She even squealed in delight when she read the response from her favorite and most trusted event caterer offering to make and send out custom signage for free. Everything was falling into place. Iris felt like she was finally breaking through the fog of Ren Anders, accomplishing task after task with ease and excitement.

The actual construction of the store seemed to be going smoothly as well. Emmett had mentioned today that the demo was officially complete and the team planned to start rebuilding walls and painting in the next few weeks. Iris had picked out the most beautiful emerald green color for some accent walls throughout the shop. She hoped it would compliment the re-stained wood of the antique pieces Sage planned to showcase.

Like she manifested it, an email from Jordan appeared on her screen. She allowed herself five minutes to freak out before she opened it.

To: Iris O'Conner
Subject: Asking forgiveness?
From: Management@ANewLeaf.com
Date: November 7th

Iris,

Sorry to have missed you at the fall festival. This project in Austin is taking up more time than I anticipated. I bet you looked incredible in whatever costume you decided to wear. I had planned to fly in on that day to surprise you in my Frankenstein costume, but something something came up with my family and then there was a massive set back in my Austin project. Hopefully I'll be able to make it back in time for the grand opening on New Year's.

Sorry again,

Jordan

She pushed down the lingering insecurity that she had been stood up, and Iris decided to give him one more chance. If he showed up for the grand opening, at the very least she'd get some answers. Was he just some overly friendly construction manager or has there been something going on between them? Her own indecisiveness made her queasy.

She responded before she had the chance to talk herself out of it.

To: Management@ANewLeaf.com
Re: Subject: Asking forgiveness?
From: Iris O'Conner
Date: November 7th

Hi Jordan,

I hope everything is okay with the site and your family. My father left when I was five so it was just my mom and I while I was growing up. If I hadn't met my best friend Sage around that time I honestly don't know how I would have made it through my childhood. Her family became somewhat of a second family to me. Sorry for oversharing, but I just wanted to say a festival isn't more important than family! (But yes, I still wore the Bride half of the costume, and yes, I looked incredible.)

Can't wait to meet you in person! I don't spend too much time at the shop right now since it's a construction zone, and I happen to like to keep my heels intact. Let me know if you end up finishing in Austin early, and I can meet you at the A New Leaf office.

Best,

Iris

CHAPTER 22

Iris

The next week went by without a hitch. Iris spent her days finalizing plans for the shop and meeting virtually with vendors for her other projects at work. With Ren leaving for Texas, it reset his need to sleep on the couch by the time he returned home. She had the bed back to herself, and she refused to allow herself to notice how large and cold it seemed without him. His smell was fading from the sheets with each passing day, and her mixed emotions remained.

Iris had been distracted by Jordan's emails all week. He typically took days to respond back to her, but this last week she had gotten multiple emails a day. Most had nothing to do with work. After she opened up about her family in her email, Jordan had started sharing his past. Turns out, they had a lot in common. Jordan had lost his mom unexpectedly when he was young, leaving him heartbroken. They had unexpectedly bonded over their tough childhoods and how they left their hometowns for college.

Iris wasn't getting her hopes up this time, though. He had yet to mention an end date on his Austin project, so they may never get a chance to meet in person before Sage's Grand Opening.

Deciding to play hooky, she gave herself the day off on a Friday to catch up on some things around the house, leaving room for an extended weekend. After allowing herself the pleasure to sleep in a bit, she took off on another morning run.

Feeling inspired by the season changing, Iris began opening the windows to crisp air when she returned to the Anders house. She threw up her hair, curls falling out regardless of her bobby pin attempts, threw on a baggy tee and boyshorts, and got to work. She dusted the living room bookshelves, amazed they hadn't toppled over with the weight of the texts they held. No one had pets which kept the overall dander to a minimum. Emmett's plea a few days prior asking them to get a dog for security led Iris to respond, "I heard Ren howling at the moon on Halloween".

Emmett responded by saying "Well, the renter's lease on his apartment will lapse on New Year's Eve, so you won't have to worry about howling for long."

Iris felt better having an organized area. She frequently picked up after Sage when she was done fucking around with whatever craft material she would get her hands on. Even the dining routine of Sage producing the healthiest, most organic dinners alongside the sweetest desserts, while Iris kept the house together really worked for them.

Maybe Sage would agree to a platonic marriage. She never snored during sleepovers, and she always smells good. Too bad neither of us are into women.

Iris's stray findings of the day included three nails on the ground, picture wire in the half-bath downstairs without a picture in sight, and a can of wood stain in the corner of the kitchen with the lid half-on. She went to vacuum, starting with the upstairs, and then worked her way back down.

Iris walked down the stairs with the vacuum, hearing it clunk behind her each step.

Sage is getting a cordless for Christmas.

Iris was a big believer of moving furniture out of the way to clean, intending to get all of the negative energy out from underneath the couch Ren spent so many nights on.

She immediately spotted a stray receipt when she nudged the couch.

Oof this might be for something Sage wants to return.

Iris uncrumpled the receipt, meaning to leave it on the counter for when she got home. She stopped in her tracks when she saw the contents. In a stupor, she left the vacuum running, almost letting it suck up the corner of the rug as she read:

Adult Frankenstein Costume x1. Adult Monster Wig x1. Face Paint: Green x1.

What.

The.

Fuck.

Iris hadn't told anyone about the matching costumes. Not even Sage. Judging by the fact this receipt was under Ren's makeshift bed, that could only leave one possible answer to the question swirling around in her head.

Iris didn't believe in coincidences, and she definitely didn't believe Ren would have just happened to get the exact matching couples costume to hers. Especially not weeks before he agreed to participate at the caramel apple booth.

No fucking way.

CHAPTER 23

Iris

Despite every prank, every annoyance, every flippant word Ren had sent her way over the years, she didn't think he would stoop that low.

What was the saying? When they go low we go lower? She hoped to god no one else was in on it. Maybe Emmett knew? I should have known better than to trust any man.

She'd been lied to.

Cheated on.

Strung along.

And now?

Catfished.

UGH! I can't believe how fucking stupid I am! I knew it was too good to be true.

Going back on her earlier decision to avoid social media investigation, she looked up "Jordan Poulter" to see if a Jordan Poulter even existed. Feeling a Regina George level of rage, she pushed open her laptop as if it were her own personal Burn Book.

Ren Anders is a fugly catfish who couldn't lock down a woman without pretending to be someone else.

Typing faster than she ever imagined, she found Jordan immediately. From the briefest search, she hurt her own damn feelings. His incredibly handsome face was plastered on the company website, and even his Instagram handle was public.

He's not even seeking work via LinkedIn because his current gig was just too good.

Looks like he actually does work for Ren and Emmett, and his current location is Austin. No wife or girlfriend or children that I can see... or at least any that he's claiming online.

Ren assumed another's identity to get close to her to what... think that she was actually worthy of a relationship? The entire idea is so disgusting. She wasn't sure if she was disgusted with herself for falling for it or if she was disgusted with him for going out of his way to do so.

Iris went back through her emails to see what signal she could have possibly missed. She scrolled meticulously, starting with the first interaction. It wasn't until a few emails in that she received something from "management@ANewLeaf.com". Her original messages were to and from Jordan Poulter. Even the email signatures were the same.

It seemed like Ren never had anything more important to do than ruining her life. She actually thought that he was trying to win her over, get back into her good graces. Now all Iris wanted to do was burn the sheets and the entire bed. And the house. And their office building. She'd put Ren on a pyre and shoot an arrow of fire into the haystack, cackling the whole way.

Iris could practically hear the bell chimes of the nunnery a few towns over. The Sound of Music soundtrack was whipping through her hair and being. Except, at the end, she would continue on with the whole convent thing and devote herself to a hot, possibly real dude named Jesus from the olden days.

Even he probably strung along Mary Magdalene.

With another heaving sigh, she slammed her laptop shut and slammed her head against the kitchen counter a few times. She opened her phone, locked it, and then opened it again. Her indecisiveness was out of control, not knowing if she should out him to everyone including his sister, or if she should plot revenge, one final time, before she left for good. No more weekend trips to Shelburne, her mom and Sage would have to visit her in Boston. She couldn't do this anymore.

Iris knew she had to run to clear her head before she made any rash decisions. She donned her bright green two piece spandex set with a black windbreaker and headed out the front door, thanking whatever god existed that she charged her headphones the night before. She would need it.

The sweaty redhead decided that her anger was going to be delivered first to Emmett Leif. If Sage was her partner in crime, then Emmett was most definitely Ren's. Without a contract binding her and Ren together, she was free to make whatever project decisions she wanted- effectively cutting Ren off from the project and her life.

She took a hot shower, threw on her favorite pair of jeans and a sweatshirt, and stole one old ass bike from the garage. Sage was gallivanting who knows where getting who knows what, and the rusty bike that they often shared in high school still had some air in the tires. Her legs were too tired to carry her after the run she took, so she took off in the direction of the office, squeaking along the entire way. While at a stop light in the bike lane, she took out her phone and started listening to one of her favorite murder mystery podcasts. Iris decided she really wanted to feel the rage and get into the mood.

Ten minutes later, she hopped off the bike and leaned it against the side of their office building. If she decided to commit double homicide, that would be the town's first crime in twenty years, so she assumed her bike would be safe.

She flung open the door, ready to rage, and noticed Emmett standing at the front desk showing someone around. She caught the ending bit of...

"...and Marjorie, please forward the latest Vintage Vixen documents to Jordan, we could use him while he's here this week to oversee the crew."

Iris was dumbstruck. The broad-shouldered man took the elderly secretary's hand in his and kissed the top of it.

"Miss me, Marge?" he said with a wink.

"Of course I did, you scoundrel," She said, returning the wink.

"Don't get too chummy again, he's going to have to go back to Austin eventually," Emmett responded with a chuckle.

"Well, I don't know man, I might end up sticking around longer if Marjorie will accept my marriage proposal," Jordan said, smiling goodnaturedly at the 75 year old grandmother of five.

"Oh Jordan, you know how to make an old gal blush!" Marjorie said, playfully putting a hand over her heart.

Iris had remained in the spot she had strutted into when she crossed the threshold of the office, watching the entire interaction like a creep.

There is a Jordan. And he's hot and real and not a liar. All of my boxes just got checked.

Both men turned around at the same time, clearly intending to walk out. Emmett and Iris' eyes locked. She found herself suddenly less pissed.

"Oh hello, Emmett, who is your new friend?" Iris attempted to keep the tightness out of her voice.

"Well I wouldn't say he's new... this is Jordan Poulter. What are you doing here, Riss?" Emmett said with a note of unease.

"Oh, just wanted to talk to you about a few of my latest proposals getting rejected," she said with clear double meaning.

"Pleased to finally meet you, Iris" Jordan said, "You must be the lovely planner who's helping coordinate Miss Ander's storefront opening? I'm sorry I had to pass the communication off after our first email, Ren insisted he take the project over for me. Then, he gave me a promotion that took me out to Austin. We just wrapped up the first phase, so here I am!" He had a fading tan and a blonde buzzcut that he ran his hand over a few times.

It was at that moment that all of the blood exited Emmett's body. She had never seen the behemoth so pale.

"Why, hello, yes I am," Iris took an extra step forward to close the gap between her and Jordan. She noted he had green eyes much like her own and a kind smile. "Pleased to meet you."

She shot a glance at Emmett, indicating she was onto something. They had people around, and she was too professional to cause a scene as much as she wanted to.

Iris extended her hand the rest of the distance, not breaking eye contact while shaking Jordan's hand. His calloused thumb brushed the back of her hand up and down, testing the waters. When she didn't flinch he just tilted his head and smiled down at her.

"Well you know, I'm about to head to lunch, would you like to join me? Emmett said he's busy hauling...?" he looked back to Emmett still frozen in place.

"A chaise lounge-a lounge that needs reupholstering, one of those fainting ones. Not that anyone will be passing out," Emmett responded suddenly alive. "I'm meeting with Sage, but actually maybe it's not that important. I am kind of hungry!" Emmett continued, rushing his words.

"Oh no, absolutely not, I think you have a furniture date with my best friend. Best not to keep her waiting, wouldn't want to be labeled a liar now would you?" Iris patted him on the shoulder, like a true younger sister who just won an argument in front of their parents.

"I don't have my car, would you be okay with walking downtown?" Jordan said with growing confidence.

"Sure! I'll just pick my bike up later. We can walk right onto Spruce Street, and grab something easy to eat. We'll swing by the shop first, though!" Iris said with perhaps a little too much enthusiasm.

Emmett shook his head in clear defeat. Iris knew he would be reporting back to Ren as soon as he got back into the truck.

Perfect.

Jordan hooked his arm around hers, and started up pleasantries beyond talk about work.

"If you live in Boston, how long will you be in town?"

"What's your favorite color?"

"What's your zodiac sign so I can know if we're compatible?"

Ah, so he's not just cheeky with Marjorie.

Clearly, the chemistry was there as they laughed all the way to the shop.

She unlocked the front door, hearing the pleasant jingle. Iris gave him the best tour she could manage, catching his crinkled eyes as he was admiring what was clearly beautiful work. She was so proud of everything she had set up so far with Sage, that she wasn't sure if the excitement was in meeting nice eye candy or if it came from herself organically.

After he took a look around and made some notes of his own, he asked if they could get pizza. Tony's was an in-and-out sort of shop that sold combos by the slice during the lunch rush hour. She toted him along the sidewalk, making sure to pass Dolly's shop. Did she just want to put on a show for everyone or was their hour-long interaction the start of something real? Which version of Jordan did she like more?

Jordan took her pizza, chip, and drink order, and proceeded to the counter to pay for the both of them. Iris's stomach rumbled, and she wasn't sure from which kind of hunger she was feeling. Getting caught up in a kiss with Ren was childish, and that wasn't what she was looking for. Iris supposed she wasn't looking for something long distance, albeit temporary, but here she was, lusting after the tall and sturdy colleague of Ren and Emmett's.

"So, when did you know you wanted to get into design?" he asked, biting into a slice of pepperoni.

"Well, design is really just... intentional structure right? I mean, if you are able to manipulate the environment around you, then you always know what you're getting yourself into. Sage, the owner, her mom died when we were younger, and my mom who was her best friend, couldn't control what happened, even though she's a doctor. I could never do something like that where I know too much. So I stick to making uncomfortable environments... more comfortable," Iris blushed.

Even though she knew that Jordan wasn't the same person in the e-mails, she couldn't stop herself from opening up.

"Wow, I'm so sorry to hear that. I didn't realize Ren lost his mom" he said, taking a long sip from his straw.

Hearing his name come out of Jordan's mouth felt wrong. It crushed the illusion shrouded over their day.

"Yeah they were a really close family. Things broke a part for a while and eventually got put back together in their own way. Sage is really looking forward to owning something of her own in this town," Iris said to bring the conversation to their mutual point of interest.

"Ah, so she doesn't own a home yet? I get it, the market is tough for people our age," he shrugged with understanding.

"Well, technically she does. Her parents left her and Ren their house in the will, but Ren choses to live in an apartment so she can have it for her projects and schemes. But, you know, she's always told me she doesn't consider the house to actually be hers," Iris admitted.

God, when did this conversation get so deep? Way to ruin the mood, Iris.

To her surprise, Jordan didn't seem put off by the heavy topic.

After finishing their meals, they decided to continue on a walk around downtown Shelburne. They passed the remaining shops on Spruce Street, down a few side streets, and before she knew what she was doing she realized she was steering him towards her favorite spot in town.

They quickly approached her secret spot. Down at the very end of town, where green grassy land met Lake Champlain, there's a bench hidden beneath a tree that looked out over the sparkling water. Iris sighed as she plopped down on the bench to take in the view.

"Wow," he nearly whispered, "I've lived here a long time, but I've never been to this spot."

She didn't look over at Jordan as he said it, she knew the magic and peace it brought.

"Sometimes I come here in the middle of my longer runs, just to feel some clarity," she said, taking a deep breath.

They sat there together, looking out at the view in a comfortable silence. She realized this was probably one of the best dates she had ever been on, so why didn't she feel excited about it? It felt more synergistic than romantic.

Iris jumped as Jordan put his arm around her behind the bench. She looked up at him, surprised to see how close his face was to her.

Oh shit. Is he about to kiss me? Do I want him to kiss me?

Her thoughts scrambled as Jordan leaned closer, now a breath away from her mouth. Could she really do this? On one hand, this had been a great afternoon and Jordan was one of the most attractive men she had ever met. On the other hand, would it be fair to do this when all thoughts led back to Ren?

Iris watched, in shock, as Jordan closed his eyes and leaned in to kiss her. Just as she was about to lean in, her hand shot out involuntarily to stop him.

"Jordan, I am so sorry. You can't kiss me," Iris said, hoping she knew what she was doing here. He was the wrong person to bring here.

"I apologize. I didn't mean to overstep. I must have misunderstood the situation," Jordan responded, blushing red. He quickly pulled his arm away from her shoulders.

"No. No, you didn't misunderstand. I had such a wonderful day with you," she said exasperated with herself.

"But?" He smiled back at her.

She blew out a breath. "But, it wouldn't be fair to kiss you when I'm thinking about someone else," she gave him a tight-lipped smile.

"Understood. You are a good person, Iris. Thank you for your honesty," He seemed a bit hurt, but not completely put off by her confession. "Can I ask, who? I can't imagine a man ruining his chance with a girl like you."

It was Iris's turn to blush.

Despite the awkward end to this day, Iris felt like she could trust Jordan. Plus, this did technically involve him in a way. She looked back up at his eyes, he looked truly interested in what she was saying.

Biting her lip, she internally said fuck it and told him everything. She told him about the original email they shared and how she had continued to respond and share personal information with him when she didn't realize someone else had taken over the account. She told him about her relationship with Ren growing up, how it had changed once she came back to town this year, and their steamy kiss. She even told him about how she found out it was Ren emailing her after Jordan got kicked off and her plan to storm into the office to confront Emmett today.

She felt lighter once she got it all off her chest.

"Wow. So Ren was a bully huh? Didn't see that one coming. I should definitely use this information to get another raise," Jordan chuckled, clearly trying to lighten the mood. She found herself laughing with him.

"Absolutely, a huge raise," she pulled her sweater tighter around herself.

"Okay, Iris. Now I'm invested. We can't let him get away with ruining my good name. What should we do to get revenge? " Jordan said, a mischievous glint in his eyes.

"No, I'm sorry. I can't let you get dragged into our shit. I can handle him," she said.

Jordan grabbed her hand lightly, running his thumb over her knuckles and said, "I know you can, but I want to help."

If she wasn't so confused with her feelings for Ren she could have seen herself falling for a man like Jordan. He was sweet, respectful, and he obviously didn't shy away from a prank.

"Are you sure you want to get involved?" she bit her lip.

"I don't offer to do anything I don't want to. Let me help," Jordan shifted on the bench to look at her fully. "What can we do to fuck with him?" She was silent as she thought. It had to be something that would make Ren angry and jealous without being too over the top. They did still have to work together on this project so they couldn't actually kill each other. She needed Ren to feel the way she did when she found out the man she was sharing personal information with was a lie.

Iris perked up on the bench. She knew just the thing to mess with him. Especially since Emmett had undoubtedly blabbed to him about her lunch with Jordan. She just hoped Jordan would go along with this without escalating anything to HR.

"Let's send a picture of us together to the groupchat with the boys and Sage," Iris giggled, already imagining how mad Ren would be when he saw it all the way in Austin with no way to get to them.

Jordan smiled back at her, seeming to understand why she wanted to do this. "Alright, let's make it a good one," he said, pulling her closer to him on the bench. Iris snapped the picture, smiling up at him on the bench like they truly were on a date. Once they were both satisfied with the picture, she pulled up her messages, selected their group chat, and sent it without a caption.

They continued that process for the rest of the day. Iris would take him to popular date spots around town, he would pull her close, they would smile up at each other, the camera would click and send. They visited Ulysses at his store, the ice cream shop, and the local park where he pushed her on the swings. Running around felt good, even if it was for revenge. By the time the sun set over the town, they had to have sent five or more photos to the group chat.

She didn't allow herself to look at any responses from the boys. She didn't need to look to know Ren was fuming. Sage had texted her separately with a simple "What the fuck? Who is that and where can I get one?"

Darkness descended on them as Iris walked Jordan back to the boutique hotel he was staying in downtown. Her cheeks hurt from smiling, and she felt so light.

It felt good to fight back. Knowing Ren had lied to her and Emmett had kept the secret from her cut deep. Despite everything Ren had done over the years, she had found herself starting to trust him over the last few weeks. He hadn't seemed like his brooding old self, and he even went out of his way to apologize to her. Maybe that's why finding out about this lie hurt more than the rest.

"Thank you for showing me around town today," Jordan leaned on a post by the entrance, arms crossed showcasing his bulging biceps. His eyes crinkled slightly as he smiled, "You sure you aren't on the market?"

This man. She wished she was more available, but despite how mad she was at him, she hadn't been able to stop herself from thinking about Ren all day. Everything they did, she wanted to do with Ren a hundred times over.

"I'm afraid so," she said, crinkling her nose.

"Damn," he let out a heavy sigh, "There aren't many girls like you out there, Iris. If anything changes, you know where to find me," Jordan said, giving her one last smile before heading into the lobby.

Iris reached into her pocket holding the receipt proving Ren's lie, rubbing it like a worry stone. She wanted to go back to Vintage Vixen to make sure she locked the door behind them earlier before heading home.

CHAPTER 24

Ren

Ren strode away from the diner on a work break midday that same Friday, sipping the current waitress/barista Jules's latest creation - a hot white chocolate mocha with peppermint drizzle. To Ren and Emmett's dismay, Jules had lost her job when the last coffee shop closed. Luckily, she stuck around to make the only innovative cups of coffee in town at the diner.

The last few times he visited Emmett, they kept trying to set her up with one of the girls on their construction crew in return for off-menu drinks she wasn't supposed to be making. She always declined, saying she had her own roster of gorgeous women. "Finally, some competition in this town!" Emmett would cheer, clinking iced coffees in the dead of winter. The boys secretly loved being Jules's guinea pig for the new flavors.

Ren was happy when he heard that Iris had taken the day off. He couldn't remember the last time she took some time for herself. He walked down Spruce Street, walking the long way to the office. He had on a bomber jacket with jeans and a beanie, finding himself perfectly comfortable against the November cold in Vermont.

What's she doing? Reading? Lounging? Binging some TV?

He was always wondering what she was up to, but too scared to text her all the same. The beginning of his week was filled with emails between "Jordan" and Iris, but she stopped responding this morning because of her day off. He took a sip, and his legs carried him on autopilot back to work.

Ren knew even though she had the weekends "off" with Sage, that still included them hounding for furniture that would match the interior of the shop. He even caught her with a sander in her hand a few days before he left for Austin. Iris was always looking at the big picture, and he found his chest tightening every time she mentioned missing Boston, no matter the reason.

His life changed the moment his lips touched hers. She was too soft, too perfect to ruin. He realized the blush he loved seeing so much also came with her arousal. Hearing her call his name out on the security camera might have been the second best moment of his life, and it happened hours after the first.

He teed up his attempts at repairing his relationship with Iris as Ren just as "Jordan" ditched her at the Fall Festival. He still couldn't believe how much of a pussy he had been. He fully intended to show up as Frankenstein, the perfect complement to his Bride and explain his fucked up thought process. But he backed out by choosing to be Count Dracula. The fair was too public, and he didn't think he could pull off what would be a massive confrontation from his breach of trust there. Instead, he tried to woo her in other ways.

He tried to seduce her rather than tell her the whole truth. He'd rather brush his hand over hers, while sharing a bottle of wine after work than admit he knew how she was feeling via email. His personal growth meant nothing in the ways that counted. He told himself he'd be different for her-better, but then his own path of self-destruction brought him right back to his sister's couch. After he got back from his trip to Austin, it was like pressing a reset button. It was completely unreasonable for her to share a bed with a liar, so he stole glances, and took his sheets and pillows back down to the couch instead of outing himself as Jordan.

Ren wasn't sure whether to declare his feelings to clear the air or to let her take the lead anymore. He wanted to fizzle what she had with Jordan and start fresh, but was in too deep.

His inner voice brought him the self loathing he was accustomed to as a teenager.

He walked into the office space, grateful for the warmth, and Marjorie stopped him.

"Hi honey, Jordan is back- did he tell you? The Austin project is done with the first phase so he'll be in town for the next week or so," Marjorie said passively.

The tip of Ren's nose went from being red from the cold to red from the heat that flooded his body.

What the fuck is he doing back? He was supposed to be there through the new year. I won't make it a permanent move if he's lucky.

"Oh, really? Go ahead and send him to my office in a few minutes, we'll have to catch up," he said coolly.

"Actually, he just left with Iris," she responded, clacking away at her keyboard.

"Excuse me? He left with Iris? Why was she here?" He knew his volume was too much, but he couldn't dampen it.

"She wanted to talk to Emmett, but then she met Jordan and it seems like they hit it off. They went to get lunch," she said. "Don't forget your next appointment" she said, and gestured to Ricky, the lead on his crew at Vintage Vixen who was seated in the waiting area.

"Be right with you, just give me a moment," he waved to Ricky.

Ren glanced down at his watch. He had exactly 5 minutes of alone time in his office before this meeting, and then he'd have to track them down. Jordan was too perfect of a guy to be left alone with Iris. She'd fall in love with him, and he'd never have a chance. Even though he'd had his chance for over a decade.

Ren's meeting went by, and he barely heard a word Ricky said. The progress seemed to be going along okay, but they were waiting on final approval from Iris on a few remaining paint color choices. He assured Ricky that he would follow up the following Monday, and shooed him off. Just then, a text came through on his phone in a group text between him, Iris, his sister, and Emmett.

What the fuck is this? Iris and Jordan. Together, taking a selfie on a fucking bench! Why are they on a bench?

He zoomed in on the background.

MY bench! Overlooking the water? This can't be happening.

Ren stormed out of his office, tossed his jacket back on, and told Marjorie to cancel the rest of his meetings that day, if he had any. His memory was hazy because his mind was filled with jealousy and possessiveness.

That's my fucking girl.

Ren walked out the front door of the office, and should have recognized the rusted yellow bike that was tilted against the side wall. He snatched it knowing Iris must have left it there, and biked to the spot he thought was a secret only to himself. He used to go there after his mom's cancer treatments just to find some solace in being alone. Looking out over the water cleared his head, and he didn't want to think about who's idea it was to go there. Ren was desperate to ruin their moment, the little devil inside of him always wanting what was his, even though he'd never claim it out loud.

By the time he rolled up to the bench they were on, they were already gone.

His phone chimed in his pocket. He quickly pulled it out, begging for another clue about Iris's whereabouts. Sure enough, another picture was sent, and his sister just had to say something about Jordan being hot. This time they were trying on clothes with Ulysses. He took the bike all the way back downtown, and of course, as soon as he approached they were gone.

"Hey, have you seen Iris with another dude? Kind of tall?" Ren said to Ulysses who was folding clothes when he walked into the clothing store.

"Yes! She and Jordan were just in here. He mentioned he needed a new jacket, so I went ahead and found him a sweater, jeans, a jacket, and a new beanie. You look like you could use one," Ulysses eyed Ren's worn expression. "You good?"

"Um, no, not really. Did they say where they were going next?"

"If she's lucky, back to his place!" Ulysses just laughed when Ren's jaw dropped.

Another text came through of them in the park, and he went.

He missed them again.

They were splitting a waffle cone in the next picture.

What the fuck is this?

Ren was nearly panicked. He lost. He lost at life, he lost something he didn't have to begin with. He was physically lost, because the cone was nondescript. Jordan won, and the guy didn't even know he was playing. He picked the closest ice cream shop, and he clearly chose wrong, because they weren't there.

He had felt defeated many times in his life, but this was one of the worst. He'd been trying to interrupt them for hours.

I'm such a fucking joke.

He walked the bike the rest of the way back to Vintage Vixen. He might as well make good on at least one thing for the day and check out the progress Ricky described.

Ren unlocked the door, and threw up his hands in exasperation. It looked like the paint got delivered, but the floors were still undone. The groundwork construction took longer than he anticipated.

CHAPTER 25

Ren

"YOU! What are you doing here?"

Ren turned at the sound.

"Well, hello Ri-" His words cut off abruptly as Iris entered the store in a fury, shoved him straight in the chest, and waved a receipt in his face.

"What the fuck is this?" She said her voice was confident but cracking.

"Ummm it looks like a crumpled up receipt? What are you doing here? Shouldn't you be on your date?" He didn't care how angry he sounded.

"Don't worry about me and Jordan. Read it. Out loud," Iris said, shoving the receipt in his hand.

She donned a gorgeous, makeupless face, freckles showing more than ever. Her thick red hair was tied up haphazardly, wearing a deep purple knitted sweater and jeans that hugged her frame just right.

"So beautiful when you're mad," Ren said darkly. "Alright let's take a look."

His heart sank.

The receipt.

I thought I tossed this.

"It's a receipt for a Halloween costume... a costume that looks like it was returned," Ren said, all blood rushing from his extremities to his vital organs. The adrenaline was kicking in, knowing she pieced it all together.

"Yes. A very specific receipt. To a costume I thought Jordan Poulter might be wearing that night," her voice quivered but eyes remained boring into him, "That wasn't Jordan at all! That was you. You son of a bitch. I poured my heart out in those emails. But you really got me, didn't you? You've been playing me this entire time, making me question what I actually feel for you," she seethed with every word, "I really thought things were different. I can't believe I missed you while you were in Austin, how fucking stupid am I?", she made an attempt to stomp away.

She only made it a few feet before Ren grabbed her wrist.

"Please, Riss, let's talk about this. I can explain this," he said, with tears filling up his eyes.

"Stop calling me 'Riss' and 'Baby' and all of it. I can't take it anymore. I was going to tell Emmett today, but I'll just tell you instead. I'm leaving in the morning. I'll come back for the opening and that's it. I am fucking done," she choked out through gritted teeth.

"I need you to listen, Bab-Iris, please I am begging you to stay. I need you here. We need to... to... go over the paint colors, and I know you need the coffee bar a certain particular way. I can't do it without you. Please," Ren sunk to his knees in front of her.

"Jesus Christ, get off your knees." She said, glaring down at him. He kept his knees planted in place, despite the sawdust and loose nails laying all around him.

"Get up, NOW, it's a Friday night and the people of Shelburne love to peer into windows," Iris huffed.

"Okay, fair point," Ren needed to pull it together.

"You should know I happened to have a lovely date with Jordan, so thanks for setting up that meeting. Come to think of it - best date I've ever had." Iris fired back at him, continuing the fight.

"Oh yes, I'm well aware. I fucking went to every stop you guys went to. I tried to interrupt you. I tried to stop you. I needed to explain and now he's involved and GOD I always do this-" Ren threw up his hands.

"You followed me? Why?"

"Because you were with someone else. I wasn't on that bench with you. He was, and I couldn't take it. I'll bring the bike back home, by the way," Ren gestured toward the bike, and the front tire was completely devoid of air.

"Great-your plan worked. You've stalked me into oblivion, and we still ended up at the same place at the same time. What could you possibly have to say for yourself?" she stood there defiantly.

CHAPTER 26

Ren
17 years old

Mom said it was gone, but it's back.

It's back.

He repeated it over and over again to himself. He was stuck in a cheap suit that didn't fit his growing shoulders. Sage rubbed his back as she sat next to him on their front steps. She almost took off her corsage, wanting to stay home with him. He knew he'd be ditching Riss, but he couldn't move off this step. His chest heaved, feeling like his world was caving in.

Ren found their mother's paperwork in their parents' room, when he went looking for a different tie in his dad's closet. The adult Anders gave up the house for the weekend, knowing it would be more fun for their kids and dates. They all grew up together so no "funny business" was expected. He didn't know what compelled him, but intuition told him to open the envelope. He had finally worked up the nerve to ask Iris to Prom. Emmett was going to take his little sister so that Iris would have a fellow freshman there. He planned the perfect night-Italian dinner pregame in the city, and cookies and cream ice cream for when they got home.

Now, the cancer had spread to her brain. "Mets" they called it. He always thought it was weird they equated the name of a great baseball team to an aggressive form of cancer.

He looked at his strong little sister through tears, "What are we going to do?"

"Well, we have two options. Wallow now, and continue until we figure out what's going on in this process. Or we can pretend you didn't read that and let her tell us when she's ready. She's keeping this from us for a reason. I'm so tired of being sad."

Sage's wisdom wasn't lost on him.

"Go if you want, I'm prepared to wallow. Riss barely wanted to go with me anyway."

"I'll go because as you can see," she spun around dramatically in the flowing purple satin gown, "I already put myself together."

"You guys should still go, and you'll even have a better time if I'm not there," Ren said.

"Well she won't be able to come because you have to be escorted by an upperclassman. Unlike you, I'll at least show Emmett some dignity and not stand him up. It's up to YOU to explain why you're being a crabby ass to Riss.

"I don't want to be around anyone, right now. I don't need to explain myself. She's always thought I was an ass anyway so I don't see the difference," Ren said, barely believing himself.

"I'm exhausted, Ren. I bought a nice dress and wanted to pretend for a few hours like life wasn't collapsing around us. But look at you, always shutting yourself off," she said indignantly, grabbing her purse. "You know what? Maybe Iris is too good for you. Wallow by yourself," she huffed and pulled up her dress stomping down the steps. "Good luck at UT Austin".

CHAPTER 27

Ren
Present Day

"I stood you up."

"No shit. I thought a knight in shining armor was out there for me. Someone who actually cared about my feelings but it was you the whole fucking time. I should have known it was too good to be true."

"No, not at the fair. Okay well yes at the fair as Jordan. But for Prom. I fucked up"

"Yeah Sage told me all about that. God, Ren. You know that my mom-my single mom-had to pick up extra shifts at the hospital to afford my dress, hair, and makeup? I stayed up all night waiting for.... Anyway. I've heard the story. You invited some buddies from lacrosse to ditch prom and threw a rager at the house. Sage had to stay the night with me instead. I've relived that night enough to know it like the back of my hand."

"No. You don't actually know," his eyes boring into her own.

"Yes, I actually do. Stop trying to fucking invalidate my experiences! You always think you have the upper hand. I was a stupid teenage girl then. I'm not her anymore. I'm used to liars and cheaters and-"

"Excuse me? Someone cheated on you?"

"That's what you care about right now? Are you so surprised I can't recognize an asshole after you conditioned me for years?"

"What's his name?"

"It doesn't matter."

He began to realize a distinct pattern of rage when it came to Iris' protection.

"His name is Dan and we dated for like 6 months... okay anyway-the point is that you left my little freshman heart damaged and unprotected after I put in so much time and effort getting ready. And then I was made fun of for it until I graduated!"

Ren was shaking his head the entire time. He had to stop her. He had to explain himself for the first time in a long time.

"What? You don't believe me? Can you say something... something productive? No jokes this time?"

She stood with her palms upright, yearning for an explanation.

"That was the night... the night we found out my mom's cancer had come back more aggressive than ever."

"That's not... That's not true. Prom was at the beginning of March, and we found...." she looked off to the side working out the timing. "The end of April... before you graduated."

"No. I found her report. It was lying on her bedside table and Sage and I kept it to ourselves. She hadn't made the decision to go into hospice or start aggressive treatment. She told everyone when you found out... but Sage and I... we knew the truth."

"She... I'm her best friend... she knew for two months and carried that with just you? Why didn't she tell me?" Iris clutched her chest like she couldn't breathe.

Ren stepped toward her, reaching out in case she needed a place to land.

"I asked her not to the day after prom. I drowned myself in alcohol that night and fucked up all around. I left her and mom. And you. I stood you up, then too. I am so, so sorry."

"Ren, I loved your mom too. She was like an aunt to me. A second mom. I can't even imagine how heartbreaking that had to have been for you and Sage. But that doesn't give you an excuse to go around treating your friends and family like shit. If you think I'm going to forgive you, you're crazier than I gave you credit for. You kissed me and then continued to be Jordan. I'm so incredibly sorry for the pain you must have been feeling then, but that hurt is still there. It might always be there," she said, shrinking in on herself.

"You opened up to Jordan more than you would have ever opened up to me. Everything that I told you was true. Everything," his eyes burned with anticipation, longing.

"I need to leave," she said, backing up, "I just can't be here... this is too much."

"Is it too much? Or are we just enough? I want to be so much more to you, as me. Not as Jordan," he said getting closer, her jasmine scent crashing into him.

"Jordan definitely isn't here. It's just you. And you're not even real," She said, inching back on the sawdust covered floor towards an exposed wall.

"Jordan was never here. It was always me. And I'm the realest thing you'll ever know," he breathed.

With the last foot between them, she tripped over a stack of baseboards that he hadn't noticed were hazardous placed in the room, getting her foot immediately stuck in a paint can.

In one quick motion, he grabbed her waist and hoisted her out of the paint can and into his body. He couldn't take one more second of distance, and his actions had to speak when words failed him.

Ren found his confidence again, and crashed his lips onto hers. She was stiff for only a moment before her hands found the back of his head in response. Iris was wrapping her leg around him, covering one side of his ass in sage green paint and giving him an unspoken second chance that he didn't deserve.

The paint that was now covering both of their legs, also now graced much of the floor.

Ren didn't give a shit about the mess. He'd take care of it himself before the crew came back on Monday. He gently pressed her against the back wall, letting his intuition about what she needed take over.

Oh, baby. If only you knew how much I've wanted this.

"You were never his," Ren said after biting her lower lip

"I was for a while..." she played.

Ren spanked her perfect bottom and laughed.

"Say you're mine, please. I will make everything up to you but say you're mine for right now."

"Not yet," she said, raising her eyebrows.

"Excuse me?" his eyes lit up at the challenge.

She just rolled her eyes and kissed him again. She held onto him like that for what could have been hours or days, not that it mattered. She made little motion to pause, giving him the chance to set her down. He looked down over her, wanting to protect her from everything that's ever hurt her. Himself included. Mustering up the most devilish smile, he picked her up once more just to lay her down, allowing himself to feel just an ounce of pressure against her. She needed to know exactly what she meant to him if she wasn't going to say he was his yet. Angry or not, she was perfect. Feeling the light pressure of nails scraping his back, he knew this was not the way he wanted her. Not fully, like this anyway.

She pulled away once, to catch her breath.

"I missed you. Where did you go?"

He knew she didn't mean physically, but instead meant where the kindness went. He used to make her snacks after school, carry her backpack, wanting to protect her from an early age. Losing his mom made him feel like if he got close to someone, he'd risk losing them too. He pulled away from Sage when he moved to Austin and she clawed her way back into his life, and against his better judgment she let him.

He knew looking at her now that Iris had clawed her way back too. Anger was no longer reflected in her eyes, only hope. It had been so long since he felt anything like that. Not since before his mom died. This perfect beautiful woman had saved him, and she didn't even realize it yet. A smile graced his lips as he responded, "I'm right here."

The ground became cold underneath them and he helped her up. She laughed that beautiful, bright laugh, and he let himself laugh along. Iris scanned him up and down after assessing herself, knowing they were completely fucked.

CHAPTER 28

Ren

Ren led Iris three stores down, ducking any glance from other pedestrians.

"Not that I don't want to show you off, but the paint is dragging the front of your sweater down, and you might need a new one," he said pulling up her sweater.

"What? I can't give a free show to the nice people of Shelburne?" she pulled it back down, showing off cleavage.

They had exactly ten minutes before Ulysses closed up shop. He grinned with that boyish charm, aiming it directly for Jared and Ulysses. The husbands were both behind the counter, looking like they just wrapped up with their last client of the day. Iris came in to shop with Sage several times since they opened, and even just last week to pick up a gorgeous white puffer jacket to keep her warm in the colder climate. Each time, they customized the shopping experience, taking measurements and asking questions to catch what styles the client was into lately. They belonged in the city, where their talents would be appreciated even more, but it was nice to have a place to get a nice outfit, even if Ren spent most of his days in work shirts and jeans.

"Well what kind of mess did you find yourselves in?" Jared said with a sigh.

"Oh honey, don't drip on the floor, the rug is new," Ulysses gestured toward the hem of Ren's sweats that Iris was still donning. "Welcome back so soon. I see you've found each other," Ulysses said with his eyebrows raised.

"Paint incident at the site," Iris broke through before Ren could spill his guts to the most fashionable folks in town.

"You struck me as a 90s girl using overalls to paint. Looks like I was wrong?" Jared said almost frustrated with himself, thinking he didn't know her vibe as well as he did.

"Usually, yes, but I was reviewing samples, and oopsie daisy there went an entire can," Iris said a little too loud, and a little too quickly.

"How about we get you into something a little more comfy-casual... and you, "he pointed to Ren, "you still need a rework top to bottom."

"I've always wanted to be styled by you guys, but we really only have a few minutes before you close. Got any jeans and a t-shirt combo around here?" Ren said, rubbing his neck already knowing the answer.

"Yeah... of course," Ulysses said, giving a full belly laugh. He got the dressing rooms prepped for them, already pulling clothes off the racks.

Ren walked out of the dressing room wearing a tan colored sweater, burnt orange slacks, and a gold chain.

Iris came out of the dressing room wearing skin tight jeans, an oversized band sweatshirt, and comfy platform sneakers. He thought she looked beautiful in comfortable things, because she was free to dance, move around, and do whatever she wanted.

"You look nice," he looked her up and down.

"You don't look half bad yourself. Who knew all it would take was a new wardrobe to make you somewhat tolerable. Should have made you come here years ago," Iris winked while not so subtly checking him out.

It did something to him. There had always been a...tension between them, but now, watching her practically eye-fucking him with unfiltered lust there seemed to be something more real and tangible going on. His cock strained in his new orange slacks and damn did it feel good.

Shit is this satin on the inside?

Checking to make sure the store owners were out of sight for the moment, Ren realized they had the dressing rooms to themselves. He couldn't resist getting one more moment alone with Iris, especially with her current lustful look and how amazing she looked in those tight jeans.

He stalked up to her in her dressing room and towered over her. Twirling a piece of her auburn locks between two fingers. He couldn't resist watching her squirm for a few seconds.

"So, before we leave our paint infumed bubble and go back to the real world I wanted to discuss something with you," Iris spoke first, staring up at him, there was a hint of doubt in her eyes now which didn't settle right with him.

"Does this discussion start with me backing you against that dressing room door and sliding those pretty little jeans off your body with my teeth?"

"Hey, I'm serious!" she swatted at him.

"So am I," he said into her ear.

Much to his dismay, she stepped back a few feet and said, "Look, I have no idea what is going on between us lately and I am guessing neither do you. That kiss was... Unexpected. And I'm not even sure if I want it to happen again. So, I think it would be best if we kept this "Thing" between us for the time being. I refuse to pull our friends into anything else between the two of us and Sage has enough going on as it is."

He bit his tongue before he could respond. He wanted to be angry at Iris for not seeing how perfect they were together, and he was angry about her plan, but he couldn't fault her for having doubts given their history. The last thing he wanted was to keep her a secret. She deserved to be worshiped every hour of every day. Especially after the taste he had gotten back in the store, how did she honestly think he could keep his hands off her? That little moan she made into his mouth had been his second coming. Still, he could play this little game of hers for a bit. He would need to get a little creative.

With a new plan developing in his mind, he resolved himself and said, "Okay, fine. For now. But baby, I think you're going to want that kiss to happen again. Oh- and I'll be coming back to bed."

She blushed bright red, spreading from her cheeks down to her neck and getting cut off by her oversized sweatshirt. Ren wanted to tear that sweatshirt off her so he could see how far it spread. He knew how much his words affected her. He also knew she secretly loved being called "baby".

Let the games begin.

CHAPTER 29

Ren

The following Monday, Ren walked Iris to the salon for her annual gossip session and haircut with Dolly. He wouldn't be surprised if Dolly managed to ruin Iris's whole "let's not tell anyone about us" plan in the first 10 minutes; that woman was like a minx when it came to pulling stories from people in this town.

Over the weekend, Iris was busy running around Vermont with Sage, and he was only able to sneak a kiss when they were unloading the Jeep together, and in bed when she let him. He could tell he wasn't fully forgiven, but he would put in however much work was required.

Ren decided to head to his makeshift office in the shop, which was just the back room that had been ripped down to its studs while they waited for the final decision on its layout. He had picked this spot for his office specifically because it would piss Iris off. This was her favorite room in the shop, he knew because he had overheard her telling Sage about it one night after they had gone upstairs to go to bed. Iris had been telling her this ridiculous plan for the room, wanting to tear down two load bearing walls to "create an open concept" for customers. Great idea, but physically impossible without causing the entire building to collapse. He still hadn't gotten the courage to break the news to her about it.

Twenty minutes later, he was still staring at the same sentence of an upcoming contract he was leading in Austin. His thoughts kept returning to how soft Iris's body had been when he lifted her out of the paint when wrapped her legs around him. Her feather soft lips. The little twitch she made when she needed him closer. The way her body fit perfectly against his. He could spend the rest of his life exploring her and it still wouldn't be long enough. His cock strained against his pants for the second time today. Fuck, what was this woman doing to him.

"Fuck it."

CHAPTER 30

Iris

The bell chimed when she walked into Dolly's salon announcing her arrival. She was excited to get to spend some time with someone she considered a friend. Dolly started doing her hair when she was five, only stopping when Iris moved away. Truth be told her hair had never been the same since she left. Her auburn curls never seemed to sit right with her new stylist in Boston, not to mention the price difference. Most of all, she missed the friendly chats. That thought stopped her in her tracks and made a little bead of sweat fall down her forehead.

Damnit. I've never been able to hide anything from this witch.

Her only hope was to keep her mouth shut about her morning and skip right over it. She would have to keep her busy with other gossip. Maybe her plans for the store, or how successful the apple stand had been at the fall festival this year. Oh! Maybe she could tell her about the time in tenth grade that she fell down the stairs and her skirt flipped up -

"Well, well, well. You look flushed my dear. Who have you been kissing?" Dolly said while motioning for Iris to sit down in the salon chair.

Shit.

"Oh, no one! No one at all!" she waved Dolly off.

"So you tripped and fell onto a man's face and smudged your lipstick? That's a new one. Even in my 60's I can still learn something new. Gonna have to tell Jim about this, maybe give it a try. Or was it a woman? You know I don't judge, honey." Dolly had started to section off her hair as she spoke.

"No! No! No kiss... Nothing exciting is going on with me." Iris could feel herself blushing. She only hoped Dolly would take pity on her and drop it.

"I can practically smell the lust on you like you're a walking sex shop," she said, fanning the air to really sell it.

There was no point lying to her. She would keep this up the entire appointment, and Iris really needed this haircut. She took one last pitying look at her split ends, sighed, and prepared herself for what she was able to say. Shit - this had to be a new record for her. *What had it been, two minutes and I was spilling my guts?*

Iris told her everything while she cut, washed, and blow dried her hair to perfection.

From the second Ren showed up and announced he was the lead contractor on the project, staying in Sage's house with them, Iris inviting him to sleep in bed with her, the surprising makeout in the bathroom, and finally the latest fight that turned intimate. She finished the story with a groan and hid her face in her hands. This was stupid. Saying it all out loud had reminded her how much history there was between her and Ren. There was no way they could get past everything they had done to each other and form a romantic relationship. Her spiraling thoughts were interrupted by Dolly throwing her curling iron into the air, jumping up from her chair, and clapping loudly. A loud crash sounded as the curling iron tumbled to the floor.

"Finally! I can't wait to tell Jim. Pretty sure he owes me $20, or maybe I had bet $50. I told him it was only a matter of time," Dolly did a short happy dance.

Her jaw snapped open, she wouldn't be surprised if it was on the floor at this point. Speechless, she watched Dolly pick up the discarded curling iron and plug it back in before she responded, "Excuse me?"

"Oh, come on. There was so much tension between you two growing up you would have to be a fool not to see it. And don't get me started on the way Ren was looking at you all night at the Fall Festival. I'm surprised you were able to keep your clothes on."

"Jesus, Dolly!"

"Hey - I'm 60, not dead. What, you think I married Jim strictly for his sparkling personality? That man bends me like a pretzel. Nothing to be ashamed of dear. With the looks Ren has been giving you I'm guessing he could do the same."

"This is by far the strangest conversation we have ever had and that is saying a lot. Remember when you had to talk me through what a UTI was? Yeah, this is worse." Iris couldn't look Dolly in the eye. Not after hearing more about Dolly and Jim's sex life than she ever wanted to know. How could she ever look Jim in the eyes? He was like her grandpa!

"Okay, okay. Sex talk aside, everyone in town knows Ren has been in love with you for years. He may have tried to hide it, or refused to acknowledge it for himself when he was younger but it was always there. I know how difficult he made your childhood so I know this has to be confusing for you. Tell me how you are feeling honey," Dolly said while sectioning her hair before starting to curl it.

This was the question that had been pinballing around her brain since the first time Ren kissed her. If she was being honest with herself, she had been questioning it long before the kiss. Ren seemed different this time. Mature, sure of himself even. When he told her about finding out about his mother's cancer relapse her heart had broken for that teenage boy she knew. That one piece of knowledge had been the puzzle piece that made everything else fit into place. It suddenly made sense why he had sabotaged their date to the dance, and why he seemed so defeated afterwards. After years of bullying and pranks, that dance was supposed to be their turning point. At least that is what she had thought when he asked her all those years ago.

Dolly was right about everything of course. Despite years of arguments, she had liked Ren all those years ago. She had even talked herself into thinking that she could put all the bullying aside if he had just showed up that night. But life has a way of laughing in your face when you want something really badly.

She couldn't let herself get that emotional and attached this time, knowing how it ended for her any other time she let herself believe she could trust someone.

"It's nothing, Dolly. Just a brief moment that we acted on. Nothing to write home about either."

Liar.

"Whatever you say dear," Dolly said with a wink. "Really is too bad. I had that boy pegged as one of those surprising possessive types. Guess I was wrong."

God - if only she knew. The way he had picked her up like she weighed nothing and grabbed her legs to wrap them around his waist. It was the hottest make out of her life. It even had her thinking about what other ways he could possess her body to do whatever he wanted. She had been so turned on she had *almost* given in and let herself say she was his.

"Guess you were wrong for once. Absolutely ordinary-" She started, hoping she was selling the outright lie she was telling but immediately slapped her mouth shut when the doorbell chimed.

What.

The.

Fuck.

Iris tried to school her expression as she watched Ren walk into the shop, knowing that Dolly was definitely watching her through the mirror in front of her. She purposely kept her eyes on his face, knowing if she would give herself away if she allowed herself to take in this new outfit. Between the cream sweater hugging his biceps and the orange slacks accentuating his lean legs and making him somehow appear even taller than he was, there was no way she would be able to keep her expression blank.

At least he waited until Dolly had styled my hair to perfection.

Ren strutted into the shop, his long strides eating up the distance between them in record time. Just as he got to her salon chair he stopped and said, "How are my two favorite girls today?"

"Well isn't this a surprise! Both of you in my salon on the same day. Ren, honey, did you come to finally get that mess on top of your head fixed? I told you last week you were due for a trim," Dolly huffed, reaching up to grab the longer strands of hair on his head. Truthfully, Iris liked his hair a little longer. It gave her something to hold onto when he was dominating her mouth on the walk over here. Not that she would *ever* admit that to Ren or Dolly.

"Unfortunately, I don't have time for that today. Just came in to remind Iris about the appointment we have tomorrow to go over the layout of the shop. She seemed a little distracted earlier."

"Wait... what? We don't have a meeting scheduled for tomorrow," she said distractedly while scrambling to find her planner in her ridiculously large bag. Honestly, why can you never find anything when you desperately need it.

Ahah! Found it.

She shoved the planner open, flipping through pages until she found the current week. Here it is! Monday, November 16th. A couple 30 minute check in's with some vendors in the morning, a video call with her boss over lunch, and then a quick check in with Sage at 3:00 PM.

"I don't have anything in here about a meeting. What did you say it was about again?" She said, never taking her eyes off her planner.

"The wall layout for the back room," Ren lifted her chin up, forcing her eyes up to his and winked at her.

Iris was tempted to call him out, feeling 99% sure Ren made up the so-called meeting on the spot, but she wouldn't let the opportunity to finally get him to listen to her about changing that wall layout go to waste so she played along. "Oh right, of course, that meeting. Must have forgotten to write it down. What time did you say it was again?" She smiled overly sweetly to really sell it.

"I believe we decided on 11:00. Don't be late," He said as he leaned in so his mouth was up against her ear. Iris felt herself shutter against him and goosebumps lined her arms. She was so mortified by her body's reaction she almost didn't hear him whisper, "Wear something you can get a little dirty, baby."

Her thighs clenched together and she felt a spark ignite between her legs. She fought the urge to rub her legs together to ease the friction. She was never more thankful for the salon cape that was draped over her body.

"Oh, almost forgot - this ones on me. Need to make sure my co-workers look presentable on the job," Ren said with an arrogant smirk as he backed up to the front door. "I'll stop by after work to pay," he yelled behind him as he sauntered out the door.

She knew before she even looked up that Dolly would be grinning from ear to ear. Gathering up some courage, she peaked up. Dolly looked like a kid in a candy store. Knowing her, she was probably scheming who she could tell this horrifying story to first. That conniving woman.

"Don't even think about it," Iris pointed her fingers in her face through the mirror as she snapped the pack buttons off the salon cape and stood up. She needed to get the hell out of here before this cunning witch wrung out any more information from her.

To her surprise, Dolly just made a "lock and throw away the key" motion over her lips and said, "Think about what?"

CHAPTER 31

Iris

The next morning went by smoothly, various vendors were successfully wrangled together for the hospital gala next month. The event plan for Vintage Vixen Espresso was mostly complete, all that was left were some small design details and charity donations. This morning Iris was able to finalize the catering menu, submit a draft of the floor plan and dance floor design, and obtain a $500,000 donation from a large technology company for one of her other projects in Boston all before before 9:00 am.

Feeling accomplished, she ran upstairs to start getting herself ready for this so-called "meeting" with Ren. She wouldn't be surprised if she showed up and he wasn't even there. He had been avoiding having this discussion with her for months. It's not so much that she wouldn't take no for an answer, it was just that she knew there had to be a way to get the layout exactly as she wanted it, some sort of beam or pole or whatever "support" buildings needed.

She settled on a simple yellow floral top, with dainty straps that tied into a bow at the top, and her favorite pair of jeans. Pulling up the weather app on her phone, she noticed it was supposed to be a little colder today so she added a black leather jacket giving the perfect combination between "girl next door" and "biker chick". Swiping a simple layer of mascara over her lashes and a quick dab of concealer, she looked herself over in the mirror. Feeling satisfied with her outfit, she slid on her favorite pair of chunky black leather boots and headed out the door.

It was mid-November, and fall seemed to be sticking to the air. There was a slight crisp chill but the sun was shining and warming her face when she walked outside. Deciding it was probably one of the last nice days before winter hit, Iris opted to walk the short distance to the shop instead of attempting to steal the Jeep. Her leisurely walk was interrupted by the shrill sound of her phone ringing. Looking down, she noticed the caller was a particularly persistent and annoying vendor.

Ugh, what does he want this time?

"Thomas- Hi, good morning. How can I help you today?"

"Iris! Oh thank god I caught you. I was just looking over the email you sent me and well... I think..."

Oh here we go, she thought. This was the third call this month, which was excessive considering all the company had to do was show up on time on the day of the event with 500 chairs. She was never hiring them again, that's for sure. Sighing to interrupt his babbling, she said, "Give it to me straight."

"Well, it appears someone mixed up the event date. Our schedule said January 4th not the 1st and umm... well... we already booked another event on the 1st, so we won't have enough chairs left over for the gala."

She could hear Thomas sputtering through the phone, likely with his boss standing right behind him making sure he got the job done. What kind of global event rental company didn't have enough inventory for two large scale events? She should have done more research before she hired them because their pricing was so great and she obviously hadn't been thinking clearly. She had been in this industry long enough to realize when a vendor was lying. They definitely had the inventory for two events, it was more likely that this guy gave her too good of a price and now the company wants her to void the contract so they don't have to lose a profit.

So much for charity.

Iris was only a few steps away from the shop and didn't have the energy to have this fight in front of a dozen construction workers so she put on her best "don't fuck with me" voice and said, "Well I'm just not understanding how you got the set up date wrong? I booked your company three months in advance and you are just now noticing this mix up? Actually it's fine I'll just call your manager later-" Iris shut up as soon as the vendor on the other line hung up.

See now would be the perfect time to have a 2000s flip phone where I could close it for dramatic flair.

Iris stopped in her tracks as she saw Ren standing in all of his Mr. Perfect glory- the tight t-shirt and newly green paint-splattered Levi's showcasing his toned frame and tan skin. Who knew a farmer's tan could be so hot?

"Where's Emmett? He said he had a few new guys he wanted to bring onto the project who could help me with the coffee bar layout." Iris got out as soon as she attempted to ignore him practically looming over her after passing the threshold.

"Emmett is meeting them at the office first to work out some logistics before doing a site viewing, so it's just me and you." He quipped, with a Cheshire-type grin.

Ren stalked toward her and locked the door behind her, getting a little too close to her ear as he passed. "We wouldn't want any nosy neighbors stealing plans for their own renovations now would we?"

She tried to ignore the chill down her spine that followed what he said.

"Well someone is awfully cocky considering this is just a small town store renovation," she said while looking everywhere except Ren's eyes in an attempt to hide the reaction she was having to his voice.

"I prefer the term 'confident', baby. Now come on-I need to show you the wall you won't shut up about in the back of the store," he gestured for her to follow him.

"Yes! Let's go look at that. Is your skull too thick to notice that I need certain things to complete the aesthetic here? You can't expect customers to get stuck in a maze while antiquing." This was her time to shine. Ren had been nothing but a pain in her ass about this stupid wall that he repeatedly states as being "load bearing", but how hard could it be to get rid of one tiny wall?

"I mean honestly Ren, if you're so successful, shouldn't you be able to take down this highly inconsequential wall?" Iris said, teasing him.

This room had always felt special to her. She lost count of the times she and Sage had snuck in the back of each store that came through here as they grew up. When it was a bakery, they took croissants and hot chocolate to the back table in the winter time. When it was a pool supply shop, the room was a dressing area to try on swimsuits during the summer. In another iteration, they helped to trim flower stems when it was a florist's workroom as a joint part-time job. Tiny in size, it was a snug 8' by 8' room, but with its location directly behind what will soon be the edge of the antique shop, it was the perfect place for a reading nook. That is, if Ren could get off his ass and remove the wall that was blocking one space from the other or else no one would know it existed.

"Okay great we made it to the room, now what do you need to show me that you couldn't have told me at the front of the shop? I have a date with a chicken salad sandwich at the deli that I can't be late for," Iris said as she looked at the newly demolished back office

Well, maybe he really is getting rid of the wall, she thought as she ran her hand along one of the wood beams.

"Now, you see, I needed you to see the wall to fully understand its importance," Ren said directly behind her. "Do you see this beam here?" he pointed at the wood beam directly to the left of her head and slowly ran his hands down her arm intertwining their fingers once they met.

"What are you doing Ren?" Iris failed to keep a bite to her tone, instead coming out raspy.

His hands came up to her shoulders, and shrugged her leather jacket off.

"This beam is supporting the entire roof of the shop. Without it, the roof would collapse," he whispered while sliding her hand up the beam and holding it above her head with his own.

Iris noticed goosebumps forming on her arms and instinctively turned around to face him. For one brief second while staring into his ocean blue eyes, she couldn't find a reason to not give into him.

"And this side of the beam over here? He quickly grabbed her right hand and placed it on the wooden beam above her head. The exposed wood lightly scratched her skin. "This beam right here is supporting the floor above us, without this, the entire attic could fall on us right now."

"Oh, I see," Iris whispered.

All thoughts had left her brain. Ren moved both of her hands together on the post directly behind her. She looked up, noticing something white in his hand a second too late as he expertly tied her hands to the post with a zip tie.

"And this post happens to be the most important one in the entire building, do you know why Iris?"

"No... No wait, why are my hands tied to exposed wood, Ren?"

"This post is the most important because it's about to be the only thing holding you up, Iris." Ren smirked as he gave her a chaste kiss and sank to his knees. He stared up at her while gently moving his hands up her legs. So slowly that Iris swore she was about to start shaking.

"What are you doing?" she said, her voice filling with need.

"Having lunch," looked up at her through thick eyelashes.

The second the words left his mouth it was like a flip had switched. There was nothing gentle about the way he popped open the buttons on her jeans and slid them off her body. All that was between her and Ren's mouth was her favorite polka dot underwear. She internally cursed, why on earth did she wear her most unflattering underwear today?

"Cute," he said while his fingers trailed lightly over the edges of her underwear.

Iris watched, panting, as they continued their assault trailing over her stomach, dipping only slightly under the fabric of the panties then moved back to her hips.

"I always loved seeing you in polka dots, but now I'm wondering if I would enjoy the sight even more if they were off," he said.

This was all too much. Ren's hands continued to explore, lightly touching her everywhere except where she desperately needed them to go. Legs shaking, she whimpered as her hips bucked.

Ren continued his leisurely pace, moving his hands up to her lace trimmed bra and squeezing her peaked nipples through her shirt all the while staring into her eyes.

An embarrassingly loud moan left her lips. Iris looked away, trying to focus on the sensations he was causing, and not trusting herself to not start begging to move his hands lower if she kept looking at him.

"Eyes on me, Iris. I'm starving and you're in your own way," he admonished gently.

In that same moment, he tugged the satin to the side and inhaled so deeply, it was like he was trying to memorize her scent.

"If you're good, and you stay still, and stay very, very quiet, no one will come knocking," he said seriously.

She couldn't even focus enough to be worried about someone coming in and seeing them when his tongue started teasing her. The slow torment continued as his tongue gently moved back and forth between her folds, completely ignoring the throbbing center she so desperately needed him to move to. With her hands tied above her head she couldn't even grab his hair to move him over to it. Iris clamped her mouth shut, refusing to allow a sound to escape to give away what he was doing to her.

"Tsk tsk. This is not going to work for me baby. I changed my mind, I need to hear you," Ren said while continuing his relentless assault.

Iris made the mistake of looking down at him while he said it.

From this angle she could see everything. Ren's hair was messy, and he was kneeling on the paint and sawdust covered floor, gripping both her legs to keep them open. She met his eyes immediately because he was still staring up at her. She could just barely see his tongue moving in a back and forth motion. The sight was dirty, she couldn't hold in the next whimper as her hips bucked up to meet his face.

"That's my girl," he muffled and then she thought he said something that sounded a lot like "Are you ready?" She felt one of his massive hands throw her leg over his shoulder, and he brought the other between her legs. He plunged two fingers deeply inside of her, thrusting relentlessly. She cried out loudly, no longer able to keep her mouth shut. His fingers continued their assault, thrusting in and out as his mouth finally descended on her clit.

For the first time in maybe forever, she had to admit she was wrong. When Ren used the flat of his tongue to slowly tease her bundle of nerves, she gripped onto the exposed beam like her life depended on it. Iris never thought passion could occur with this much filth around, but there she was, getting the best head of her life. Lost in the pleasure of the moment, she shamelessly started grinding her hips up to his face. If she was thinking clearly she may have been worried she was suffocating him. Apparently he didn't mind suffocation, because she heard him moan into her, vibrating straight to her core and causing her to black out momentarily from the new sensation. She had never heard a man moan while doing this. Come to think of it, had Iris ever seen a man so enthralled with her own pleasure? Thoughts of anyone else quickly floated out of her mind when he abruptly stopped to catch her eyes, using his grip on her ass to pull her even closer to his wanting mouth.

He let her build and build until she was straining so hard against the beam she thought the tie was going to snap. He drew back ever so slightly to look at her again, almost as if he was looking for an unspoken permission. Even when he demanded the kiss, it was him taking control. Even though she was the one tied up, she knew this was different. Was she, Iris Alberta O'Connor the one who finally had the upper hand?

Before she had time to dwell on it, his tongue joined his fingers, creating the most deliciously full sensation. She started to feel a pressure building inside of her, begging to be released. She whimpered when he removed his fingers and desperately started grinding her hips more aggressively.

"Oh god, please," She whimpered.

"What was that, Iris?" Ren said, teasing her clit again with his tongue.

"Please, please, please," She chanted. She didn't care that she was begging. At this point, she would do anything he asked.

She could sense Ren's smirk, and he gripped her other leg in response, wrapping it around his shoulder so he was completely supporting her. He was like a man possessed. Pressing three fingers back inside of her, he clamped onto her clit and sucked hard. Iris detonated. That was the only word to describe what happened next. She felt like she might have heard herself screaming his name, but she was too far out of her body to know for sure.

CHAPTER 32

Ren

Ren's eyes were shut tight, lapping up what seemed like the Last Supper while Iris screamed out his name. God, he could listen to that sound every moment and it still wouldn't be enough.

In truth, he hadn't planned on doing any of this today. He had a whole afternoon of teasing and tormenting Iris about these wall designs planned out. He had approved her design months ago, working out a way to add a support beam so they could tear down these walls, but she didn't need to know that yet.

All his plans for the hour went out the window the second he saw Iris walk in. He'd been so mesmerized by those thin straps tied in a bow peeking out at the top of her shoulder, begging to be tugged loose, and the way her jeans hugged her hips displaying a perfect outline of her ass. It was impossible for him not to notice that those straps had barely been able to hold up her breasts. Before he even processed what he was doing he had her tied up and waiting for him like a Christmas present.

He looked up now, eyes skimming over the outline of her. Her top was still in place but one strap had slipped slightly, causing it to drop lower and showcasing more of her chest. Iris had the kind of breasts that could bring a man to his knees. Round, plump, almost spilling out of any tops she wears.

How easy would it be to just slide those straps down her shoulders a bit and continue this....

"Hold still, Iris," Ren gasped after she finished bucking against his face.

He gently put her back on her feet. "God, baby. Do you have any idea how perfect you taste?" Ren tried to hide his smile watching how shy Iris was acting. Didn't she realize his face was literally just between her legs? "I can't tell you how long I've wanted to do that for," he admitted.

Iris sounded like she was attempting to control her breathing as she reoriented herself to the room.

"Just admit that you've wanted to know what my stubble felt like between your legs," he said with a purr.

That was apparently not the right thing to say, because she seemed to come out of her post orgasm daze.

"Was that what this was? Some ploy to give me an orgasm and hope I forget about everything else and run off into the sunset with you? Ren, please untie me right now."

"No. This was me paying respect to the best event planner in town," Ren said, trying to lighten the mood. Unfortunately, Iris didn't seem to be in the mood for flattery.

Reluctantly, he stood back up to retrieve her pants. He ignored the bulge in his pants begging to be set free. He got back down on his knees to help her back into them, grazing her smooth skin with his fingers as he lifted her leg up to slide them back on one foot at a time. Needing this moment to last, he slowly inched his hands up her legs, resting them on her hips. Without thought, he latched onto her zipper with his teeth and zipped it back up. He heard her gasp, but he wasn't done.

Standing back up was painful, he wanted nothing more than to stay down there and worship her forever. He slowly moved his hands from her hips back to the center of her jeans to fasten the button. Iris looked flushed. Her eyes were slightly glazed as if she was looking right through him. Her cheeks still had a slightly pink hue and he could see her breathing heavily from the rise and fall of her chest.

Oh, my girl is still turned on. Let's see if she'll admit it.

"Do you need something?"

He felt her legs clench from where his hands were still resting above the button of her jeans. Between that and the deep shade of red her cheeks and chest just turned, he knew she was lying when she squeaked out, "No. I think that was more than enough."

"You sure? Nothing you want to beg for?" Ren smirked. He wanted nothing more than to grab her hips and fuck her senseless against the wall. All she had to do was ask for it.

"Nope," she responded shyly, not looking him in the eye.

She always was a shit liar.

"Okay then," Ren responded dryly in an attempt to hide the disappointment that she wouldn't admit was she so clearly wanted. He wouldn't be able to avoid finishing the job for himself in the shower later.

That's okay, I can wait.

He could see her eyes were coming back to focus and knew their moment was up.

Reaching behind his back he grabbed his pocket knife. Ren watched her eyes snap open with amusement.

"Ren, what the hell are you doing?" Iris said, a little startled.

Ren said nothing as he slowly trailed the unopened pocket knife up her legs, stomach, and over both breasts. He stopped to swirl the knife over both nipples, watching them harden and peak through her top. He continued his trail up her throat, gently tickling her ear and then finally reaching up over her head.

He angled his head in the crook of her neck, giving it a gentle nip before resting against her ear and whispering, "Giving you what you need," right as he snapped the tie holding her hands together. Ren caught her as she stumbled forward.

Without a word, Ren settled her back on her feet and walked over to the primary work station, immediately putting on his respirator mask.

Ren couldn't resist the urge to inhale deeply, the tight seal of the mask trapping Iris's sweet floral scent mixed with her juices on his tongue. He looked right in her eyes as he did it. Ren was lucky he didn't buckle to his knees with the look of lust she returned.

Now that he had a taste of her he didn't know how he would ever be able to stop. He would gladly die between her legs. His cock jumped, just as excited by her smell as he was.

"What are you waiting for?", he asked through the mask, "You said you had a pastrami waiting for you across the street?"

"Oh... yeah... um it was a chicken salad sandwich, and I..." She trailed off dazed and next-level confused. As soon as she heard the whirring of equipment, she picked up her purse, and headed straight for the door.

CHAPTER 33

Iris

Iris was so parched that she didn't think twice when she slammed the empty glass of ice-water down at the counter of the diner and gestured, "another one" to the waitress behind the bar. She noticed a name tag that read "Jules", right after she noticed the stripe of purple hair that came out of a ponytail.

"You sure are thirsty. But you look tired. Need something to get you jazzed, instead?" Jules looked expectantly. She reminded her of a bartender who knew your order as soon as you stepped inside. Despite the outdated candy striper-type uniform, Iris had a feeling she could be friends with this girl.

She was tired. And still confused. And a little high off of that orgasm. She couldn't remember a time she had felt this carefree. Her tension had been released, so she giggled in response.

"Yeah, actually, you guys have drip right?"

"If you don't tell my boss, we have a lot more than just that," Jules wiggled her eyes conspiratorially.

"Even though it's noon... I could go for a martini right now, but-" Iris got cut off.

"No! No, I mean if you want a latte or a mocha I can make those!" Jules responded with a light in her eyes.

"Ohhh! Wait," Iris looked back at her name tag. "Why does your name sound familiar?"

"You're Sage's friend, right? She used to come by the coffee shop all the time when I was a barista there," Jules said with a smile.

"Oh my god, were you there when the pipes exploded?" Iris responded, chuckling.

"Okay, maybe that was me! It all happened so fast!"

"I heard you had to give Mrs. Trevitt a free coffee. Not that she deserved it" Iris whispered conspiratorially. Jan Trevitt always had her nose turned up at folks who were less than ultra-conservative.

"Tell me about it," Jules replied pointing out the small pride flag pin on her apron. "You look like a caramel latte kind of girl," she pivoted and pointed back, "With oat milk. And let's make it iced so you can take it to-go. I hear you've been working on revamping my old place of work."

"How did you know my exact order? That sounds fucking perfect! And a chicken salad sandwich to-go too, if you don't mind!"

Jules called out "Got it!" to her as the swinging door to the kitchen closed behind her.

Iris's level of enthusiasm wasn't exactly welcomed as she turned left and right. A few elderly couples were staring at her, rolling their eyes at her profanity.

"What, you've never been hungry before?" she scoffed in response before remembering these could be potential customers for Sage.

Five minutes later, Jules came back with the largest, most decadent caramel latte she'd ever seen. Caramel drizzled down the side, and there were even dried strawberries at the top of the cup.

"Holy hell, that's what I'm talking about! I'm gearing up for more interviews with vendors for the grand opening. I can't decide between an ice sculpture or a balloon artist..."

Jules started blankly back.

"Too much?" Iris responded, pulling the latte near for her first big drag.

"Maybe a little?" Jules shook her head. "Maybe free coffee for the first 25 guests would be a bigger draw?"

"Okay, I'm loving that," Iris made a guttural sound that once again attracted the attention of the elderly diner patrons. "And I'm loving this even more. Can I ask what they're paying you? Because whatever it is, it's not enough."

"I was definitely making more at the coffee shop because I could take home tips too," Jules said, glancing longingly across the street at Sage's storefront.

Sage did say she had some creative liberty, right?

"Well. It's a few months out and I'd have to talk to Sage... but..." Iris said as the chicken salad sandwich was slid to her, "This is the best fucking latte I've ever had. Would you be interested in working at the shop-"

"Yes! Immediately yes! When do I start? Get me out of this fucking place," Jules started to untie her apron to throw it down on the counter.

CHAPTER 34

Iris

"And I swear to god, you guys, just like that, she tore off her apron right there and then! It felt like it was out of a movie," Iris said, relaying her conversation with Jules the other day. The car continued its drive into Burlington to celebrate the latest advancements of the shop. Emmett, Emmett's latest fling Cassidy, and Ren were entertaining the conversation Iris struck since she had gotten in the backseat of Emmett's truck with Ren.

"Well good thing you did an impromptu pre-screening with her. The next best barista Sage could find was a retiree at the Starbucks in Hinesburg. When she called him for an interview, he kept asking 'so will there be lines on the cups for me to use'? Just pour with your heart, Gerald!" Emmett laughed, turning around briefly at the light to meet Iris' gaze and then coughed uncomfortably when he found her stricken.

Why does Emmett have so much intimate knowledge about this? I thought Sage was alone when she interviewed that dude.

"Do you guys think I overstepped? I know it's Sage's place, but I remember how she talked about her drinks and couldn't help myself!" Both boys had been extra-occupied with the project lately, so this was Iris' chance to catch them up.

"I'm not sure Sage realized Jules was still in town," Ren chimed in eyeing Emmett in the front seat, "She could use someone who's been in the coffee industry more than any of us have."

"Jules is really phenomenal to work with! She was only with us a few months, but it's clear that she's missed at the diner. Our main line cook Jeff keeps asking me to make the iced mochas she used to smuggle him, but I can barely get past hot coffee with cream and sugar," Cassidy chimed in cheerily.

"Sorry I had to poach her, please tell Jeff to not spit in my omelet next time I come in," Iris said back, only half-kidding.

Cassidy seemed content to look out the window, staring directly at the sun. The girl was consistently kindhearted, even a loyal customer of Sage's. Sage refurbished a couch for her after she finally moved out of her parents house and into a cute townhome. Beyond blind loyalty, there really wasn't a thought behind those eyes. Like a really nice golden retriever. Iris was surprised she held appeal for Emmett, because beyond being gorgeous and blonde, she didn't have many hobbies known to the group.

Iris truly hoped she didn't over-assert herself by inviting Jules for an interview with Sage set for the next week. She was the artistic vision behind this project, after all, while Sage galavanted all over the Northeast, searching for rare pieces. Sage left Iris alone more than she would have liked. Not nearly enough cock-blocking.

Iris couldn't be luckier that Sage understood the importance of positive intent at the end of the day. Sage had worked for a lobster shack, pastry shop, and at a dive bar that occupied the same space over the years, so she had some semblance of an idea about supply chain. Iris discovered that Jules came with a business degree and a willingness to work.

Finally, the crew had finalized the infrastructure, so Sage was able to focus on getting the shop in order. Sage had been working so hard on flips and finding the best furniture possible, that Emmett and Iris decided that the foursome needed to get away for a night. Sage declined the invitation almost as quickly it left Iris's mouth.

Turns out, reupholstering the barstools had to be done immediately. The trio was upset but understood that when Sage got fixated on a project, she had to finish what she started as soon as possible. Iris thought back on the conversation they had earlier in the day.

"It's fine, really," Sage had said when Iris begged her to celebrate her hard work, "Emmett can just bring along that Krista chick in my place."

Sage waved around the staple gun a little too flippantly.

"You mean Cassidy? The same girl who's been working at the diner since she graduated a year ahead of us?" Iris tentatively approached, and flipped up her own goggles, damning eye safety at the behest of attempting to convince Sage to indulge a little.

"Right, sure, that one. I'll barely be missed! We can celebrate again when everything is finally done." Sage plopped down under the bar stool cross-legged.

"Why can't we celebrate the little wins, though? It feels like you haven't taken a break, and none of us would even be here if it weren't for you. You brought us all together. You deserve it." Iris plopped next to her, keeping the fabric taut while Sage stapled with tight-lipped concentration.

"No, I'm sure. Just drop it, Iris." The girls had worked with 90s synth pop blaring in the background, until Iris needed to get ready.

Iris refocused in the backseat, suddenly intent on bringing her back some dessert at the very least. Emmett dominated the driver's seat, kicking back his chair until he hit Ren's own knees.

"Oh sorry man, almost forgot you were back there!" Emmett said pretending he needed to readjust.

"You're such an asshole," Ren responded. "Are you sure you don't need me in the front to give you directions? You're a little challenged in that department. " Ren started messing with Emmetts jet-black hair from the seat immediately behind him.

Emmett turned around briefly to slap Ren's hand away before he entered the on ramp.

Iris watched Emmett's chocolate brown eyes immediately zone in on Ren's hand that was resting just inches away from Iris's thigh. She said nothing, but glanced back at Emmett in the rearview while he raised an eyebrow in question.

Feeling Emmett's eyes on her was making Iris nervous. Her heart started to beat louder as she wondered how much Emmett knew of their relationship. Whatever that looked like.

Sweat beaded on her forehead and she continued to convince herself that Emmett somehow had figured it out even if Ren didn't tell him. Unable to take it anymore, Iris did the only thing she could think to do in this situation and that was continue to talk.

"Oh, and then when I came home, I canceled my call with the balloon animal guy and switched it to a different lady who does balloon arches. I mean, who knew there were two different balloon niches like that here? All of the places I worked with in Boston just did everything. I'm also still debating on the design for the ice sculpture. I thought something in the shape of a typewriter could be cool. You know, like really vintage." Iris could simply not shut the fuck up. She rambled on and on for the next ten minutes while they headed north to dinner.

She grew hotter and hotter as Ren's gaze slid toward her. She could feel him take her in from head to toe. Suddenly her nervousness had nothing to do with Emmett's knowing gaze.

Ren bent down, appearing to anyone else to be grabbing something from the floor of the truck. Iris jumped as his hand connected to her thigh instead. Goosebumps erupted over her whole body with just one touch. God, how could a simple touch feel so good. Her body responded to him like he owned it.

Trying to remain unfazed despite the growing ache between her legs, Iris kept her eyes focused on anything but Ren as he inched his fingers up her thigh any chance his best friend and his random date weren't looking their way. Luckily and unluckily for her, Emmett and Cassidy weren't paying any attention to the backseat. Ren's fingers gently stroked her thigh, up and down, and side to side. She clamped her mouth shut to keep a moan from escaping when two of his fingers slowly ascended up her thigh to the side of her panties. Iris had never regretted wearing a dress more than this moment.

"I can still smell you," Ren whispered in her ear, as Cassidy and Emmett attempted small talk about the weather.

"Wow, I really love these clouds. So fluffy!" Cassidy said. The smiling golden-haired girl rolled the window down and stuck her head out of the window.

"Yes, that's very... nice, Cassidy. It's a nice day. Really cool," Emmett said, staring straight ahead.

"What do you mean?" Iris whispered back to Ren, fixing a smile on her face so as to not get caught up in whatever game he wanted to play. He'd been strictly business this past week, only asking her things related to the shop. The only time she felt close was when she'd feel the weight of him sneaking into her bed late at night after she was already half asleep. He also hadn't mentioned anything about plans for Thanksgiving in a few days, so she decided to cater a buffet to the hospital her mom worked at. Her mom worked most holidays, so she tried to make the time to go to her when possible.

"What I mean," he said low in her ear, "is that this is going to be very hard for me."

"What's hard? Just a group of friends at dinner, celebrating our progress," Iris said, her body shuddering as his fingers resumed their relentless teasing strokes just outside the area she so desperately needed them to be. She fought the urge to scoot her body closer to his.

With his hand still up her dress, Ren started peppering questions about the crew's next steps.

"Did you add that extra security to the front lock like we talked about?" Ren's hand inched closer to her middle spot that he worked over so easily just seven days ago.

Iris couldn't believe he was so collected pivoting back to group conversation.

"Yeah, I had Jim take a look because he has some of the latest security systems."

"Will there be any cameras in the shop?"

"Of course. Can't let any of the hottest merchandise in the store get taken," Emmett shot back, a little defensive.

The last few minutes were filled with awkward silence while she stifled her whimpers.

"Here! Let's grub," Emmett said hungrily and Ren quickly pulled his hand out of her dress. Iris was glad her mouth was still clamped shut so no one could hear her gasp when she caught him licking the fingers that touched her before he opened his own door to step out.

God, he edged her all the way here. Her thighs rubbed together as she climbed out of the car and her legs almost buckled. Shit, how was she supposed to make it all the way through dinner like this? Ren was already walking up to the restaurant door by the time she got herself out of the truck. Iris glared at the back of his head.

Her body was coiled tight from his teasing hands. It was totally bullshit that he got her all worked up just to leave her hanging. Hell, even a light wind might push her over the edge at this point.

Iris blushed, feeling how wet her panties were under her dress as the four of them walked into the restaurant.

She didn't know which was worse, coming in the backseat of her hookup buddie's friend's truck while everyone was there, or not getting to come at all.

Emmett approached the host first, stating "Leif, party of four."

The host clearly found both men attractive, giving her best saccharine smile. Iris could have gagged, and even Cassidy appeared less than pleased.

Ren and Emmett mimicked their best gentlemanly stances, pulling out the girls' seats at the same time. Ren assumed the chair to the left of Iris, resting his hand on her thigh once more under the table. Sweat started trickling down her back when it became clear his hand was going to remain unmoving on her thigh. She barely resisted the urge to fidget in her seat and rub her thighs together to relieve her growing need and the deep ache in her core.

"So Iris, do you have any projections on sales for the first month?" Ren said calmly.

"I would project that we break even. I doubt Sage will see any significant profit for the first few months, actually. I do have a few events planned out for her when I go home to Boston," Iris looked up from the menu nervously.

"Hmmm... Going home. Well, that's to be expected, but I'd like to continue to invest in the dream," he cocked his head at Iris. "And I know it's yours too. We can talk about numbers in the next few months but the longer I'm in this, the more I want to help."

"I don't think that will be necessary. With the events I have lined up for the next 6 months, I'm sure we'll hit our goal."

It was true. Iris had set up a dream list of six events-one for each month. In January it was the Grand Opening with a massive balloon arch and a variety of activities. February would sport Valentine's card-making, each of the cards going to the local senior center. The winner of the big March Madness event would win a one-on-one coffee class with Jules, hosted at the shop, and so on. There was no doubt in Iris' mind that her friend's shop would be a success. There was so much opportunity. Iris' job was to help harness it. She felt herself relaxing and was finally able to focus on the conversation as she walked them through her different event plans.

"Don't you think Sage should be here to talk about this, man?" Emmett interjected.

"Don't you think I already talked to my sister about this?" Ren furrowed his brow back.

"Here's the deal. Vintage Vixen Espresso will be successful. So successful, which is why we want a percentage in the company, not to just help with it's construction," Emmett explained.

"Are there going to be plants there, as well? Gosh! A plant shop, coffee bar, and antique all in one! How exciting!" Cassidy clapped her hands together.

"Wow, you guys. That's definitely something Sage will have to think about-" Iris got cut off when the waitress approached.

"Hello, there, first time in?" The waitress trained her eyes on Ren. "What drinks can I get you?"

God, what was it with the women in this restaurant?

"Yes," Iris said sharply "And I'll actually take the house red."

"I'll take the white, please!" Cassidy said, pointing at the drink menu simultaneously.

"Martini, extra olives," Emmett added.

"A scotch for me, neat," Ren said, rounding out the order. "Thanks," he said shortly.

"Perfect, I'll be back to take your order after the drinks are out," the waitress responded, looking notably dismissed.

Several minutes later, the waitress returned with drinks and complimentary bread rolls in hand.

Iris and Cassidy telepathically communicated to each other how excited they were over the basket. The girls started in on the yeasty goodness. The steam billowed out when Iris pulled back the napkin. Cassidy chatted her up to see what life was like in Boston. She completely forgot Cassidy kept up with the foursome on social media. So weird to be disconnected from high school in most ways, yet still so connected in others.

"You posted the most insane looking bagel I've ever seen a few months ago and I drooled!" Cassidy said, redeclaring her love for carbs. Iris went for a second roll, deciding to like Cassidy more than she intended to. The boys started to kick off on their own side tangent.

"So how was finishing up the coffee bar? I know it's important, it's the first thing everyone sees when they walk in. Then BOOM, stunning refurbished antiques courtesy of our little entrepreneur," Emmett raised his martini as a silent toast to Sage.

"Well, you know when I started to sand it, I was so distracted," Ren said, gripping her thigh almost uncomfortably. "You started to do that by yourself? Why were you so distracted?" Emmett asked with genuine curiosity.

"Well, this smell kept wafting around my mask. I kept inhaling and inhaling, but it wouldn't go away. It even stuck around after I switched masks," Ren stroked her skin with just one finger, back and forth.

Iris almost spit out her wine. Which was a shame because it was damn delicious with notes of cherry and dark chocolate.

"You okay, Riss? I still finished it up that same day, sanded it and everything," Ren looked at her with a silent dare in his eyes as he spoke.

"Totally fine! Feeling good thanks, just went down the wrong pipe." She felt a deep blush forming on her cheeks as Ren resumed those torturous movements that started in the backseat. Only this time she was already turned on so every movement he made had her body twitching. She took another sip of her wine, willing her body to keep it together for the duration of the dinner.

"Was there a gas leak? I thought you guys made it past the leaking pipes, hence dinner?" Cassidy said with genuine concern.

Emmett just shook his head in dismissal, restating how many times the crew checked on the infrastructure. "We've exceeded all of the building code expectations you could imagine."

CHAPTER 35

Ren

Ren let his mind wander back to the other day with Iris as he sipped his scotch. He couldn't believe the spell he had been put under. On the outside, he could not have appeared more nonchalant if he tried. He knew when he swaggered over to his mask, that Iris would be the slightest bit lost and confused. He hadn't meant to send her on her way so quickly, but if she had spent one more moment in his presence, there would have been much more to clean up than just her jacket on the floor.

It had taken him another 15 minutes to prepare himself to sand the coffee bar down. He had been so mesmerized and distracted by her scent on his skin, so intoxicating under the mask he put on to protect himself from particles while he sanded.

Ren felt drunk just a few sips into his scotch, remembering the moment. He could have spent so much longer between her thighs, torturing her the way she deserved. His desire to see that pink flush crawl up her chest and making her come with urgency were constantly at odds with one another. He yearned to sink his teeth into the bare flesh of her ass and make sure she knew what she meant to him.

The annoying waitress came back to take their orders, with an even stronger attempt to eye-fuck him. There was no way to get her off his back, knowing Iris was growing increasingly more upset with her.

Guess I'll just have to show her what's really on my mind.

He could barely focus on anything with how soft her skin was. Luckly, Emmett was so busy trying (and failing) to flirt with Cassidy that they weren't paying attention to his side of the table.

With Ren's hand already drawing lazy lines up and down her leg, he began slowly inching his fingers higher. With that pretty little slit up the left side of her dress, it was easy to get his hand where he needed to be.

He could see how worked up Iris was when they got out of the jeep earlier. Judging by how tight her posture was and how often she was clenching her thighs together under the table, he could take a guess that she was feeling...unsatisfied.

He hadn't planned to do anything when they first got into the jeep but that slit up her dress went so high it was like an arrow pointing you in the direction you needed to go.

I have to feel her again.

He trailed his fingers up between her legs and held them there. Keeping his eyes intentionally blank, Ren slid Iris's chair closer to his and spoke softly into her ear. "Are you already wet for me, Iris?"

She actually squeaked. Damn, that sound was cute but she was going to need to do a little better than that. Moving her panties to the side, Ren started rubbing his index finger between her drenched folds and said, "Answer me."

He watched Iris frantically look at the opposite side of the table. When she noticed Emmett preoccupied with gaining Cassidy's interest by discussing the intricacies of lacrosse, she shifted her view to look over the entire restaurant. Seeming to assess every patron in the restaurant, she must have been satisfied with what she found because she finally turned her eyes back to him and said so quietly he almost didn't hear, "Yes."

"Good girl. Now, tell me what you need."

"Ren, we're in public. We can't," she gritted out.

He could tell she didn't mean it, just a half hearted attempt to do what she believed was the right thing. Her breathing was shallow and frantic and she was subtly scrunching her dress up higher so her legs could go wider. Meanwhile, Emmett went on and on about the logistics of operating heavy machinery, and Cassidy was fascinated. The music in the restaurant was also getting louder as time went on, giving Iris and Ren a bit more coverage for the perverted behavior.

Seeing that she needed a little motivation, Ren inched a finger into her at the same time his thumb circled her clit. She clamped her mouth shut and her arms lined with goosebumps.

"Say that again baby, I couldn't quite hear what you said."

Instead of responding, Iris moved her legs wider apart.

That's all the invitation he needed. With this new angle he was able to move his hand completely over her now exposed pussy. Unfortunately, this was going to have to be quick.

Ren pushed two fingers into her pussy up to his knuckles while his thumb continued to circle her clit. Her walls clenched around his fingers, god she was so tight. So tight he could barely pump his fingers in and out of her.

Knowing she was still close from earlier in the car, it wouldn't take long. Her legs started to shake next to him as he continued his rhythm.

"Do you think the people in this restaurant can see how well you take me? How wet you are and how tight this pussy is squeezing my fingers right now?" Ren whispered in her ear.

"Spinach and artichoke dip for the table," the waitress interrupted.

"Thank you" Cassidy responded for the group. The girl really loved bread and cheese.

A small moan escaped her mouth.

"I. Feel. The. Same. Way," Cassidy said, punctuating each word by dunking the tiny toast into the dip. She shoved it in her mouth like a cheese connoisseur. "Yum!"

Iris' walls were clenching around his fingers even tighter now. He pushed his fingers in deeper and started rubbing harder on her clit.

She was so close. Her cheeks were flushed, and her breathing was so erratic it was making her breasts bounce slightly in her dress.

Tearing his gaze away from Iris, Ren moved his attention back to the others at the table. "So, Emmett. What other jobs are you working on at the moment?" Ren said, hoping to distract the table, not willing to risk anyone else hearing her pretty little moans.

"Just a few small builds in town and then one apartment complex in Burlington -" Emmett stopped himself, "Whoa Riss, you ok? Is that wine not sitting well? You look super flushed."

Ren smirked, watching Iris' eyes go wide as she forced her mouth open to respond. "Oh, um. Yes. Yes. Yes. Oh my god, yes I'm fine." As she spoke, Ren added back his thumb to rub harder on her clit. She was so wet her juices were dripping down his hand. Circling her clit once, twice, a third time. That was all it took. He felt her orgasm roll through her. Her walls spasmed, and her legs snapped closed around him as she rode his fingers.

Ren coughed loudly, pretending to choke on an ice cube and forcing everyone's attention on him as she rode out her orgasm at the table.

"Shit! Ren are you okay? What is going on on that side of the table tonight, did someone poison both of you?" Cassidy said frantically.

"I'm fine! Just went down the wrong pipe." Ren said once Iris' legs unclamped from around him and he was able to safely place it back on her thigh. "You sure you're okay Iris? You do look a little flushed."

God, she was so beautiful like this. Her cheeks were still pink, eyes slightly glazed over in pleasure and there was still a slight sheen on her skin. He would gladly spend all day between her legs to see her look like this everyday.

"Sorry! I am fine. You're right, there must be something in this wine." Iris responded, chugging the rest of her glass of the wine. Standing up from the table she continued, "I think I just need to splash some water on my face, if everyone will please excuse me."

Cass looked unconvinced and called after her, "Want me to come with you? What's the saying... oh! I'll powder my nose!"

"No, really it's okay. I'll be right back!" Iris said with a forced smile.

He wanted to follow after her to see what she was thinking but knew that would be way too suspicious with this group.

The waitress decided to return with their entrees as Iris walked away, giving him yet another suggestive look as she set down his steak. Even Cassidy was rolling her eyes at her blatant attempts at this point. He ordered everyone at the table another round and sent the young waitress on her way without another glance.

The rest of dinner went by smoothly. Iris got back to the table looking like she had actually splashed water on her face but appeared more composed after what they had just done. Her and Cassidy spent most of the night reminiscing on old high school memories. When the check came, the girls thought the guys were going to fight like they did during their lacrosse days. Something about not paying for Iris's meal didn't sit right with Ren. The group hadn't been onboard with it until he lied and said he was charging it as a business expense. It also got Emmett out of paying for a date he didn't seem too keen on keeping around.

On more than one occasion during dinner Ren had caught Emmett giving him a knowing look which he pointedly ignored. He would likely be getting an earful from him later if he noticed what happened tonight but fuck it. Watching her come undone next to him in a room full of people was the single hottest thing he has ever seen. That, and her coming undone on his tongue earlier this week. Hell, anything involving Iris was his undoing. He could only hope she would let him do it again.

CHAPTER 36

Ren

Emmett worked in reverse order, dropping Cassidy off first. She gave a shy wave "goodbye", and Emmett didn't get out of the car.

"You're really not going to walk her to the door? That's messed up, man. She was nice... enough," Ren chastised.

"I'm exhausted, leave me alone," Emmett retorted, "Besides I haven't seen you be super chivalrous lately. You didn't open the door for Iris when she got in!"

"Oh yeah well Iris and I... we're not even..." Ren trailed off, turning to her.

"We're not what, Ren?" Iris darted back, in challenge.

"We're not anything, Emmett, so give it up," Ren said laughing uncomfortably.

He noticed Iris shift closer to her door, saying nothing. He knew he fucked up immediately.

They drove the ten minutes back to Sage's in a more comfortable silence now that Cassidy wasn't pointing out every building asking, "Did you guys work on that project?"

Emmett pulled up to the familiar two-story on the corner. Ren admired the way that the front yard of his childhood home was always maintained the way their mom liked it thanks to Sage. He'd have to thank her for that soon. He wondered if he ever gave his sister enough kudos for holding everything together when shit constantly hit the fan. He also wondered if helping out on this project would ever be enough repayment.

"Thanks for the ride, Emmett. See you soon," Iris said, patting him on the shoulder from the backseat.

"No problem Riss. Will you tell Sage that I'll make sure there's a 'next time'?"

"Um... Sure. I'll let her know. I doubt she'll be as upset as soon as she sees this," Iris lifted up the to-go box filled with every type of dessert Emmett asked the restaurant to make.

Emmett nodded with a tight smile in response.

"Coming?" Iris said to Ren, sliding down and out of the truck.

"I'll be home later, I'm thinking we need some quality guy time," Ren said.

"Oh... okay. No worries. See you later then," Iris nodded curtly.

Emmett drove off as soon as they saw her get inside the house safely.

"Are you going to start talking or should I?" Emmett spoke up.

"Honestly, you're my best friend. No friend who has ever been my friend has been more of a friend than you," Ren slurred.

"No man. Hear me out. I feel the same," Emmett looked back with his eyes glazed over.

The boys were absolutely shit faced. Ren had fully intended on making sure he came clean about what had been happening between him and Iris. He got the nauseating feeling that something was going on between his best friend and his little sister, too.

I'm not a hypocrite. Hypocrite. Hippo. Crit. What a fun word.

"Listen man, Riss is gorgeous. I get it. I surrreee do. But don't you think that maybe this is a bad idea," Emmett said, doing his best to push through the conversation.

"She let me have a taste of her, but all I want to do is piss her off. It does something to me to get a rise out of her," Ren nearly shouted.

"Hahaha, you are so right. She looks even better when she's all pinked up," Emmett said.

Ren sobered up for a moment. Of course his best friend could also appreciate a beautiful woman. But he didn't realize how a statement like that would affect him.

"Chill out, man! I'm not womanizing your girl. I actually am a little preoccupied in that department already," Emmett said casually sipping yet another martini.

"Yeah, Cassidy is a nice girl. Do you think you'll see her again?" Ren said cautiously.

"Not sure... Maybe," he says.

"Yeah," Ren said, staring straight ahead. "I think you're fucked in the relationship department."

"I think we're both fucked."

They clinked glasses.

They only felt comfortable getting belligerent because they were the only two left in the bar. Besides Ernie, of course. They had some semblance of a reputation to uphold, after all.

"Getting blasted for fun or is it because of everyone's two favorite girls in this town?" Ernie questioned with mirth behind his eyes.

"Both" they said in unison before giggling like teenagers.

Ernie shoved the two best friends that anyone could have into the back of an Uber. Emmett found his keys and made four attempts to unlock his apartment door before the boys stumbled in.

"Night" Emmett nodded, tripping into his own room.

Ren trudged to the massive couch. Feeling suddenly very grateful that his best friend is a behemoth, he fell face first onto the cushions, remaining in the same position until the sun came up.

CHAPTER 37

Iris

Iris tossed and turned until 2:30 in the morning. Her head was spinning with what happened at dinner. She was sweaty, hot, and anxious. Ren left her on read when she tried to send him a "goodnight" text, and he still wasn't home yet.

By 3:00 AM, she got a blurry selfie from Emmett hugging Ernie and an audio message.

"Heyyyyyy girl! How are you? Dinner was so fun. You are such a good friend. We love you. Don't we, Ren? Anyway, please please give Sage a kiss from me please. No reason at allllll! It's a boy's night and Ren will be home-" *Click.*

Oh boy, they were really getting after it. Only one thing left to do.

Iris tiptoed down the hall and creaked open the door. She lifted up the left side of the comforter, where she knew Sage wouldn't be, and slipped in. The tired auburn-haired girl inhaled Sage's familiar cinnamon and honey scented body wash and nuzzled close.

"Iris, that you?"

"How'd you guess?"

"Well you didn't make the bed dip like a huge man so I figured it was you and not my latest dream. Can't sleep?"

"You guessed it, sister."

"Alright sleepyhead, come here," Sage patted the bed beside her.

Iris pressed a kiss on the top of Sage's head.

"What was that for?" She grunted from sleepiness.

"That was from Emmett," Iris whispered

"Hmmmm," Sage hummed pleasantly.

The two girls drifted off into a dreamless sleep knowing that they'd always keep each other company. Even if a couple of idiots didn't know what they wanted out of life.

CHAPTER 38

Iris

Iris woke up more content than she had been in a while. She and Sage always sought solace with one another, snuggling up in each other's beds or on the couch with a massive blanket when the hardest winters came for them.

When Sage's mom died.

When Iris had her first breakup.

When they got fired from the flower shop for sneaking free flowers to girls who looked like they needed it. Boys will be boys, but chosen sisters are forever.

She looked over to her best friend power stretching, doing sun salutations while still in bed. Iris started laughing at her friend who was always ready to go.

"What are you laughing at? I can smell your morning breath from here," Sage said, cracking one eye to look back at Iris.

"Oh nothing, I just pity the man who has to keep up with you in the morning," Iris retorted.

"Well with the dry spell I've had, no one's been having to keep up with me! The most action I got was the little smoochie I got from you slash Emmett last night," Iris jabbed Sage in the rib. "Let's attack this day. Just you and me. No boys, no stinky crew. Just us. I'll start with grinding some beans," Sage actually somersaulted out of the bed.

"She stuck the landing!" Iris said, sticking her arms out and then clapping the sides of her thighs, as she was also only wearing an oversized t-shirt she stole from Ren.

What are dudes for if not massive sleep shirts?

"It's a ten across the board for the amazing gymnast!" Iris gave a literal round of applause clapping her hands in a circle.

Sage took a bow leaning forward, putting the full-ass underwear on display to her best friend and traipsed down to the kitchen, hounding for a cup of joe.

"I'm putting our go-go juice into big ass to-go mugs. We're going shopping, bitch, so take a shower!" Sage yelled back up the stairs.

Iris cracked a massive smile. Nothing couldn't be made better by her best friend. Her smile faded from remembering why she crawled into bed with her in the early hours of the morning to begin with. She tossed the blanket over her face, wondering how she would ever work her way around talking about the fact that the best orgasms of her life came from her best friend's brother.

I can't believe Ren fucking Anders might be the best- worst thing to ever happen to me. Time to put on a smile and work out keeping a secret from Sage. I ruined her surprise Sweet 16 birthday party, what makes me think I'm a secret-keeping mastermind? Does Ren want to be kept a secret?

Iris scrubbed and scrubbed in the shower. Images of his fingers plunging into her. The look of his face almost defeated as she exited the car. The blush that was on her chest when she looked in the mirror, washing her makeup off when she got home. No amount of scrubbing washed away the fact that she needed to get even with Ren. She let the citrus-blend body wash aroma fill her nostrils, thinking it would block out the lingering scent of his cologne that was laced with notes coriander and juniper berries. Her fingers trailed down her stomach wanting to relieve the frustration, and she stopped.

The last thing I need is to think about feeling that hard length press up behind me when we were in bed.

Iris turned the shower on cold last-minute, hoping it would bring her to her senses.

Fuck a cold plunge, this shower will do just- fuck FUCK fuck nevermind.

She jumped out of the shower and quickly began lathering herself head to toe with an orange blossom lotion when she toweled off. Iris went back to resorting to choosing to feel good and smell good for no one but herself. Donning her best push-up bra, long sleeve black t-shirt, and cropped jeans with booties. Iris gave herself a once-over. Feeling insecure in relationships was nothing new to her, but she never would have imagined it would be Ren making her doubt herself this time. She thought back to his response to Emmett last night. Nothing. He said she was nothing to him. Was she not up to his usual standards? Was he embarrassed by her?

Sage had already finished getting ready, choosing flowing cream linen pants and a brown sweater. The two girls stood appreciating the other's outfit.

"First stop, Buster's Antiques," Sage said, holding out the extra large to-go mug to Iris, as promised.

"Okay, I'm looking for a giant rodeo clown painting to put right above my dining room... Thoughts?" Iris said, ribbing Sage.

"Yeah fucking right. And I'm suddenly into still life photography featuring a bowl of apples and bananas."

With that, the two were off with the intent of finding the rest of the necessary opening pieces of furniture and artwork for the shop.

"So he kind of ghosted you... but kind of didn't? Explain." Sage picked up a lamp shade, inspecting if the undone threading was worth the effort to repair.

"Well. Yes and no. We're still emailing."

Liar.

Truth be told, Jordan had texted her after their impromptu meeting while he was still in town. His parents convinced him to stick around for Thanksgiving, and he even invited her to some festivities. A simple, "I had fun tonight, let me know if you want to do it again." She didn't respond. Honestly, too wrapped up with Ren to even think about another man.

"Ah, I see you're still smitten with him then."

Oh perfect. This was my out. I'm going to pull the trigger and tell her. How mad could she actually be? She did steal my favorite sweater in 8th grade and got paint all over it, so that makes us basically even right?

"Yeahh, so actually about Jordan-", before she could finish Sage interrupted. "Hmm... even his name is hot. Damn, I need to get laid. I'm getting turned on by a name that starts with J what the fuck is wrong with me."

Okay. This could still work, I can tell her the truth.

Despite the lame pep talk, when she opened her mouth all she could respond with was, "Yeah, totally. Totally a hot name. Smitten as hell, that's me."

Fucking coward.

"So when are you going to man up and ask him to come visit again?" Sage was practically vibrating with excitement beside her. Always the best sidekick and friend, making Iris feel even more guilty about what she was doing.

"Oh look! Let's check out that model car. I have always wanted one of those," Iris was racking up the lies at this point.

"Ummmm... Didn't know you were into model cars these days Riss. Sure, lets go take a look."

After successfully dodging a million follow up questions about her soon to be fake boyfriend Jordan, Iris led Sage to the Cafe for a quick lunch before they headed back to the house with their purchases, sans model car.

It felt good to spend time together just the two of them even if she was drowning in guilt over her secret situationship. There were too many questions in her head to even begin to tell her best friend what she was currently doing with her brother. If she was being honest with herself, she wanted more with him. The things he could do to her body aside, she found herself drawn to him. She couldn't deny that she was starting to open up to him. Ren always had been able to walk up and with one look tear down all her carefully placed walls, and this time has been no different.

She was unsure exactly when it happened, but she realized somewhere along the way that she had started to trust him. He brought out a new side of her. A side that was unafraid to be her most authentic self. He never batted an eye at her need to excessively plan out every aspect of her day, or her need to check in on the build every chance she got to make sure it was going as planned. In fact, he had been going out of his way to reassure her whenever he could. There had even been a few days where it seemed he had been reading her mind because he sent her updates before she even had the chance to ask. He understood her. He accepted her. And she was starting to feel the same about him.

CHAPTER 39

Iris

Iris yelled a lame excuse to Sage about needing to head into town, jumped in the car, and was now pulling up to the boys' office. She refused to spiral about her relationship with Ren any longer.

She was lucky enough to borrow Sage's obnoxious hot pink Jeep for the day. Iris simply couldn't bring herself to think about buying a car. She walked practically everywhere in Boston, and the parking fee at her brownstone apartment had been astronomical. Even though she missed the foot traffic running errands, it was fun to drive something commanding on the road.

Today she found herself on a mission of sorts. On one hand, she was hoping to persuade Ren to change out the coffee bar's countertop shape to a funky semi-circle instead of the original design they agreed upon months ago. How could she have people lining up begging to get in if the space didn't flow the way she wanted?

On the other hand, she was there to confront the man who's been invading her dreams, and seems adamant on pretending nothing happened between them in the middle of the shop's construction site and a buzzing restaurant during a full dinner service.

It had been a full week since the group dinner and subsequently the same amount of time since she last spoke to Ren. She had already committed to bringing food to her mom's hospital staff for Thanksgiving and Christmas, so there wasn't exactly enough holiday cheer to go around. Every morning she woke up expecting to find him in bed next to her only to be greeted by pillows instead. The "goodnight" text she sent him during his night out with Emmett sat unanswered in her phone.

So much for open communication.

It shouldn't bother her, Ren had never come out and said what they were to each other but after the mindblowing public orgasm she received during dinner she hadn't seen this new ghosting session coming. Who was he to get to call this thing off without speaking to her first?

Even with his radio silence she hadn't been able to focus all week.

She noticed Emmett coming out of the building and gave him a meaningful wave "hi" as she walked toward him.

"Here to give Ren a hard time about something?" Emmett asked cheekily. She wondered if Ren had told his best friend anything about the romp that definitely violated more than a few laws.

Despite Sage's crankiness toward him, Iris maintained a soft spot for Shelburne's hottest playboy. She knew he was just giving her a hard time, so she threw him a wink and said, "Why else would I be here?"

Emmett only raised his eyebrows in response and asked if he could pick anything up for her too while he was out for lunch. She shook her head "no" at the kindness and mentioned that she wouldn't be there long. Emmett climbed into his truck, laughing to himself.

It was too cold for Iris, even though her blood stayed thin living on the East coast. She kept herself wrapped tightly in a bundle as she walked through the office of construction bros. The office doors were unmarked, but she knew that fake knee-slapping laugh anywhere. Anyone who knows Ren knows that he chuckles so hard he snorts if he actually means it. Uncaring that he was on a call, she opened the door to find him standing there staring at her with surprise and awe. She knew he was staying at Emmett's but she couldn't figure out why he was looking at her like this.

Had she been too loud or embarrassing while he was giving her two of the most earth-shattering orgasms of her life?

Was she supposed to be polite and quiet? What fucking fun would that have been.

What could I have possibly done differently? That fucker was the one who tied me up and practically begged for my scent to be all over him. And for someone so unwilling to talk to me, he sure seemed to be marking his territory last week.

Never one to back down from a fight with him, Iris kept her stance staring right back at him. Ren challenged her, beckoning a finger for her to step closer.

Please-it's like he's never met me before.

She closed the door and locked it behind her.

Two can play at that game.

The lock clicking piqued his interest that was shown in raised eyebrows, even though he continued his phone conversation.

Iris manhandled the chair so she could stand in between his legs and mimicked hanging up a phone. He shook his head, so she shrugged off her fuzzy overcoat, revealing a deep V-cut long sleeve sweater, a leather skirt, and tights to match.

Leaning over the desk she half-whispered, "Put the phone down. Now."

His eyes widened in question as he concluded the call, "Hey, Jim, I'll give you a call back-one of my most important clients just walked in for an impromptu meeting."

"What can I help you with today, princess? Here to demand something unreasonable again? Or is it to try and plan another chick flick movie night with my sister and not invite me? Because if that's the case I'll have you know How to Lose a Guy in 10 Days is one of my favorite movies," Ren said, feigning sadness and running his hands up from her knees to the inside of her thighs.

Clearing her throat Iris said, "No I'm here for a few different reasons. First off- I need that coffee bar sign to be something vintage, maybe in white pen off of a fucking dusty mirror or something. And also, you haven't emailed me back about the new coffee counter design I sketched. I want the coffee to seem like it's always flowing. I don't want it to look like an actual bar."

Iris didn't allow herself a second to breathe before tumbling into the real reason she was here.

"Secondly- I cannot believe you're such a child and have been avoiding me. Can you be an adult for one second in your life so we can have a conversation about whatever this," she gestured between them, "is? she spilled the words out. With less fervor she threw in, "And thirdly, I pictured you as an American Psycho or Fight Club kind of guy."

Before he could respond, his phone rang again, and he motioned to pick it up. As soon as his hand grasped the receiver, she tossed it off the side of the desk.

"Why did you leave Sage's house after our... our thing? Why won't you sleep in our bed anymore?"

Ren's blue eyes turned into the harshest ocean as he stood up from his chair in one swift movement. Banging a fist on the table, he whisper-yelled, "I can't sleep next to you because I am already consumed by you. I don't need a reminder of your smell every single morning I wake up. I can't wake up with your perfect fucking leg wrapped around my body and keep up this facade of being respectful. I can't be near you because then people will know what's going on. Emmett already suspects something is up between us, and I can't let this compromise Sage's project." Defeated, he sat back down with his head in his hands.

"Oh, don't give me that crap! You don't think I know how important this is? This is my project too! Why do you think I'm even here and care so much? After your mom died, that shop was a safe haven for us to go, no matter what it turned into year after year. I am just as invested in the project and Sage's happiness as you are," Iris whisper- shouted and jammed her finger into Ren's chest for emphasis. He didn't move an inch even when she switched tactics and used her whole hand to try to shove him away from her. Much to her dismay, even in her anger, all she could focus on was how solid his chest was pushing up against her hand.

When he remained silent, Iris huffed and said, "I'm not running away this time. I'm tired of pretending this isn't real. I'm tired of pretending you aren't important to me. I'm tired of waking up in the morning only to realize you aren't there next to me. Just this once, you are going to sit here and be quiet. I need to do something," Iris proclaimed. If she touched him just one more time, it would be out of her system. She slunk to her knees, and crawled underneath the desk.

"Oh God, Iris, what are you doing?", Ren said, straining to get the words out past his teeth.

"I'm running a very important experiment. Now sit back down," she commanded.

He did as she asked, looking down at her through open legs.

She ran both of her hands up his calves toward his thighs, tugging briefly on the back of his knees so he had to brace his hands against the desk. Iris thought that maybe because she couldn't see him this time, their connection would be less erotic.

She was wrong.

He grew right in front of her eyes, and she started to rub through his jeans. She used her lithe hands to undo his belt and zipper quickly, knowing she didn't have much time.

At least, not nearly enough for what she had set out to do.

When his length popped out in front of her she realized there were clearly things she didn't know about Ren Anders. She had felt him before, just a few times in the morning when she pretended not to notice, but seeing and feeling it first hand was an entirely different experience. Even under the darkness of the desk, she could tell he was above average.

There was no way she was fitting all of that inside her.

Her fingers trembled slightly as they trailed up his length, paying extra attention to the vein running up to the tip. Her mouth started watering as she gave a slight squeeze at the top. Needing a moment to collect herself now that she understood the sheer size of him, Iris peeked up at Ren from under the desk.

That was a mistake.

Ren's eyes penetrated her, holding her hostage under the desk. His jaw was clenched and his hands were gripping his chair so tightly she thought he might break it.

Despite his appearance, he was utterly calm as he spoke. "You have two seconds before I lose control and bend you over this desk and make you scream my name."

His filthy words unlocked a switch and calmed her nerves. Iris kept eye contact as she took him inside of her mouth, inch by inch. She involuntarily moaned at his taste, not remembering a time when she felt herself getting wet while getting someone else off. Iris loved giving head almost as much as she loved getting it, but feeling him come undone because of her was going to be an otherworldly experience.

With the first few drops of precum pouring out, Ren tried to stifle his grunting as he gripped her hair. It was too gentle for Iris, too intimate, so she pulled his hand harder into her hair giving him the signal that it was okay to take a little of the control back.

That seemed to be all the encouragement he needed. The hand gripping her hair tightened to the point of pain as he angled her head exactly where he wanted her. She watched, transfixed as he lifted his hips off the chair and started fucking her mouth. Iris relaxed her jaw, moaning as he hit the back of her throat.

"Do you feel how hard I am for you? Do you feel what you're doing to me? You are fucking incredible," Ren said trying to keep his breathing even.

She couldn't have responded even if she wanted to, too lost in this moment. She had never been this turned on in her life, between Ren's filthy words and knowing someone could walk in and catch them at any moment.

Her core clenched and she couldn't take it anymore. Iris moved her hand down to the edge of her skirt, just inches away from relief.

She looked up as she slipped two fingers into her panties but stopped when she saw the dark look in Ren's eye.

"Well, well, well. I thought this was about getting even?"

He wasn't fighting fair. Even in her lust filled stupor she knew she was too stubborn to give in now so she lifted her hand out of her panties and started stroking him instead.

Her pussy clenched, wishing it had a toy of its own to ride when he said "Are you going to be a good girl and swallow every last drop of me right now?"

Crazed, she used both hands to stroke him while her mouth suction cupped the tip. She felt him pulsating on her tongue and couldn't help the involuntary moans she let out as she quickened her pace.

"God, Riss, this feels so fucking good," he said, gripping her hair tighter.

She felt tears hit her eyes when she took his cock as deep as it could go, nothing short of the apocalypse would stop her from feeling that sweet, hot liquid from hitting the back of her throat. She just stopped herself short of fingering herself, because the need was almost too much.

"Don't you dare stop, I'm going to-,' Ren let out a grunt, and Iris felt him melt underneath her as he released into her mouth. Pleased with herself, she gently pulled up his boxers and pants, helping him get situated before she got out from under the desk, adjusted her skirt, and turned to leave as she had before. He stood up and stumbled after her, grasping each side of her face. He slammed his lips onto hers, his earthy taste mixing with his own release in her mouth as he explored for an answer that couldn't be found in words. She pulled away from him and they stared at each other in dumbfounded silence.

A knock at the door startled them both as he gently moved her behind the door so whoever knocked would think he was alone. Luckily, Emmett wasn't back yet from picking up his takeout order, and Ren found himself slamming the door a little too hard on one of the guys asking him about the timeline for supplies and production on one of their new projects.

"I know we don't have time right now but we are going to talk about this," Ren turned to Iris suddenly frenzied. He was terrified that she would just leave not understanding what she meant to him. He knew he wasn't the bravest but he needed more from her. Teasing her for years was one of his favorite pastimes, but feeling her body was a drug he'd never be able to quit.

"We are way more than a so-called "thing" as you put it. I told you before and I'll say it a thousand more times if I need to," Ren started to back her into the door he just slammed. "Fuck giving you space and fuck being afraid of other people finding out. I have always run away from everything important but not this time. Iris, you deserve better so that's what I want to be. Better."

Gently stroking her face with the back of his hand he whispered, "You. Are. Mine. Time to get that through your pretty little head, baby. Fuck everyone else, I can't stay away from you a second longer. Are you good with that?"

Seconds ticked by as she stared up at him, seeming at a loss for words for the first time. He would have made some smart ass comment about that if this wasn't the most important conversation he had ever had with her.

After what felt like an hour but was probably five seconds she responded, "I'm good with that, we just can't tell Sage yet. Not when so much is riding on this for her. And I still need time to figure out where my head is in all of this," she said smiling but nervous.

He watched her face transform into a grin that could only mean trouble as she continued, "Who knew all I had to do was give you a blowjob to get you to talk to me. Honestly I should have thought of this sooner. How very typical."

"Baby, I was a goner the second you walked in here. Now shut up." His lips met hers before she could respond. One hand gripping the back of her neck so he could angle her mouth exactly where he wanted her. Her lips parted for him, giving him complete control.

Reluctantly, he pulled himself away from her.

"As much as I would like to finish what we started here, I do need to get back to work."

He watched her eyes dim slightly and his body almost buckled. She covered it just as quickly and responded, "Of course. I'll see you around then?"

"I meant what I said to you. I'm done staying away from you. I'll see you tonight."

That must have been the right thing to say because she visibly relaxed.

"Oh and Iris- We will be finishing what we started."

CHAPTER 40

Iris

The next few weeks went by in a haze of stolen moments together. Ren had stayed true to his word, having been back in bed with her every single night. He was careful to ensure Sage was asleep when he creeped up the stairs toward Iris's bedroom door for their forbidden slumber parties. Sure, the adult thing to do would be to tell people, but neither of them wanted the attention off Sage during such a critical time for her. Despite their new proximity overnight, they had barely gotten any time alone together during the day. Iris knew they would need to define whatever was happening, but she chose to live in the moment, focusing on the way his breath hitched when he kissed her. The grimace she would see in candle light when he'd stop them before having sex.

Besides, between Christmas upcoming and the Vintage Vixen Espresso grand opening on New Years Day, every waking moment was planned with activity and finalizing the interior. Iris was up at dawn, talking with each party vendor, and Ren was always out the door shortly after.

They had managed to sneak away for a few quick makeout sessions here and there, but the two always seemed to be interrupted by something. Sage yelling about the wrong stain dried into a drip pattern on her latest antique flip.

Emmett yelling at Sage for leaving said wood stain open and wait-ing right in front of the door when he came over to help her move the pieces to the shop.

Sage yelling that Emmett's feet were too big for him to see any-thing of importance in front of him.

Iris had to imagine this is what hell felt like- never ending blue balls.

Today, Sage had called Iris in a frenzy, saying something about an emergency and her not being able to drive into the city to pick up a dresser that she "desperately needed to complete a bedroom set". Iris had immediately offered to pick it up for her.

When she realized her only mode of transportation was a rickety bike with one fucked tire, she knew just who to call.

Iris and Ren drove down a deserted stretch of road, staring out at the snow capped mountains and sprawling grassy fields. Iris rolled down the passenger side window despite the frigid air, and felt the wind on her face. She felt right at home, and that's what terrified her the most. Ren's strong arms made light work of getting the dresser securely in the back of his work truck, and they were headed back to drop it off at Sage's at-home workshop. Just when Iris had a moment to let go of her stress in the serenity of the wind against her face, she heard a loud pop and squeal.

Ren snapped his neck, slowing the truck as he turned his head to see where the sound came from.

As the truck pulled to a bumpy stop on the side of the two lane road, he turned and asked, "Are you okay?", with genuine sincerity.

"Wow Ren, you're looking at me like you give a shit if I live or die," Iris chuckled. "I'm fine. Can we look to see what made that sound? It's getting dark," Iris asserted as she flung open the passenger side door.

Iris glanced at the still intact furniture set as she rounded the truck. She was all for being dramatic, but this particular antique set was truly fucking ugly. It looked straight out of a scene from beauty and the beast- all beast no beauty. The once beautiful wooden dresser set had been painted a distinct vomit green, with gaudy brass finishings and large chicken foot shaped dresser legs. All signs of the original 1970's vintage French Provincial bedroom set were hidden. She wouldn't even be surprised if a candle stick jumped out at her from one of the brass polished drawers.

Ren puffed out the air gathering behind his cheeks as he took in the scene in front of him. His breath made little clouds of smoke against the cold air. He had managed to get to the popped tire first, because it was on the driver's side. As he bent over to inspect the damage, Iris couldn't help but notice his baby blue tee riding up just a little bit from underneath his jacket. There was just enough for her to catch a glimpse of his muscle corded lower back and wonder what the rest looked like.

He had been wearing a t-shirt to bed, and even through their previous rompings together she never got a good look at his body because it was always dark in her room when he entered. Now, she had an unobstructed view as it stretched over taut muscles. While grappling with the idea that she might have cared as much about his physique as he did her safety, he popped up a little too close to her face to report that the tire needed to be changed.

"Where's the spare? A big strong man like yourself will have no problem fixing this thing up. Let me know if you need anything," Iris said, using both hands to hoist herself onto the back of the truck to settle in, pulling out her phone in an attempt to call her best friend about the blow out. Surprise- she had no service in the mountains.

"I can't get through to anyone, so you might want to check to see if your carrier will let you make a call," she said to Ren, trying to avoid the anxiety creeping in.

"In the meantime do you, like, need anything? Because I think this is one you'll have to figure out. I'm good with timelines, not wrenches and wheel wells," She said, peering down at him from the truck bed. She strained her neck to see another inch of skin.

"Yeah, like the knowledge of how to change a tire from a YouTube video that isn't loading," Ren said, tossing his own cell to the side to chastise her simultaneously.

"You don't know how to change a tire? What happened to the rugged, sexy contractor? That's embarrassing." she goaded him. It felt good for a second to get back to teasing him. Every time he came near her in public, a flush rose up from inside her, and she fought like hell to dampen it. She felt it happen again as she recalled him leaning over her to secure the dresser in place in the back of the truck.

"Hey look-this strapping young contractor just happens to call his insurance for roadside assistance when things go awry. The past couple times I've been... wearing a suit! And I don't want to get those dirty." Ren said, his eyes darting around. He started to ruffle around in the back to see if the car jack was there, but then turned around looking defeated.

He looked at her, shrugged his shoulders, and grumbled about the gas station they passed a half mile back to get some help. Ren turned to head back that way.

"Hey! So what? You're just going to leave me here all alone? The sun is going to set soon, and that's exactly how people die when they're not careful," Iris yelled after him, jogging to catch up. Huffing slightly by the time she caught up because his over 6'4" frame carried him twice as far as she could have gone in the same amount of time. She had never been so grateful for Ren making her switch into her running shoes before the trip.

Ren chuckled at her remark and simply stated under his breath, "No one would be able to get close enough to you to hurt you, baby".

Iris stopped in her tracks for a moment, while he kept going. Despite everything that Ren had done to her in the past, Iris found herself wanting to completely let down her walls and let him in. But her mind betrayed her in unhealthy ways. What if he changed his mind about her and left her like everyone else ended up doing? Iris stared at Ren's back as he continued to walk down the now dimly lit road. She could feel that this was the moment she needed to decide once and for all, let the walls crumble and put all her trust in a man who used to bully her, or keep them up and lose something she was beginning to think could be truly wonderful. Despite their shaky past, Ren had been nothing but honest and kind to her since the meeting in his office. There was no sign of the past bully he once was. Maybe it was time Iris finally let go of the past.

They walked together in silence for about thirty minutes, Iris still lost in her thoughts, until they approached the gas station.

"Okay so if you had one day left on Earth, and you had to make a meal of only things at the gas station, what would it be?" Ren asked, approaching the door handle.

"Well when I'm thinking about my last day on Earth, I wouldn't be spending it with you making fun of me so I won't say."

"Are you so sure you wouldn't want to spend time with me like that?' Ren said, holding the door open, "Just entertain me while we're here and tell me what you'd have."

"Okay. Fine. It's gotta be Bugles, a Diet Dr. Pepper that's in a styrofoam cup and not a bottle, and a 100 Grand Bar."

Ren was immediately off to find all of those snacks, plus more, before ending up at the cashier's station, laughing it up with the guy even though they just met. Iris caught up to the conversation after perusing the latest InStyle, hearing a simple "Thanks, have a good day" while watching Ren slide a 100 dollar bill toward the cashier without asking for change. He got plenty of snacks and drinks, but there's no way they were that much.

"So wait, what did he say?" Iris asked, starting the small trek back to the car.

"He told me he was running a sweet deal on snacks," he said, holding up a bag.

"What does that have anything to do with helping us fix a tire?"

"It doesn't. I just wanted to make sure you were fed before I started to work on the car."

If the Diet Dr. Pepper wasn't so bubbly and refreshing, she would have spat it out all over his face.

"You had us walk all the way over here so I could get a freaking snack? And it's basically dark out and-"

Ren shoved a 100 Grand bar right into her mouth, and continued on their trek back to the truck. Momentarily distracted, she accepted the fact that her blood sugar was dipping to dangerously low levels and welcomed all of the Red 40 and carbonation the gas station had to offer.

They finally approached the truck, and Ren pulled out a stash of tools from the back.

Confused as hell, Iris started "Wait... was that jack and tools there the entire time?"

"Did you actually think that I'd drive around town unsafe and un-equipped for an accident? I need you to understand something. Everything I do is for a reason. And right now I need you to tell me what's going on in that head of yours."

Ren pulled a blanket from the backseat of his truck, popped open the tailgate, and gently placed the blanket down. He wordlessly gestured for Iris to sit on it, and she obliged. Mostly because she could just make out a glimpse of his ass in jeans from where he started working on the tire. What would it be like to get her claws into him? What would his breath taste like as they were coming together? She wasn't sure she would ever know at the rate things were happening.

Iris couldn't remember the last time she had a moment to herself, a moment to breathe and close her eyes without the pressure of life caving in.

CHAPTER 41

Ren

He glanced over to this perfect creature parched on the back of his truck as he finished lowering the car jack, so fiery and full of spirit looking completely at ease. Ren's breath caught in his chest just staring at her. He was glad he reminded her to bring a few extra layers on this side quest in case she got too cold.

He knew he had to come clean about what happened all those years ago.

Right as he opened his mouth, Iris' eyes fluttered open and she beat him to it.

"You know, I forgive you," she said, simply.

"Forgive me? For which thing exactly?" he said nervously.

"All of it. I've been wondering if I was unfair to you and should have given you more time to prove yourself as my friend, and not my enemy. Sage was never my enemy, but I made you into one because I was just so... isolated without having other trusted people around me. And when your mom died, she felt like family to me too. Even though she wasn't my mom, I thought we could come together to comfort each other, but maybe that was stupid of me," she finished in a hushed tone.

Jumping up from where he was crouched down fixing the tire, Ren laid down his tools and said. "No! No, please don't talk about yourself like that. I need you to know that I'm embarrassed by my actions.

I was a stupid kid trying to do anything to make friends and I turned into a bully in the process. If it wasn't for Emmett coming along and telling me what an asshole I was about five million times, I'm not sure I would have gotten out of the habit. I never should have treated you so poorly. I wish I could go back to that first day on the playground and take that moment and every other moment back. I wish I would have told you how I really felt, how it took every ounce of strength to not punch those boys when they pushed you down or how much your presence helped keep me standing when my mom passed away. I have admired your strength and resilience through the years, you always got back up and fought me no matter what I did or said to you. God, Iris you are the most incredible woman I have ever met. I don't deserve a second chance with you, but I'll keep begging for one anyway," he felt himself tear up for the first time in years. This woman brought him to his knees, and he would do anything to rectify his past mistakes.

CHAPTER 42

Iris

Tears flooded her eyes as she listened to Ren finish speaking. These were the words she had always secretly wished he would say to her, but never believed he would. Even though she had already forgiven him for his actions, she felt a weight lift off her shoulders when he finished. She couldn't bear the idea that she could go without him for one more second.

She watched Ren wrestle with himself from a few feet away. His feet shuffled back and forth. She could tell he was waiting for her to say it was okay for him to come to her. Iris couldn't hold back a second longer. Reaching up, she tugged him the rest of the way to her by his jacket. That was all the invitation he needed. He wrapped his massive hands around both sides of her head and pulled her away for a moment to take the briefest look at her. In that split second, she wasn't sure if he thought she was real or not. He pulled her face to his with such intensity that they nearly knocked teeth. He flipped her on her back, crushing her with his weight.

"I missed you. I haven't been able to get your smell, your taste out of my head. I'm desperate to feel you come apart every way possible, and that starts tonight," Ren said against her lips. "But first, I need to get us somewhere a little safer. I can't have anyone seeing what I'm about to do to you. Get in the car, baby."

Iris whimpered. She didn't think her body could wait another second. Ren seemed to read her thoughts and said, "Don't worry, it's not far."

Iris forced her body to move off the back of the truck and slide into the passenger seat. Ren was seconds behind her jumping into the driver's side. She wasn't sure how he had the time to put all the supplies away but she wasn't going to stop and ask. Ren pulled the truck back on the road and quickly turned off on a nearby dirt road. After a few minutes of driving, they came to a deserted field, void of all light except what was being emitted from the stars above them. Iris quickly climbed out of the truck, staring up at the stars above. When was the last time she could see them this clearly? It was one of the most beautiful things she had seen. Thousands of stars twinkled down at her, creating a dim lighting enough to almost see in front of you.

She tore her eyes away from the sky, realizing she hadn't even heard Ren get out of the truck behind her. She could just make out his silhouette in the middle of the field. Walking over to him, she gasped. There in the middle of the field was their very own oasis. The checkered blanket had been laid down on the ground, a few pillows on either side with two large knit blankets laying next to them. There was even a portable heater to keep them warm. She stared down at Ren, completely speechless. "How?" Was all she managed to get out.

Ren smirked at her from the ground, picking up one of the blankets and motioning for her to sit down by him. "I packed a few things in case something like this ever happened. Can't say I ever thought I'd be lucky enough to be with you when it did happen though. Come here, sit with me."

Iris did as she was told, sitting down next to him and letting him wrap the blanket around her. "Are you cold?" He asked.

Truthfully, she wasn't chilly in the slightest. Actually, she was burning up. Iris slowly removed the blanket from around herself, then removed her winter coat. "Actually, I'm not cold at all," She responded, praying Ren would understand what she was trying to say. She was still worked up from what happened on the truck and she didn't think she could wait a second longer. Luckily, Ren must have felt the same way.

Ren closed the space between them. He started kissing her neck, lifting her shirt off without stopping. Iris held her breath as his eyes traveled down her body, seeming to memorize every inch of her. Her breath caught as he began placing kisses on her clavicle, both breasts, her stomach, and finally down to the edge of her jeans. Ren was panting, placing his mouth over her core, heating her from the outside, in. He wrapped his fingers around the top seam and started to pull her pants down in such a frenzy that she thought her jeans might come apart at the seams. Iris could feel the rough texture of the blanket underneath her ass, but with Ren's fingers gripping her thigh, and his day-old stubble rubbing against her most sensitive area, it slipped her mind.

"The gas station was for you, this snack is for me," Ren said with a devilish grin. Ren locked eyes with her for a moment before he dove his tongue in and out of her, fucking her with it. He laughed to himself, and she was so turned on that the vibrations from that alone almost sent her over the edge. He was punishing with his tongue, giving her the sweetest torture she could imagine. His hands joined soon after and his thumb began rubbing her clit in a circular motion while two fingers entered her. She was squirming beneath him, begging but she didn't even know what she was begging for.

"Oh my god, please don't stop," Iris was so close, she was feverish and could feel her core clenching. She had to bite her tongue to keep herself from begging him again. He was an expert at eating her out under the covers, but she wasn't sure why he'd always stop there. She'd returned the favor several times, but they never went all the way.

Her encouragement spurred him on, and his fingers pressed up and out over and over. Iris met him with each stroke, greedy for an orgasm. She used his fingers like a toy and fucked herself on them while he reached one hand up to squeeze both breasts in one massive hand. She came with a cry so loud, she was worried cars passing by on the highway would stop to think it was a woman in distress. Ren barely gave her a moment to recover as he slipped his jeans off. He released his length from his boxers, clearly too desperate to enter her. He appeared unconcerned that the rest of his clothes stayed on considering how cold it was outside.

He started to stroke himself over her. Iris was at awe with his length every time, even though she would frequently use her tongue to memorize every inch of him. His balls looked so tight, needing release as soon as possible. He stretched his neck side to side, using the pre-come as lube. Now, his entire member glistened and pulsed with just moonlight to shine down on them. He pushed open her legs with his own, and used the tip of his cock to grind against her clit. The cold air hit her sex, and she sucked in a breath.

"I can't hold back now that we're truly alone," he said, rubbing her entrance, finding her already wet. "I need to hear you say you want this," Ren said, keeping up his torturous pace on her clit. Iris felt tears prickle her eyes, so turned on by the man in front of her. There was zero hesitation as she said, " Yes, a million times yes. I want this. Please." He teased her entrance, giving her just an inch of himself. Iris needed to get accustomed to his size, and quickly. The stretch felt so sweet, as he went slowly at first, watching her breach hitch with each added inch. He leaned over her so that his hot breath warmed the cold skin around her collar bone.

"You're here, you're real," he said as he thrust inside of her, "you're mine," Iris screamed in delight and disbelief at how perfectly he fit inside of her. He slowly punctuated each thrust by pulling all the way out, just to go right back in, grazing her clit with each entrance.

The build was so unbearable that she lost her senses of time and direction. The singular feeling of togetherness made her feel so whole, so wanted, that she wasn't sure how to place the feeling.

She hated the barrier his jacket provided, but loved it all the same for being the one thing she could hold on to. When they got home, she'd need to sink her claws into the carefully sculpted stone she'd been admiring all day. Ren's breathing was becoming more erratic, the tighter she held onto him. She hooked her heels around to his ass, giving him permission to drive her further and further into the ground. On instinct, one of Ren's hands curled around the back of her neck protecting her, while the other had a firm grip on her hip.

"Don't ever look away from me again, please baby, look at me. Look at me so you know who's your undoing," he said.

Ren knew exactly what he was doing with keeping their eyes locked. He stuck his thumb into her mouth and he pulled it out with a pop. He applied light pressure to her clit, running it up and down, matching each stroke. He only increased the pressure when she started to plead.

"Please, Ren. Please," she gasped.

"Please, what? Use your words," he responded languidly.

"Please make me come. I'll do anything, anything for you," she begged.

It wasn't until then that she realized he wasn't using his full length. He went to the hilt, hitting her in places no one had before. Iris came so violently she almost kicked him off of her. She used the waves of her own pleasure to milk Ren's cock for all it was worth. Seconds later he roared into her ear, following her into new, unknown territory.

CHAPTER 43

Sage

Today is the first day of the rest of my life. Or some shit like that, right?

Sage and Emmett reached across the gorgeous new coffee bar to snag the to-go lattes Jules whipped up. Emmett insisted on driving to the shop with her once more to make sure "everything was up to code".

Obviously, it was.

She couldn't help but be in awe of the beauty around her. Vintage Vixen Espresso showcased every piece so lovingly and intentionally. The aroma of the freshly brewed coffee could allure the most disinterested customer from across the street. Everything was coming together exactly as Sage intended. Well, maybe not perfectly because there was still some tension between her brother and best friend. Hopefully now that Christmas passed without them killing each other, tonight would go smoothly as well. She even spied them exchanging gifts when they thought no one was looking.

I bet Iris gave him a can of farts.

"What's this one called?" Sage said, wide eyed when a burst of cinnamon hit her mouth.

"I've been so focused on the flavor profile, I haven't gotten any further than calling it Cinnamon Surprise," Jules said with a weak laugh.

"I'm sure you'll come up with something clever! We have plenty of time over the next few weeks to build out a menu system where you can interchange the letters so you can change them every day if you want to," Emmett reassured her.

"I'm not worried about getting the names right just yet. I really appreciate you getting set up so early. I know you were probably up late getting a New Year's kiss," Sage winked.

At least someone was getting some.

"Not this year! Just me and Milo resting up in preparation for today," she said, and pulled out her phone to show Sage a selfie she took the night before. It featured Jules and her orange tabby wearing matching party hats.

All she needed now was a shower, and to get officially ready. Jules wanted to test out the fresh syrups she made from her patio garden on them this morning before the grand opening tonight, and Sage couldn't have been more grateful as soon as the smell of freshly ground beans hit her nose.

"Thanks Jules! Have I told you you're my favorite person?" She said with the biggest smile she could muster. She really meant it. Caffeination was the closest she could get to feeling high without losing track of time and projects.

"Wait, I thought I was your favorite person?" Emmett looked at her with hooded eyes and the slightest grin.

"Oh leave it, Leif. Let's drop this coffee off to Iris while it's hot and you can do whatever else you need to do to stay out of my way today."

She wasn't sure if she said this for herself or because Jules was still behind the bar, staring between the two of them.

"I prefer to be in your way, but it's your day, business owner!" Emmett said, elbowing her side.

Sage clinked her coffee with Emmett's in a "cheering" motion, and nodded toward the door to head out.

"See you in a few hours, Jules! The place smells so... aromatic!"

Jules just laughed in response and set up the remaining bottles of lavender syrup on the back counter.

She tried to turn her back to the door to open it with her butt, but Emmett caught it instead. He was being too chivalrous, which made her and everyone around them suspicious. Maybe they were suspicious. None of it mattered because nothing was actually happening between them. As long as the store didn't need any major maintenance, there were plenty of handymen around town who would be able to do minor repairs. And finally, maybe Emmett would leave her alone.

Do I want him to leave me alone?

She wanted to drive herself to the store, but he insisted on picking her up early this morning to run over the order of operations for the rest of the day. Final touches happened days ago, but he was relentless in helping set up the shop. The project was finished and paid for. She guessed the extra help was a good promotion for A New Leif.

She rounded to the passenger side door, and before she could set one of the coffees down to open the door, Emmett took both from her into his massive left hand, and opened the truck door with his right.

"In you go, little lady."

Emmett glanced around him like he was her own personal security. What a joke. There's no crime in Shelburne.

She slid into the passenger seat, trying to take the coffees from him.

"Buckle up, first!"

"God, okay, Dad! Let's get this show on the road," She tried to do her best teen rebel impression by cranking up the whining in her voice and crossing her arms over her chest. She looked up at Emmett, expecting some sort of childish jab to be flying from his mouth but instead she was met with his smoldering eyes glaring back at her.

"Dad? I prefer daddy, actually," Emmett didn't laugh like she expected him to.

His hands were curled so tightly he was dangerously close to crushing his own coffee.

No surprise there.

To the town of Shelburne, he was the golden boy, the cheerful happy go lucky guy that everyone wanted to be friends with, but Sage had caught a few glimpses like the one he was currently giving her and knew beyond a shadow of a doubt that there was more to Emmett Leif than met the eye.

Her house was a short five minute drive from Spruce Street, and for that she found herself to be very grateful. Being this close to Emmett in the car was almost overwhelming. He smelled like the sort of spice that sticks to your clothes this time of year.

She found herself yapping all the way home to fill up the silence. She was never comfortable just... sitting. Emmett pulled into her driveway soon enough, and Sage never felt more relieved to exit a vehicle. She had the smallest bladder known to man, and was more than used to the feeling of needing to exit just as quickly.

She noticed Ren's company truck parked outside, eager to say hi to him again and to thank him for his help.

"Hey why don't we just go back to my place and get something to eat, honestly do you need to go home yet?"

Is he sweating?

"No, I need to shower and start getting ready for tonight," she insisted.

"You look perfect as you are," he said stubbornly.

"Okay..? Why are you trying to hold me hostage? Like I said I'll see you in a few hours," she said, pulling down the passenger side mirror to inspect herself.

Sage could still smell her own morning breath, and hated the feeling of grimy old clothes. She and Emmett practically stayed up all night working on the finishing touches of the front signage back at his office overnight. She slept on the couch in his office, waking up with a blanket over her. He was awake when she woke up. She didn't feel embarrassed... just seen. Maybe for the first time in a long time. Her hyperfixations didn't usually have any place to be except for her head. He took the time to change the entire color of the outline with her, and then they affixed it to the front, finally giving the store permanence in the way it deserved.

"No! You look great as you are!"

"Shut up, Emmett!" She rarely used his first name anymore. It felt too personal. She used it now to put emphasis on her point of needing to move along with her day.

"At least let me grab a few donuts before we leave?" he asked hopefully, with worry and anxiety filling his eyes.

"Yeah, sure, just don't bother coming upstairs. I'll be naked, taking arguably the best 'everything' shower of my life."

Sage trekked up her porch steps, while Emmett followed with the entire breakfast.

At least I have a hand to look for my keys.

She unlocked her door with ease and noticed the house was completely silent.

"Iris! Ren! I know you're in here I saw the truck! I have sustenance!"

"YES! Iris and Ren WE ARE BOTH HERE! The BOTH of us! EVERYONE in the same HOUSE!" Emmett was literally shouting right behind her eye. "Wow, didn't realize you were so excited to see our friends all of a sudden." She was momentarily distracted by the giant scene Emmett was causing. He slammed the food down on the counter, kicking the chair out and accidentally throwing it on the ground.

Sage started to get a little nervous when there wasn't a response.

This is supposed to be the greatest accomplishment of my short life. Where the fuck are they?

CHAPTER 44

Iris

"Oh shit! Oh shit! oh shit! Did you hear that?" Iris silently slapped Ren's chest.

They were sweaty and completely tangled up in each other.

"It's nothing baby, I'm busy right now," Ren said coyly, sliding his finger back into her, so slowly in and out.

"No, I'm serious" she panted, "I think Sage might be back already."

"It's fine, let me continue my good work down here and be extra quiet. She won't come in, we're still sleeping," the little Devil winked at her and dragged himself down between her legs. He inhaled deeply, smelling her sex after he fucked it. This wasn't the first round of the morning. Iris couldn't get enough of the feel of his stubble between her thighs. He was clean shaven a few days ago at the final inspection, really putting on a show of professionalism for his sister and best friend.

A truck engine cut off, and just as she was about to hit another glorious climax, the front door opened.

"Iris! Ren! I know you're in here- I saw the truck!" she heard Sage wail from downstairs.

"YES! Iris and Ren, WE ARE BOTH HERE! The BOTH of us! EVERYONE in the same HOUSE!" Emmett's booming voice was over hers, in clear warning.

"I'm waking your asses up, it's time to start the day! I don't care if it's 6:30 in the morning!" Sage emphasized every step she took up the stairs.

"Oh god you HAVE to put on a shirt! And underwear! And a chastity belt!" Iris whispered.

He grabbed the closest thing to him- one of Sage's old robes Iris was borrowing, right as she flung the door open.

"Good mor- what the fuck?"

Iris made a quick assessment of the room.

"Why does it smell like sex? Iris... you don't sleep naked."

Emmett came barreling up the steps after her.

"Hey guys. Look at you. Two friends. Hanging out super early in the morning. Just like us. There's breakfast downstairs!"

"You're right! Just friends! Naked friends! I actually have a mole on my ass that I thought Ren should look at!" Iris clamored.

Ren sighed, looking up at Sage. "It's actually exactly what you think, and I've been in love with your best friend for the past- how long have we known you?" he turned back to Iris still in the bed, covering herself with the comforter, redder than the hair on her head. "Yeah, however long that is."

"YOU LITTLE BITCH," Sage yelled, directing her anger at her brother, "I ALWAYS KNEW SOMETHING WAS SUSPICIOUS. AND YOU," she targeted Iris next, "YOU DIRTY LITTLE LIAR. WHEN I SAID GO GET HIM I WASN'T TALKING ABOUT MY BROTHER!"

"Okay everyone, let's all calm down, we have a store opening to attend!" Emmett interjected all the while holding Sage back from going airborne. Iris noticed the exact moment he realized Sage wasn't going to give up the fight. He just sighed, easily flung her writhing body over his shoulder, carried her into her room, plucked the outfit and undergarments out from her dresser and pleaded that they needed to leave.

"THIS IS MY HOUSE AND I DEMAND AN EXPLANATION!"

Sage yelled from the other room and back into the hallway. Each word was jostled with Emmett's massive footsteps.

"So here's the thing, Jordan was never real! The date was real," Ren coughed loudly, clearly upset, "but all of the advice you gave me was actually for Ren. We're so sorry we kept this from you, we didn't want to take any attention away from the shop's progress!"

Emmett put his back to them in the doorway, allowing Sage to see them one last time for the day before he marched her back down the steps.

Iris opened her hands out to Sage, almost dropping the comforter, giving the entire friend group a show.

"I'm very excited to be your sister-in-law, because that better be where this is heading!" she pointedly eyed her older brother, trying to stay menacing despite remaining tossed over Emmett's shoulder like a sack of potatoes, "BUT IF YOU DON'T PUT SOME CLOTHES ON-"

"Alright little missy, let's just get ready at my place," Emmett inspected the bag of clothes that he got, appearing to be convinced that whatever he grabbed was worthy of her grand opening, and finally headed down the stairs.

"PUT ME DOWN RIGHT NOW EMMETT LEIF OR I SWEAR TO GOD YOU WON'T BE ABLE TO SOW YOUR SEED IN THIS TOWN A SECOND LONGER!"

Iris watched as Sage beat her hands against Emmett's ass walking down the stairs. After what felt like eternity she forced her mouth to function and tried to make peace the best way she could by yelling back, "We love you! See you soon!"

She noticed Ren physically cringe beside her.

"Well...that was not ideal."

She couldn't stop the snort that came out of her. "Ideal would not be the word I would use for that. That was a catastrophe. Sage is my best friend. I owe her everything and she has never in our entire friendship lied to me. She is never going to forgive us for this."

She couldn't stop the tears from building in her eyes, soon they were traveling down her cheeks. Iris tried to blink them away but more kept falling. Ren's hand grabbed her chin lightly forcing her to meet his eyes. Only love shown in them, the kind she knew mirrored her own.

"What do we do?" Ren softly wiped the tears from her cheeks, planting soft kisses in their wake.

"Here's the plan. We are going to go to the store opening early and explain everything. This is not some dumb fling or short term relationship. You are it for me, baby. There is not a single doubt in my mind that you are mine and this is the end game. I will do anything for you, including talk some sense into my younger sister for not seeing how much I was in love with you sooner. Sage talks a big talk but she loves both of us and I have to believe she will come around."

"But what if she doesn't?"

"Then we will spend the entire store opening being so disgustingly in love that she will have to change her mind. Sage is a romantic at heart, I know she wants both of us to be happy and baby, you make me the happiest man in the world."

Tears were flowing freely down her cheeks now. Ren was looking at her with such honest hope in his eyes she couldn't resist a second longer. Before she registered what she was doing she flung herself at him, wrapping her arms tightly around his neck in a way that had to be suffocating and alternating between plastering him in kisses and whispering I love you.

"It's funny really, I used to think the saying 'there is a thin line between love and hate' was so incredibly dumb. I could never imagine a scenario where one could turn into the other. But I realize now, even back then, I was always thinking about you. I tried so hard to hate you, I would force myself to relive each moment where you were cruel to me but even then I couldn't get myself to give up on you. I love you Ren, I've loved you through every moment of our lives, even the messy parts where I probably shouldn't have," Iris admitted.

"I love you too, Iris. I've loved you forever. Since the first moment I laid eyes on you," Ren said. Iris opened her mouth to argue that there was no way in hell he loved her even back then when Ren stopped her. "I know you don't believe me, I can see you wanting to argue with me over what I just said. But it's true. I loved you then, and I never stopped loving you. If you don't believe me, take a closer look at my tattoos."

Iris grabbed Ren's shoulder, almost pulling it out of its socket trying to get a closer look at his full arm sleeve. She had noticed it was larger this year, but everytime she had tried to get a closer look at it in the past he pulled away. Now she could see why.

There, in the middle of his bicep was a giant iris flower. It was beautiful. The flower itself was stunning, perfectly drawn in painstaking detail. All the petals were in full bloom. But what she was most drawn to was next to the flower. Written so small she had to squint to see it, and she probably would have missed it if she wasn't staring so hard, it was a date. Not just any date. It was the date that Iris had moved into the house next door from the Anders. Tears were flowing again and Iris couldn't stop them if she tried. This meant more to her than any words or gifts ever would. This was proof that Ren had always felt the same way she did. She could feel the tiny remaining walls crumble inside her. There was nothing that could come between them this time.

They stayed like that, wrapped in each other's arms and just holding one another.

Iris wanted to stay in this bubble forever but knew there were things they needed to do. This thing between them wouldn't feel real for her until her best friend was on board.

Peeling herself off Ren was more difficult than she anticipated, mainly because he was refusing to let her go. After twenty minutes of negotiating with sexual favors, she was off the bed, showered, and ready.

❦

The store officially opened at 5:00 PM, so Iris and Ren walked hand in hand into the store at exactly 10:00 AM to begin setting up. They had decided to text Sage together, using the group chat name "friends and lovers" to try to lighten the mood. She had messaged back agreeing to meet them here so that was a good sign right?

Sage walked into the store exactly fifteen minutes later, sticking to her rule of arriving fashionably late. Iris flinched at the hurt she saw in her best friend's eyes when she walked in. Even more unsettling was the fact that Sage wasn't saying a word. That didn't stop her from glaring at Iris and Ren's conjoined hands though.

After a few minutes of awkward silence, Iris realized she was going to have to start this. "Sage, I am so sooo sorry. We never should have kept this from you. You are my best friend, and it has been killing me not to tell you. The truth is, Ren and I didn't know what was happening between us at first so we decided to keep it a secret until we could put a name to it. We should have told you. You have every right to be angry at me." Iris blew out a long breath, her stomach was in knots and she felt like she couldn't breathe properly with how Sage was staring blankly ahead.

Finally, Sage spoke but it wasn't directed at her. "And you -" she said, flicking her eyes up to Ren, "What do you have to say?"

Ren pulled Iris's hand up to his mouth and pressed a small kiss on it before continuing. "I meant what I said earlier. I love her, I think I always have and I know I always will. I will continue to love her even if you don't agree with this, but I really hope you do because Iris and I love you too. This relationship between us wouldn't have formed without you. You are the glue that holds us all together."

Iris watched Sage's blank mask crack. A tear slipped down her best friend's face as she seemed to really look at them for the first time since walking in. "Wow. So this is really real isn't it?" She said, waving her finger between the two of them.

Ren responded before she could. "Afraid so."

Sage sighed but Iris knew her well enough to see the joke behind her eyes. "Guess I should have figured this shit out when you got a giant fucking tattoo of an iris on your arm. Alright. Look, I feel like I don't know which one of you to give this speech to so I am just going to say it to both of you. If either one of you breaks the other one's heart I will punch you. There, that should do it. Sister and friend duties fulfilled." Sage made a big show of slapping her hands together in an "all finished" motion.

"Don't get me wrong, I'm still angry you both lied to me but I also understand why you did it. I can get over this if you both promise never to lie to me again. Oh, and I better be the maid of honor AND best man at the wedding." She winked at Ren and Iris felt him laughing beside her.

Iris couldn't stand the distance between them any longer. With Ren still holding her hand, she pulled everyone together in a giant hug. This was it, no lies or secrets left between them. She felt lighter than ever as a laugh fell from her lips.

"Alright! Now that we are all friends again we better get to work! Sage, where would you like us to start?"

The three of them spent the next few hours cleaning and organizing everything they could get their hands on in the shop while vendors began trickling in the doors. There wasn't a speck of dust or an antique out of place by the time the clock chimed 5:00. Iris grabbed three champagne flutes filled to the brim courtesy of her favorite alcohol vendor and rushed over to Sage right as she was flipping the door sign to "open".

"Are you ready?" She said while handing Sage her first drink of the night.

"I hope so," Sage said, taking a big sip of the tart martini.

CHAPTER 45

Iris

Despite the last five months of planning and this being her actual full time job, Iris still felt nervous. She needed this event to go perfectly. Everything had been hand picked to Sage's standards, from the color of the walls (Sage green, duh), the custom coffee bar (obviously a beautiful reclaimed wood that had been sanded and stained dark to offset the white marble countertops), to the arrangement of each custom piece Sage spent the last few years finding and refurbishing. This was her best friend's dream and Iris refused to be the reason anything went wrong.

Sage's nerves became more and more obvious as the clock ticked on. It was now 5:10 PM and there wasn't a single customer in the store.

Iris was getting angry, they had spent the last four months going up and down main street convincing every shop owner that this shop was going to be the turning point of this cursed location. After ten failed shops, Vintage Vixen Espresso was going to stop the cycle. They had managed to convince every shop owner and town local to give the store a chance, so why wasn't anyone here?

Iris and Sage were so busy staring at the door willing it to open that neither of them realized when Ren picked up the largest custom painting from the center of the store and carried it over to the checkout.

A bell chimed, causing Iris to just about jump out of her skin. She turned around the same time as Sage and gasped at what Ren was carrying.

There, in Ren's hands was the most beautiful painting Iris had ever seen. The painting was huge, big enough that it would cover the majority of a large wall and be the centerpiece of the room. The painting itself was beautiful, using only muted hues of green, ivory, and light pink around the edges, but it was what was in the center that always made Iris stop and stare. There, in the middle of the painting was an iris, titled up as if it was reaching to find the sun. She remembered the exact moment Sage found it at an estate sale in the richest neighborhood in Burlington years ago. Iris had thought about buying it from her everyday since but knew it held a special place in Sage's heart too. Dozens of people had tried to buy it from her over the years, even offering her twice the asking price, but Sage had never even considered it.

Now, Ren stood at the counter but he was staring at her with a huge smile on his face. Iris couldn't bear to look at Sage, knowing she was about to break his heart by saying no to the sale.

She stood completely immoble watching Sage walk up to the sale counter and stare expectantly at Ren. She was surprised she remembered how to speak at all when she finally said, "Ren, you know Sage won't sell that painting. She has a huge not for sale sign right below where it was hanging."

"I think she has just been waiting for the right customer to come along. Plus, I promised myself I would be Sage's first sale of the day," he said, shrugging.

Iris couldn't believe her eyes when she watched Sage start ringing in the order. Ren and Sage were whispering so low to one another that she couldn't even hear them negotiating the price. Next thing she knew, the sale was complete and Ren was marching the painting up to her with a smirk.

"I'm going to go bring this home quickly before anyone can steal it," Ren said to her. He walked by, stopping to whisper, "This would look perfect in our new place together, don't you think?" in her ear before planting a quick kiss on her cheek.

He was out the door before she could respond.

She let herself imagine them moving in together and realized it didn't sound bad, not at all. Seeing him every morning, waking up together in each other's arms. Laughing together. Coming home to him cooking for her. It sounded perfect. She would admit to herself that it was everything she wanted. The voice in the back of her mind reminded her of their current timeline and the fact that she would be returning to Boston soon. She had never done a long distance relationship before, is that where they were headed? Would she be able to walk away from him knowing she wouldn't see him for weeks at a time.

Iris forced herself to focus on one dilemma at a time. Tonight, she had a store to run with her very best friend who was back staring at the unopened door.

"Do you think everyone got the time wrong?" Sage said, a hint of vulnerability in her voice. "Or maybe they all changed their minds about supporting the business."

Despite those same thoughts rolling around in Iris's head, she wouldn't allow that doubt to spiral. Iris squared her shoulders, "I bet everyone is just going for the fashionably late vibe. They will be there. Also, where the fuck is Emmett? Shouldn't he be here early too?"

"Oh. I um... I told him to just come with everyone else. There was no need for him to be waltzing around here early." Iris caught a strange expression in Sage's eyes but wasn't sure what it meant.

"The store sign looks beautiful by the way," Iris said, admiring the giant store sign hanging above the front door. "How the hell did you get it done in time? You didn't even know the name this time yesterday." Iris chuckled despite the heavy atmosphere.

"Emmett and I actually finished it last night, or early this morning I suppose is more accurate." Sage wouldn't meet her eyes.

Interesting. Now who's keeping secrets?

Iris could tell there was more to that story but decided not to pry today. If her watch was correct, which she hoped it wasn't, it was now 5:35 PM and the store was still empty. Sensing they both needed a distraction, Iris grabbed two more glasses of champagne and handed one to Sage who promptly downed the entire glass.

By 5:45 PM Iris was ready to go grab whatever random fools were walking the street and force them inside.

Luckily, there must have been some god watching that wanted to spare her from that embarrassment because the door finally swung open.

That was the moment everything changed.

It was like the floodgates had opened, people began spilling into the store. Iris looked down and saw one of their fliers had been tossed on the ground in the chaos and bent down to pick it up before anyone could trip on it. By the time she stood back up there had to have been at least fifty people in the store.

She caught Sage's eye across the store and smiled. Sage was in the middle of a group of twenty old ladies showing them some custom vintage jewelry boxes. The ladies were staring at her like she hung the moon, soon every single one of them had a box in their hands.

Iris looked back down at the flier in her hand. She hadn't been involved in the final edits of this and was curious to see what they had come up with.

Her eyes zeroed in on the invite.

"Come see the new store on the block! If you love vintage finds, or the best espresso in town, check out the Ander family's best renovation yet. Doors open at 6:00 PM"

"Shit."

Well that explains why no one had shown up for the last hour.

The next few hours flew by. Sage was born for this, she was running around the store non stop showing each customer a piece that ended up being exactly what they were dreaming of. The store was actually beginning to feel pretty empty with the amount of items she had sold. It seemed like the entire town of Shelburne had shown up to support Sage as the night went on. Ren had returned shortly after the first crowd filed in. All her Boston friends had driven in together to help support the store. Even Jordan had flown back in to support Sage and the store. Iris did a double take when she saw Emmett walking in with the blonde from their double date in tow.

What was her name again? Claire..? Clarissa? Kleine?

What was even more strange was the way Sage had looked when she noticed Emmett's surprise date. Iris had caught her staring at them, a look of disgust and hurt in her eyes as she grabbed another glass of champagne. Soon after, she had been swept up into another sale and Iris hadn't gotten the chance to corner her about it.

"This was a success. The store looks perfect, Iris." Ren said, sliding up beside her at the coffee bar.

"I agree. We make a pretty good team, Anders."

"Come here, I want to show you something." Ren said, grabbing her hand and pulling her through the store.

They reached the back at record pace. She hadn't been back to this side of the store much since their not so subtle moment back here when this was still his makeshift office. Iris's cheeks heated thinking about what happened back here.

Ren led her to the bookshelf and small reading nook, patting the cushioned bench in a "sit down" motion.

"This is my favorite part of the store," Ren smirked beside her. She had to guess he was thinking about the same things she was.

"Do you think this will be enough to get everyone to support Sage and her business?" Iris said, changing the subject.

"I hope so. I think she has sold most of her work already so that has to be a good sign. I overheard Jim talking to his buddies earlier saying this was his favorite store on the block and you know how hard it is to get his approval. And I heard the knitting club over there raving about the event you have planned for them next month."

"Wow, never thought I would see the day Jim would give any

of us his approval," Iris chuckled. "Should have known Sage would be the first."

A comfortable silence distended as they watched people shuffle through the store. Iris had never felt this with anyone before, the sense of belonging and freedom to simply be herself. She looked up, staring at Ren's profile as she watched him looking over the crowd hating that she was going to ruin this moment.

"So.... about the painting." She started

She watched Ren tear his eyes away from the store to look at her with such love and happiness she couldn't imagine spending even a day away from him.

"Listen. I know how hard you and Emmett have worked to make A New Leif successful. Shelburne is your home and Boston is mine. I would never ask you to give that up. So- I've been thinking about asking my boss for a more permanent remote position. It will be a lot harder to meet with clients and vendors from out of state but I think I could make it work and only have to travel a few weeks a month. That is, if you even want me around. We haven't talked about moving and I totally understand if you aren't ready for anything like that I just-"

Iris was cut off by Ren grabbing her face and kissing her. It started innocently, a soft kiss against her lips but instantly turned heated as his hands found the nape of her neck. Using his grip on her hair, he pulled her even closer to him on the bench, plunging his tongue into her mouth at the same time. Her toes curled, Iris grabbed his shirt and pulled her body against him.

A couple coughed nearby pulling Iris's thoughts back to where they were. Ren must have remembered too because he gave her one last kiss and pulled away.

"Iris, baby. It's cute that you think I could be away from you for that long," Ren smiled smugly. "I already spoke with Emmett and called the office. Turns out, the company is doing well. Very well actually, and we have been planning on opening a new office for awhile now. Boston wasn't the original city in mind but with some number crunching we determined there is quite a market for us. They have already acquired a building and construction is scheduled to start next week."

Iris was speechless.

The thought of having to leave Boston had been weighing on her since she came up with the idea. Ren had to have known that she didn't want to leave and was uprooting his whole life for her, for them. Her heart swelled impossibly larger. Suddenly, their future was no longer muddy or filled with doubt. She hadn't thought it was possible to love him more, but he was once again proving her wrong.

"That is, if that is what you want?" Ren said, suddenly looking worried.

Iris realized she had been staring at him in silence for longer than what is socially appropriate when someone tells you they are moving for you.

"Yes. Absolutely yes." Tears building in her eyes again today.

"Thank god." Ren whispered as he pulled her into him again, placing a kiss on her forehead, then her cheeks, nose, and finally her mouth.

When they finally broke apart Iris realized the store had cleared out. Everyone had gone outside to watch Sage flip the sign to say "closed".

Iris smiled for what seemed like the millionth time today. "What now?"

Ren intertwined their hands, grinning back at her and said, "Now you let me love you for the rest of our lives."

"Only if I can love you back," Iris grinned, never one to back down.

Epilogue

Iris

One year later...

"Hey! Watch where you're going!"

The biker appeared as though the entire road was theirs for the taking, swerving back and forth. She sat down on a nearby bench to catch her breath, heart pounding out of her chest. You would think after living in Boston for the last ten years she would be used to the high-traffic areas. Although, maybe her mind wasn't as sharp today.

Her thoughts wandered back to the man she left in her bed this morning and the reason she wasn't able to watch where she was going. Ren had woken her up with a "goodbye present" for their last day living in the tiny one bedroom apartment they had called home for the last year. Iris had never been one to shy away from a gift, and this morning had been no exception.

Ren's idea of a present had been waking her up with his head between her thighs. At first, she thought she was having the best dream of her life. She had been on the brink of climax when she finally forced her eyes to open, looking down to see Ren staring up at her while his tongue circled her clit and two fingers plunged in and out. Just the sight had her clenching around his fingers and screaming his name.

Ren had packed up and moved to Boston shortly after his sister's antique shop opened. Iris had settled herself back in a few days earlier following their four month stay in Shelburne. There had been no discussion about living arrangements at the time. Ren had shown up at her apartment straight from the airport with his bags and never left.

Iris loved that apartment and the life they built together, but after an entire year of living within 850 square feet with another person taking up too much closet space, they decided it was time to take the next step.

The next step happened to be a beautiful three bed, three bath craftsman style house right outside the city. Iris fell in love with the way the light twinkled through windows and how easily she pictured them there, working in tandem in an at-home office.

They officially closed on the house last week, but despite Iris's protests Ren wanted to stay in the apartment a bit longer. In true engineer fashion, he needed to complete some minor renovations in order to prepare for the housewarming party tonight. Iris nearly had a heart attack when Ren informed her that he wanted to plan the party without her help. After about six hours of questions about the theme, vendor selection, and invite list, he finally relented and allowed her to be in charge of the food catering. This is how she found herself on the busiest street in Boston over lunch hour.

After picking up the catering and narrowly avoiding getting hit by a car, pedestrian, or cyclist, Iris found herself back at the apartment.

How many times do I have left to approach this door, by myself? What will it feel like to walk through the doors of something I own?

She passed through the threshold and slogged the bags onto the counter. She made quick work of putting the cold items away and proceeded to get ready.

Iris smiled to herself, and picked out her favorite emerald green scoop neck maxi dress and a pair of nude heels, remembering how Mrs. Anders said that green was her best color. Iris completed the look by curling her long red locks, pinning back one side with a pearl floral hair pin. She applied her trusty pinky-nude lipstick at the very end. All that was missing was her date. And the matching pearl necklace that accompanied the hair pin, but that was bequeathed to Sage in the will. She had a strange feeling Sage would be wearing the other piece of the set tonight. It would go against her personal style, but this was an occasion after all.

She swore Ren told her he was going to be home all day today. She wondered if he was having issues planning the event without her...

Iris silently cursed herself, she should have tried harder to get him to let her help, after all she considered herself one of the best event planners in Boston at the moment. After she returned from Shelburne, her inbox had been overflowing with event requests. Seems word had gotten out about the antique store's success. First-time business owners in the Boston area wanted Iris's event planning help to make their new stores a success as well. Iris realized that to achieve her version of success she needed to venture out on her own. She quit her job right then and started up her own event planning company. After a whirlwind year, Iris and her new team of event planners had helped over 50 new businesses launch and the requests were still coming.

Snatching her phone out of her clutch she went to dial Ren's number. She instead found a text from him saying he got caught up at the house and to meet him there.

Iris slowed her car to a crawl as she pulled into the driveway 20 minutes later. The house sat on an acre of land, nestled back in the trees giving it a private feeling. As she drove up to the house she noticed there weren't any cars in the driveway.

Okay that's weird...did he forget to send out the invites? I swear to god I told him to do the electronic invites so this wouldn't happen!

Her internal panick was cut short when she spotted Ren standing on the front porch. Her breath got caught in her throat. Her boyfriend always looked attractive, but tonight he was breathtaking.

Ren wore a fitted navy suit, so dark that it almost looked black if you weren't looking closely enough. It fit perfectly, so much so, that she knew he had to have recently gotten it tailored. His golden brown hair had been styled back out of his face, giving him a professional appearance. Ren was most often put together for business meetings in the city, not usually this formal for a gathering of close friends and family.

Iris snapped her mouth shut and hopped out of her car. She had been sitting in her car peering into those blue eyes at a distance. She hopped out of the driver's side and around to the trunk to collect the food for the evening.

"Hey baby, where is everyone? Did we have another mishap with the arrival time on the invites?" She raised her voice so she could be heard behind the car.

"Oh you know our friends, always fashionably late," Ren chuckled nervously.

The shakiness of his voice caught her off guard. Ren was never nervous, his unshakeable confidence is one of the things Iris loved the most about him. She left the food in the trunk momentarily and came back to face him.

"Hey," she said, placing both hands gently on either side of his face, "Even if no one shows up tonight we still have each other."

His shoulders slumped, and he relaxed into her touch. Taking that as a sign that her words had helped, Iris placed a soft kiss on his lips then said, "Show me this party you insisted on planning without me."

"Okay, but don't get jealous when you see that I can plan events better than the world famous Iris O'Conner." Ren smirked as he grabbed her hand to lead her inside. Twisting the knob, he opened the door to a completely dark room.

"Oops, I must have turned the lights off before I came outside. Would you mind switching the light back on? Should be on that wall to the right of you." Ren informed her.

Iris's hands fumbled all over the dark wall until she finally found what felt like a light switch. Flipping it back on she was instantly blinded with the sudden contrast in color.

Her eyes adjusted to the light and she looked up at their new living room and screamed.

There, in the center of their new home stood everyone she loved smiling and waving welcome home signs with drinks in hand. Iris felt tears sting her eyes as she looked at everyone who had taken the time to celebrate with them. Everyone they cared about had shown up, Sage was in the corner sipping a drink, Emmett was at the complete opposite side of the house staring straight at her best friend. Iris and Ren's collective work friends were mingling together in the corner. The Monday coffee crew from Boston were assessing the decor in appreciation. Even her mom took the day off from the hospital to make the trip out.

Her curls shook with disbelief when something caught her eye. There, in the middle of the living room, hanging up on the wall was the painting Ren had bought during Vintage Vixen Espresso's opening night. She hadn't seen the painting since then. Every time she asked Ren about it, he told her he was waiting until he found the right space to hang it.

She went to grab Ren's arm next to her but her hand grasped the air. She tore her eyes away from the group in front of her, searching for Ren. Iris moved her gaze down, finding him kneeling on one knee smiling up at her.

"Wh...what is this?"

The excited crowd hushed at his movement.

"Baby, I have loved you since the second I saw you. Now, we all know I didn't handle that knowledge well at the beginning, but I am determined to make it up to you and prove how much I love you every day of my life. You are kind, smart, and painfully stubborn in a way that constantly keeps me on my toes. I can't imagine my life without you, challenging me, making me a better man. And I know you could have planned this event a thousand times better than me, but this was one event I needed to plan for you. So here, in our new home, in front of all the people in this world who love us I need to ask you. Will you make me the luckiest man in the world and marry me?"

Tears were streaming down her face and she couldn't even try to stop them. Ren had spoken about how lucky he was, but it was her that was the lucky one.

She watched Ren reach into his pocket and pull out a large emerald stone that sat on a thin white gold band. It was the most beautiful ring she had ever seen and the exact ring she had imagined every time she dreamt of this as a girl. Getting down on her knees in front of him, Iris cupped his face with both her hands. "I can't imagine my life without you by my side. Yes, a million times yes! I will marry you." She couldn't hold back a second longer and apparently neither could Ren because he grabbed her behind the neck and slammed their mouths together. The kiss was desperate and passionate and probably not appropriate for the thirty or so people watching. Neither of them cared.

Behind them, champagne was popped and glasses were being passed around. Iris finally pulled her lips from Ren and stood up from the floor. Ren wiped the tears from her cheeks then interlocked their hands.

All at once the spell she was under was broken as Sage slammed into her, crushing her body in a hug.

"Congratulations, Riss! I'm glad he finally worked up the courage because I have been dying to tell you every time we talked the last few months. You know I can never keep a secret from you." Sage was practically vibrating with energy. "You have always been a sister to me, glad we can finally make it official."

Iris laughed, unable to conceal how happy she was a second longer. "I couldn't agree more," she responded as Sage handed her a glass of champagne and they clinked glasses.

"Oh, and good job to you too, I guess, brother." Sage said to Ren, not even slightly managing to hide her smirk when Ren rolled his eyes back at her. These two never missed an opportunity to mess with each other.

Iris made eye contact with Emmett across the room as he raised his glass to her. She noticed he had been keeping his distance while they were with Sage. "What's going on there?" Iris looked to Sage, flicking her eyes between her and Emmett.

"Nothing. What? Why do you ask?"

"Just seems like you two are avoiding each other? You never did fess up and tell me what happened between you two the night before the store opening when you stayed up to make the storefront sign." Iris raised her eyebrows in a silent question. Sage avoided eye contact as she responded, "Nothing worth writing home about. I see his blonde friend didn't come with him tonight."

Iris definitely caught some bite to her tone. She was also one hundred percent sure Sage knew Emmett's former girlfriend's name but figured it best not to call her out.

"Cassidy? Oh, did Ren not tell you? They broke up last month." Iris kept her tone purposefully blank.

Iris caught the flash of joy in Sage's eyes before she masked it.

This should be interesting.

"Well, anyway. Enough about that man child. This is your engagement party! You need to go mingle, we wouldn't want all your guests thinking you two only want to talk to me" Sage winked.

"Okay, okay you are right. We should go make our rounds. Oh! You're still staying here tonight, right? Feel free to grab either of the guest rooms, they are right next to each other in that hallway to the left. Emmett is also staying so first come first serve." Iris said before Ren started dragging them into the crowd.

"Cheers to the happy couple! Now where's the food? I'm starving!" Emmett said a little too loud from the back of the living room, beelining for the front door.

"Actually, I'll get it," Sage said tersely.

They nearly collided on the way back out to the car.

After hours of catching up with everyone and more congratulatory drinks than Iris could count, the party was finally winding down. She spied Sage and Emmett slinking off to their chosen bedrooms on the first floor, right before the remaining guests left.

Ren grabbed her waist and swung her to face him. His lips were on hers a second later. His tongue met hers as the kiss grew heated, like it always did between them. She wrapped her legs around his waist, unlocking their lips to pepper kisses on his neck.

"So I was thinking," Ren started as he backed her up against the front door. "Since our first contract together went so well, I think we need to make another one."

She was distracted by his fingers digging into her thighs dangerously close to her center so it took her a moment to realize what he was saying.

Forcing her mind to focus, Iris replied "And what would that contract say exactly? You better not start emailing me using a false persona again or I will kick your ass, Ren Anders."

Ren chuckled against her neck. "Got it. No fake names this time. This contract will be shorter, and hopefully a lot easier for you to say yes to." Ren removed his lips from her neck to stare into her eyes. "Just you and me, Iris. Promise me this is forever."

Iris didn't even need a second to respond.

"I think I can agree to those terms. But this time, let's sign it with something other than a pen," Iris said, guiding him up the stairs.

She had no fear in her heart this time around. She gazed down at the emerald ring on her finger, its deep green hues shimmering with the promise of a future together. When she looked back at Ren, his eyes were filled with a love so profound that it made her heart swell. In that moment, she knew without a doubt that she would commit herself to him in every way possible - no contract or vow felt like enough to capture the depth of her devotion.

Now where's that dotted line?

THE END

ACKNOWLEDGEMENTS

First and foremost, we would like to extend our gratitude toward the many hands that helped bring our first novel to life.

To start, thank you to Sheri Potter for her diligent editing, formatting, and belief in our work. The guidance and support offered is more than we could have hoped for during our first publication. She transformed our manuscript into what you see on the page, and we could not be more grateful for her diligence on this project.

Next, we would like to thank our fantastic cover artist Gowtham Thangaraj. Because of you, we know people will understand the meaning of our words, making it love at first sight. Unlike our main characters.

A special thanks goes to Courtney, Bri, Erin, Hannah, Emily, Sheila, and Amanda, for your input on the very first draft. Your feedback was incredible, and we are so glad you all got to be a part of this journey from the very beginning.

To our partners, who make us feel seen every day. It's not every day that the woman in your life writes a smutty romance novel. To Henry-thank you for giving us the male perspective on this project. Your wit, coffee deliveries, and never-ending support never went unnoticed. To Devin-thank you for being a sounding board and safe space during the writing process and for the countless hours you spent listening to us ramble on and on about our favorite characters. Without your support and vision this book would not be what it is today.

Finally, we want to thank the readers for making all this worthwhile. Without your time, energy, and excitement, we wouldn't be able to pursue doing what we love so much.

Our words, our love, is all for you, you little cheeky devils.

ABOUT THE AUTHORS

Zia Tyree is a first-time novelist and Registered Nurse. After spending countless hours devouring fantastical worlds and romance on pages, she decided to take matters into her own hands by crafting novels for other feisty romantics on her rare days off. When she's not writing, she's planning the next group get-together, sipping a coffee, or casting some sort of spell. She resides in the Southwest, with her loving fiance and three perfect rescue dogs.

Kristen Sandmann is a first-time novelist and a Registered Dietitian. After spending her workday running around hospitals educating patients she spends her nights immersed in the world of fiction. After years of reading other brilliant authors' work, she decided it was time to venture out into the world of book writing herself. When Kristen isn't at work, she can be found running, rewatching her favorite TV show (again), and gallivanting around Cincinnati, OH with her two wonderful dogs and husband.